Daniel Defoe, George Saintsbury

Selections From Defoe's Minor Novels

Edited by George Saintsbury

Daniel Defoe, George Saintsbury

Selections From Defoe's Minor Novels
Edited by George Saintsbury

ISBN/EAN: 9783337001445

Printed in Europe, USA, Canada, Australia, Japan

Cover: Foto ©Andreas Hilbeck / pixelio.de

More available books at **www.hansebooks.com**

SELECTIONS FROM DEFOE'S MINOR NOVELS

EDITED BY

GEORGE SAINTSBURY

LONDON

PERCIVAL AND CO.

1892

CONTENTS

INTRODUCTION

Although Defoe has never been edited as a whole, and is, unless a great change takes place in the habits of English book-buyers, very unlikely to be so, he has had his fair share of partial collections in greater or smaller extent. I am not aware, however, of any attempt to deal with him in the way here proposed. The nearest thing to it is the **rather** abundant bundle of extracts given in Mr. Arber's *English Garner*, vol. vii., in which the selections are wholly political. Of such matter I have myself included nothing, the ever famous *Shortest Way* being reprinted in another volume of this series. The whole of my excerpts here will be from the works of fiction by which Defoe gained his greatest popularity, and in which his unrivalled talents for description and narrative appear. A selection from the lighter passages of his miscellaneous work may follow.

afterwards set up as a hosier or hose-factor.   He tried the foreign, especially the Peninsular, trade a little, but had to compound with his creditors, and to abscond for some time. Then he became partner in and manager of some tile and brick works at Tilbury—an enterprise which was ruined by his pillorying and imprisonment for the *Shortest Way*.   After his release his occupations, which had always been partly, became almost entirely literary, a practical connection with politics being also opened by his becoming an agent of Harley's.   During the rest of his life he was always more or less a political journalist, and some of his engagements in that way are not over creditable.   He had from time to time fresh troubles about his old or new debts.   One of his most respectable employments was the advocacy of the Union with Scotland, for which purpose he both wrote and travelled, residing in the north for a considerable time.   But he never quite gave up his fancy for dabbling in business.   In 1712 he made a fresh venture of some sort, of which little is known, but which seems to have had some reference to his old connection with the clothing trade; and ten years later he speculated in land.   Although seemingly well-to-do he was never far from prison, and sometimes in it; and though he had a handsome house at Stoke Newington, he died, apparently in distress, on 24th April 1731, lodging in the same parish where he was born.

A mere catalogue, without comment, of the certain work of Defoe would occupy far more space than is available for this whole introduction, and would be of very little service for the purpose of this volume. It is sufficient to say that he wrote everything—prose and verse, novels, histories, religious and moral treatises, sketches of manners, works on political economy, periodicals, tours, memoirs, pamphlets, lampoons, essays, sermons. He achieved the feat, extraordinary even now, and still more extraordinary then, of starting and keeping up with his single pen for nine years a tri-weekly newspaper, entitled *A Review of the State of the British Nation*, without allowing this to stop, or greatly to decrease, the volume of his miscellaneous production. Imprisonment, hiding, wandering, business of all kinds, had no effect on the quantity of his writing, and apparently not much upon its quality. And last, but not least, his most imaginative as well as his most masterly works were the product of his declining days, *Robinson Crusoe*, with the satellites here represented, all dating from the last ten or twelve years of his life.

This is, however, more surprising at first sight than on examination, for the distinguishing and effectual quality of Defoe's work is the same everywhere—a point in which he differs from almost every other writer.   No one perhaps with such an entire absence of what is commonly called literary quality of mind has achieved such a peculiar literary character of writing; and the perfection of **his** expression is **as** much the secret of his popularity with purely literary critics as the peculiar character of his thought and sympathies is the secret of his vogue with the un-literary.   There is in Defoe absolutely nothing high-flying or transcendental.   His verse is exceedingly bad—its badness being sufficiently accounted for by **the** fact that his thought was prosaic in kind, and that, unlike some other writers who share this disadvantage with him, he had neither time nor fancy for supplying the deficiency by elaborate attention to form. His prose is nearly, if not quite, of the first class, because the criterion of the excellence of prose is the direct and faithful transfer, with only a certain varnish of art, of the purpose, sentiment, information, idea, or what not of the writer.   In his faculty of representation **Defoe** was a consummate no less than an unique artist, accomplishing the 'disrealising,' as it has been called, which is necessary to art, with such a marvellous and unerring economy of means that he has sometimes been taken for a mere Realist. His work, generally speaking, has the character as nearly as possible of spoken rather than of written style,—the nature, the freshness, the spirit, the unadorned grace of the best conversation of a certain kind. And this accounts to a certain extent for his wonderful fertility. But this is only half the mystery; the other half lies in the immense variety, combined with the peculiar pitch, of his thoughts and interests. He is, as it were, sublimated commonplace; he is the eternal and consummate example of the truth, constantly formulated by critics, that what pleases is that which is just above—not too insolently or conspicuously above—the mind and taste of the reader. Defoe had a vast number of interests, but he never urged any to that pitch of crotchet, of *engouement*, which offends. He had an abundance of plain common-sense, and could argue very well indeed; but he was never seduced by his logical faculty into paradox, into subtlety, into any of those abuses of syllogism which irritate and perplex the ordinary reader. He had an abundant and prolific fancy, which never by any chance became fantastic; which seldom, indeed, reached even the borders of imagination proper. He was a sincerely religious man—one who could take persecution for conscience' sake; but he was not in the least what his own day called an enthusiast, and could perfectly well understand and practise trans**action** and compromise. **He** was a good plain moralist, sturdy and English in his morality; but he was quite able to make both ends meet, and was not at all troubled by any eccentric point of honour. In fact he was the shrewd, fairly-educated, prosaic, Philistine, middle-class Englishman in quintessence,— endowed, moreover, with the literary faculty which, while it is commonly supposed to be denied to the English race in general, has in individuals given us a literature second to none of ancient or modern times. His Philistinism might at times disgust if it were not expressed with such genial simplicity— for it is a pity that we have left the adjective of genius in its proper sense to Germans and Frenchmen, who certainly have no better right to it than ourselves. His garrulity might offend if it were not for its astonishing combination of truth to nature and adaptation to artistic ends. His prolixity might weary if it were not that it is entirely free from any combination of pretentiousness. As it is, he is literally, as I have called him, unique. No language **has** his fellow; and it is excessively improbable that either this or any other language will ever produce one. The adjustment of limitations and endowments was made once and for all.

It was, as has been said, in the last twelve years of Defoe's life that the extraordinary series of fictions here laid under contribution was published. From **the** first and greatest of them, which appeared in **1719** and the years immediately following, nothing **has** been taken; for *Robinson Crusoe* is not so much in every one's hands as in every one's head, **and** woe to England when it ceases to be so. The second in order (1720) was *Captain Singleton*. **1722** **saw not** merely *Moll Flanders*, the *Memoirs of a Cavalier*, and *Colonel Jack*, but the well-known *Journal of the Plague-Year*, and the very characteristic *Religious Courtship*—perhaps the most extraordinary turn-out for a single twelvemonth that any man of letters has to his name in the bibliography of the world. *Roxana* appeared in 1724, and the *New Voyage round the World* next year. From this last I have taken nothing, for it has less personal interest than **any** other, and may not improbably be a mere working up of some actual voyage of the half-trading, half-piratical character then common. **Its most** striking passages, dealing with mutiny **and the** like, bear a curious resemblance to others much more dramatically **worked up** in *Robinson Crusoe*, and may very possibly represent the originals of these. **Of the** other five—*Captain Singleton*, *Moll Flanders*, **the** *Memoirs of a Cavalier*, *Colonel Jack*, and *Roxana* —extracts will be found. Susceptibilities which deserve respect, if not full sympathy, have required a very little "editing" here and there, and have still more conditioned the selection; but I think it will be found fairly representative for general reading. Like a great deal else in Defoe's work, these novels are to some extent literary puzzles; and **it** cannot be said to be exactly certain in even a single case how much of them is frank and imaginative invention, how much dexterous vamping and setting off of matter previously existing and representing actual experience. What is certain, however, is that, as in the somewhat similar case of Dumas, there is such a personal, singular, and uniform touch visible in all the best passages of them, that a wise critic will be very little concerned with questions of origin. What we admire in them is beyond all question Defoe's, and no one else's—the marvellous reality of touch, the strange idiosyncrasy of character, **the invariable** fidelity to one scheme and one sphere **of** life, not very lofty, **not in the** least **romantic,** but possible, literary, and true.

Those who are not satisfied with these generalities (between which and an impossible excursion **into** detail **there** is no third way) **may be** invited **to** consult my own article in the ninth edition **of the** *Encyclopædia Britannica*, my friend Mr. Minto's volume in the *English Men of Letters*, or, **if** they wish to go still further into the matter, the biographies of Wilson, Chadwick, and Lee, and that prefixed to the younger Hazlitt's **edition** of part of the works. Of the most **attractive** portion **of** those works this little volume will, I think, give **a** sample not ungrateful to the taste, and hardly to be obtained otherwise except by loading the shelves with cumbrous volumes; yet if it sends any reader to those volumes themselves I shall be even better pleased than if **he** remains satisfied with what I have **given.**

I.—'CAPTAIN SINGLETON'

(The interest of Captain Singleton, *which is considerable, is twofold. One part lies in the remarkable account of the journey across Africa, which Singleton executes with his comrades from Mozambique to Lower Guinea, and which, long thought to be a mere* voyage de fantaisie, *has been seen (since Central Africa has been in the last quarter of a century explored) to be so much more close to the truth than the notions on the subject prevalent even in our own day, that it is thought Defoe must have got at the accounts, or at least the maps, of some Portuguese traveller. From this part I take my earlier excerpt, which wants little explanation. Singleton, a foundling, after various adventures by sea in his early youth, is, with others, marooned for mutiny from a Portuguese ship in Madagascar. They build a vessel, make for the mainland, and then cross it. They fight their way through the coast fringe, capturing a 'black prince,' who goes with them, and using* pagazis, *or negro carriers, like all African travellers, with a*

few buffaloes to help. They have just had a sharp fight.)

From this part of the country we went on for about fifteen days, and then found ourselves obliged to march up a high ridge of mountains, frightful to behold, and the first of the kind that we met with; and having no guide but our little pocket-compass, we had no advantage of information as to which was the best or the worst way, but were obliged to choose by what we saw, and shift as well as we could. We met with several nations of wild and naked people in the plain country before we came to those hills; and we found them much more tractable and friendly than those devils we had been forced to fight with; and though we could learn little from these people, yet we understood, by the signs they made, that there was a vast desert beyond those hills, and, as our negroes called them, much lion, much spotted cat (so they called the leopard); and they signed to us also that we must carry water with us. At the last of these nations, we furnished ourselves with as much provisions as we could possibly carry, not knowing what we had to suffer, or what length we had to go; and to make our way as familiar to us as possible, I proposed, that of the last inhabitants we could find, we should make some prisoners, and carry them with us for guides, over the desert, and to assist us in carrying provision, and perhaps in getting it too. The advice was too necessary to be slighted ; so, finding by our dumb signs to the inhabitants that there were some people that dwelt at the foot of the mountains, on the other side, before we came to the desert itself, we resolved to furnish ourselves with guides, by fair means or foul.

Here, by a moderate computation, we concluded ourselves seven hundred miles from the sea-coast, where we began. Our black prince was this day set free from the sling his arm hung in, our surgeon having perfectly restored it, and he showed it to his own countrymen quite well, which made them greatly wonder. Also our two negroes began to recover, and their wounds to heal apace, for our surgeon was very skilful in managing their cure.

Having, with infinite labour, mounted these hills, and coming to a view of the country beyond them, it was indeed enough to astonish as stout a heart as ever was created. It was a vast howling wilderness, not a tree, a river, or a green thing to be seen ; for as far as the eye could look, nothing but a scalding sand, which, as the wind blew, drove about in clouds, enough to overwhelm man and beast : nor could we see any end of it, either before us, which was our way, or to the right hand or left : so that truly our men began to be discouraged, and talked of going back again ; nor could we, indeed, think of venturing over such a horrid place **as** that **before us,** in which we saw nothing but present death.

I was as much affected at the sight as any **of** them; but, for all **that, I** could not bear **the thoughts of** going **back again. I** told them we had **marched** seven **hundred** miles of our way, and **it would be worse** than death to think **of** going back again; **and** that, if they thought the desert was not passable, **I** thought we should rather change our course, and travel south till we came to the Cape of Good Hope, or north to the country that lay along the Nile, where, perhaps, we might find some way or other over to the west sea; for sure all Africa was not a desert.

Our gunner, who, as I said before, was our guide, as to the situation of places, told us that he could not tell what to say to going for the Cape; for it was a monstrous length, being, from the place where we now were, not less than fifteen hundred miles; and, by his account, we were now come a third part of the way to the coast of Angola, where we should meet with the western ocean, and find ways enough for our escape home. On the other hand, he assured us, and showed us a map of it, that if we went northward, the western shore of Africa went out into the sea above a thousand miles west; so that we should have so much, and more land to travel afterwards; which land might, for aught we knew, be as wild, barren, and desert as this. And therefore, upon the whole, he proposed that we should attempt this desert, and perhaps we should not **find it** so long as we feared; and, however, he proposed **that** we should see how **far** our provisions would carry us, and, in particular, our water; and that we should venture no farther than half **so** far as our water would last; and if we found **no end of** the desert we might come safely back again.

This advice was so seasonable that all approved of it; and, accordingly, we calculated that we were able to carry provisions for forty-two days, but that we could not carry water for above twenty days, though **we** were to suppose it to stink too before that time expired. So that we concluded that, if we did not come at some water in ten days' time, we would return; but if we found a supply of water, we could then travel twenty-one days, and, if we saw no end of the wilderness in that time, we would return also.

With this regulation of our measures, we descended **the** mountains, and it was the second day before we quite reached the plain, where, however, to make us amends, we found a fine little rivulet of very good water, abundance of deer, a sort of creature like a hare, but not so nimble, and whose flesh we found very agreeable; but we were deceived in our intelligence, for we found no people; so we got no more prisoners to assist us in carrying our baggage.

The infinite number of deer, and other creatures

which we saw here, we found was occasioned by the neighbourhood of the waste **or desert,** from whence they retired hither for food and refreshment. We stored **ourselves here** with flesh and roots of divers kinds, **which** our negroes understood better **than** we, and **which** served us for bread, and with as much **water as** (by the allowance of a quart a day to **a man for our** negroes, and three **pints a** day a man for ourselves, and three quarts a **day** each for our buffaloes) would serve us twenty days ; and thus loaden for a long miserable march, we set forwards, being all sound in health, and very cheerful, but not alike strong for so great a fatigue, and, which was our grievance, were without a guide.

In the very first entrance **of** the waste **we were** exceedingly discouraged ; for we found the sand so **deep,** and it scalded our feet so much with the heat, **that,** after we had, **as** I may **call** it, waded rather **than** walked through **it** about seven or eight miles, **we were** all heartily tired and faint—even the very negroes **lay** down and panted, like creatures that had been pushed beyond their strength.

Here we found the difference **of** lodging greatly injurious to us, for, as before, we always made us huts to sleep under, which covered us from **the** night air, which is particularly unwholesome in those hot countries ; but we had here **no** shelter, no lodging, after so hard **a** march, for here were no trees—no, not a shrub near us—and, **which** was still more frightful, towards night we began **to hear the** wolves howl, the lions bellow, and **a** great many wild asses braying, and other ugly noises, which we did not understand.

Upon this we reflected upon our indiscretion—that we **had** not, at least, brought poles or stakes in our **hands,** with which we might have, as it were, palisadoed ourselves in for the night, and so we might have slept secure, whatever other inconveniences we suffered. However, we found a way at last, to relieve ourselves a little. For, first, we set up the lances and bows we had, and endeavoured to bring the tops of them as near to one another as we could, and so hung our coats on the top of them, which made us a kind of sorry tent. The leopard's skin, and a few other skins we had put together, made us a tolerable covering, and thus we lay down to sleep, and slept very heartily too for the first night, setting, however, **a** good watch, being two of our own men with their fusees, whom we relieved in an hour at first, and two hours afterwards ; and it was very well we did this, for they found the wilderness swarmed with raging creatures of all kinds, some of which came directly up to the very enclosure of our tent. But our sentinels were ordered not to alarm us with firing in **the** night, but to flash in the pan at them, which they **did,** and found it effectual, for the creatures went off always as soon as they saw it, perhaps with some noise or howling, and **pursued such** other game as they were upon.

If we were tired with the day's travel, we were all as much tired with the night's lodging : but our black prince told us in the morning he would give **us some** counsel, and indeed it was **very** good counsel. **He** told us **we** should be all killed, if we went on **this** journey, and through this desert, without some covering for us at night ; **so** he advised us to march back again to a little river side, where we lay the night before, and stay there till we could make us houses, as he called them, to carry with us to lodge in every night. As he began a little to understand our speech, and we very well to understand his signs, we easily knew what he meant, and that we should there make mats (for we remembered that we saw a great deal of matting, or bass there, that the natives made mats of) ; I say, that we should make large mats **there** for covering our huts or tents to lodge in at night.

We all approved this advice, and immediately resolved to go back that one day's journey, resolving, though we carried less provisions, we would carry mats with us, to cover us in the night. Some of the nimblest of us got back to the river with more ease than we had travelled it but the day before ; but, as we were not in haste, the rest made a halt, encamped another night, and came to us the next day.

In our return of this day's journey, our men, that

made two days of it, met with a very surprising thing, that gave them some reason to be careful **how** they parted company again. **The** case was this. The second day in the morning, before they had gone half a mile, looking behind them, they saw a vast cloud of sand or **dust** rise in the air, as we see sometimes in the roads in summer, when it is very dusty, and **a** large drove of cattle are coming, only very much greater ; and they could easily perceive that it came after them ; and it came on faster than they went from **it.** The cloud of sand was so great that they could not see what it was that raised it ; and concluded that it was some army of enemies that pursued them ; but then considering that they came from the vast uninhabited wilderness, they knew it was impossible any nation or people that way should have intelligence of them, or the way of their march ; and therefore, if it was an army, it must be of such as they were travelling **that** way by **accident.** On the other hand, as they **knew** that there were no horse in the country, and that they came on so fast, they concluded that it must be some vast collection of wild beasts, perhaps making to the **hill** country for food or water, and that they should be all devoured or trampled under foot by their multitude.

Upon this thought they very prudently observed which way the cloud seemed to point, and they turned a little out of the way to the north, supposing it might pass by them. When they were about a quarter of a mile, they halted to see what it might be. One of the negroes, a nimbler fellow than the rest, went back a little, and came in a few minutes, running as fast as the **heavy** sand would allow; and by signs gave them to know that it was a great herd or drove, or whatever it **might** be called, of vast monstrous elephants.

As it was a sight our men had never seen, they were desirous to see it, and yet a little uneasy at the danger too : for though an elephant is a heavy, unwieldy creature, yet in the deep sand, which was nothing at all to them, they marched at a great rate, and would soon have tired our people, if they had had far to go, and had been pursued by them.

Our gunner was with them, and had a great mind to have gone close up to one of the outermost of them, and to have clapped his piece to his ear, and to have fired into him, because he had been told no shot would penetrate them ; but they all dissuaded him, lest, upon the noise, they should all turn upon, and pursue **us :** so he was reasoned out of it, and let them pass, which, in our people's circumstances, was certainly the right way.

They were between twenty and thirty in number, but prodigious great ones ; and though they often showed our men that they saw them, **yet** they did not turn out of their way, or take any other notice of them, than, as we may say, just to look at them. We that were before saw the cloud of dust they raised, but we thought it had been our own caravan, and so took no notice ; but as they bent their course one point of the compass, or thereabouts, to the southward of the east, and **we** went due east, they passed by us at some little distance ; so that we did not see them, or know anything of them, till evening, when our men came to us, and gave us this account of them. However, this was a useful experiment for our future conduct in passing the desert, as you shall hear in its place.

We were now upon our work, and our black prince was head surveyor, for he was an excellent mat-maker himself, and all his men understood it ; so that they soon made us near a hundred mats ; and as every man, I mean of the negroes, carried one, it was no manner of load, and we did not carry an ounce of provisions the less. The greatest burthen was to carry six long poles, besides some shorter stakes ; but the negroes made an advantage of that, for carrying them between two, they made the luggage of provisions which they had to carry so much the lighter, binding it upon two poles, and made three couple of them. As soon as we saw this, we made a little advantage of it too ; for having three or four bags, called bottles (**I** mean skins or bladders to carry water), more than **the** men could carry, we got them filled, and carried **them** this way, which was a day's water and more, for our journey.

Having **now** ended **our** work, made **our** mats, and fully recruited our stores of things necessary, and having made us abundance of small ropes and matting for ordinary use, as we might have occasion, we set forward again, having interrupted our **journey** eight **days** in all, upon this affair. To our great comfort, **the** night before we set out, there fell a very violent shower of rain, the effects of which we found in the sand ; though the one day dried the surface as much as before, yet it was harder at bottom, not so heavy, and was cooler to our feet, by which means we marched, as we reckoned, about fourteen miles instead of seven, and with much more ease.

When we came to encamp we had all things ready, for we had fitted our tent, and set it up for trial, where we made it; so that, in less than an hour, we had a large tent raised, with an inner and outer apartment, **and** two entrances. In one we lay ourselves, in the other our negroes, having light pleasant mats over us, **and** others at the same time under us. Also, we had a little place without all, for our buffaloes, for they deserved our care, being very useful to us, besides carrying forage and water for themselves. Their forage was a root, which our black prince directed us to find, not much unlike a parsnip, very moist and nourishing, of which there was plenty wherever we came, this horrid desert excepted.

When we came **the** next morning **to** decamp, our

negroes took down the tent, and pulled up **the** stakes, and **all** was **in** motion in as little time as **it** was **set** up. In **this** posture we marched eight **days, and** yet could see **no end, no** change **of our** prospect, but **all** looking as wild and dismal as **at the** beginning. **If** there was **any** alteration it was that the **sand was** nowhere **so** deep and heavy, as it was **the first three days.** This we thought might be, because, for six months of the year, the winds blowing west (as for the other six, they blew **con-**stantly east), the sand was driven violently to the **side** of the desert where we set out, where the mountains lying very high, the easterly monsoons, **when** they blew, had not the same power **to** drive **it** back again ; and this was confirmed by our finding the like depth of sand on the farthest extent of the desert to the west.

It was the ninth day of our travel **in** this wilderness, when we came to the view of **a** great lake of water ; and you may be sure this was a particular satisfaction to us, because we had not water left for above **two** or three days more, at our shortest allowance ; I mean, allowing water for our return, if we had been put to the necessity of **it.** Our water had served us two days longer than expected, our buffaloes having found, for two or three days, a kind of herb **like a** broad flat thistle, though without any prickle, spreading on the **ground, and** growing in the sand, which they ate **freely of, and which** supplied them for drink as well as forage.

The next day, which was the tenth from **our** setting out, we came to the edge of this lake, and, happily for **us, we came to** it at the south point of **it ; so we** passed by it, and travelled three days by the side of **it, which** was a great comfort to us, because it lightened **our** burthen, there being no need to carry water when we had it in view. And yet, though here was so much water, we found but very little alteration in the desert; no trees, no grass or herbage, except that thistle, as I called it, and two or three more plants, which we did not understand, of which the desert began to be pretty full.

But as we were refreshed with the neighbourhood of this lake of water, so we were now gotten among a prodigious number **of** ravenous inhabitants, the like whereof, it is most certain, the eye of man never saw : **for, as** I firmly believe, that never man, nor any body of men, passed this desert since the flood, so I believe there **is** not the like collection of fierce, ravenous, and devouring creatures in the world ; I mean, not in any particular place.

For a day's journey before we came to **this** lake, and all the three days we were passing by it, and for **six** or seven days' march after it, the ground was scattered with elephants' teeth, in such **a** number as is incredible ; and, as **some of them** may have lain there for some hundreds of years, so, seeing the substance of them scarce ever decays, they may **lie** there, **for** aught I know, to the end of time. The size of some of them **is,** it seems, to those to whom I have reported it, as incredible as the number; and I can assure you there were several so heavy as the strongest man among us could not lift. As **to** number, **I** question not there are enough to load a thousand sail of **the** biggest ships in the world, by which I may be understood to mean, that the quantity is not to be conceived of; seeing, that as they lasted in view for above eighty miles travelling, so they might continue **as** far to the right hand, and to the left as far, and many times as far, for aught we knew; for it seems the number of elephants hereabouts is prodigiously great. In one place in particular we saw the head of **an** elephant, with several teeth in it, but one of the biggest that ever I saw: the flesh was consumed to be sure many hundred years before, and all the other bones; but three of our strongest men could not lift this skull and teeth: the great tooth, I believe, weighed at least three hundredweight; and this was particularly remarkable to me, for I observed the whole skull was as good ivory as the teeth; and, I believe, altogether weighed at least six hundredweight; **and** though I do not know but, **by** the same rule, all **the** bones of the elephant may be ivory, yet I think there **is a** just objection against it, from the example before me, that then **all the other** bones of this elephant would have been **there as well as** the head.

I proposed **to our** gunner, that, seeing **we** had travelled **now** fourteen days without intermission, and that **we had** water here for our refreshment, and no want **of** food yet, nor any fear of it, we should rest **our** people **a** little, and see, at the same time, if, perhaps, we might kill some creatures that were proper for food. The gunner, who had more forecast of that kind than I had, agreed to the proposal, and added, why might we not try to catch some fish out of the lake? The first thing we had before us, was to try if we could make any hooks, and this indeed put our artificer to his trumps; however, with some labour and difficulty, he did it, and we catched fresh fish of several kinds. How they came there, none but He that made the lake, and all the world, knows; **for,** to be sure, no human hands ever put any in **there,** or pulled any out before.

We not only catched enough for our present refreshment, but we dried several large fishes, of kinds which I cannot describe, in the sun, by which we lengthened out our provisions considerably; for the heat of the sun dried them so effectually without salt, that they were perfectly cured, dry, and hard, in one day's time.

We rested ourselves here five days; during which time we had abundance of pleasant adventures with the wild creatures, too many to relate. One of them was very particular, which was a chase between a she-lion or lioness, and a large deer ; **and, though the deer** is naturally **a very nimble** creature, and she flew by us like the wind, having, perhaps, about three hundred **yards the start of** the lion, yet we found the lion, **by her** strength, and the goodness of **her** lungs, got ground **of her.** They passed by us within about a quarter of a mile, and we had a view of them a great way, when, having given them over, we were surprised, about an hour after, to see them **come** thundering back again on the other side of us, and then the lion was within thirty or forty yards of her ; and both straining to the extremity of their speed, when the deer, coming to the lake, plunged into the water, and swam for her life, as she had before run **for it.**

The lioness plunged in after her, and swam a little way, but came back again ; and, when she was got upon the land, she set up the most hideous roar that ever **I heard in my life,** as if **done in the rage of** having lost her prey.

We **walked** out morning and evening constantly ; the middle of the day we refreshed ourselves **under our** tent : **but** one morning early we saw another chase, which more nearly concerned us **than** the other ; for our **black prince, walking by the** side of **the** lake, was set upon by a vast great crocodile, which came out of the lake upon him ; and though he was very light of foot, yet it **was** as much as he could do to get away : he fled amain to us, and the truth is we did not know **what to** do, for we **were** told no bullet would enter her ; and we found it **so** at first, for though three **of** our men fired at her, yet she did **not** mind them ; **but** my friend the gunner, a **venturous** fellow, of a bold heart and great presence of mind, went up so near as to thrust the muzzle of his piece into her mouth, and fired, but let his piece fall, and ran for it the very moment he had fired it : the creature raged a great while, and spent its fury upon the gun, making marks upon the very iron with her teeth, but after some time fainted and died.

Our negroes spread the banks of the lake all this while for game, and at length killed us three deer, **one** of them very large, the **other** two very small. There was water-fowl also in the lake, but we never **came** near enough to them to shoot any ; and, as for **the** desert, we saw **no** fowls anywhere in it, but at **the lake.**

We likewise killed two **or** three civet cats ; but their flesh is the worst of carrion.   We saw abundance of elephants at a distance, and observed they always go in very good company, that is to say, abundance of them together, and always extended in a fair line of battle ; and this, they say, is the way they defend themselves from their enemies ; for, if lions or tigers, wolves, or any creatures, attack them, they being drawn up in a line, sometimes reaching five or six miles in length, whatever comes in their way is sure to be trod under foot, or beaten in pieces with their trunks, or lifted up in the air with their trunks: so that if a hundred lions or tigers were coming along, if they meet a line of elephants, they will always fly back till they see room to pass by to the right hand or to the left; and if they did not, it would be impossible for one of them to escape; for the elephant, though a heavy creature, is yet so dexterous and nimble with his trunk that he will not fail to lift up the heaviest lion, or any other wild creature, and throw him up in the air quite over his back, and then trample him to death with his feet. We saw several lines of battle thus; we saw one so long, that indeed there was no end of it to be seen, and, I believe, there might be two thousand elephants in a row or line. They are not beasts of prey, but live upon the herbage of the field, as an ox does; and it is said that though they are so great a creature, yet that a smaller quantity of forage supplies one of them than will suffice a horse.

The numbers of this kind of creature that are in those parts are inconceivable, as may be gathered from the prodigious quantity of teeth, which, as I said, we saw in this vast desert; and indeed we saw a hundred of them to one of any other kinds.

One evening we were **very much** surprised ; we were most **of us** laid down **on our** mats to sleep, when our watch came running in **among** us, being frightened with the sudden roaring of some lions just by **them,** which, **it seems,** they had **not** seen, the **night** being dark, till they were just upon them. There was, as **it** proved, an old lion and **his** whole family, for there was the lioness and three young lions, besides the old king, who was a monstrous great one : one of the young ones, who were good large well-grown ones too, leaped up upon one of our negroes, who stood sentinel, before he saw him, at which he was heartily frightened, cried out, and ran into the tent : our other man, who had **a** gun, had not presence of mind at first to shoot him, but struck him with the but-end of his piece, which made him whine a little, and then growl at him fearfully ; but **the** fellow retired, and, we being all alarmed, three of our men snatched up their guns, ran to the tent door, **where** they saw the great old lion by the fire of his **eyes, and** first fired at him, but, we supposed, missed him, **or at** least did not kill him, for they went all off, but raised a most hideous roar, which, as if they had called for help, brought down a prodigious number of lions, and other furious creatures, we know not what, about them, for we could not see them ; **but** there was a noise, and yelling, **and** howling, and **all sort** of such wilderness music on every side of us, as if **all** the beasts of the desert were assembled **to** devour us.

We asked **our** black prince what we should **do** **with** them. 'Me go,' says he, 'and fright them all.' So he snatches up two or three of the worst of our mats, and, getting one of our men to strike some fire, he hangs the mat up at the end of a pole, and set it on fire, **and it** blazed abroad a good while, at which the creatures all moved off, for we heard them roar, and **make** their bellowing noise at a great distance. 'Well,' says our gunner, 'if **that** will do, we need not burn our mats, which **are our** beds to lay under us, and our tilting to cover us. Let me alone,' says he. So he comes back into our tent, and falls to making some artificial fireworks, and the like; and he gave our sentinels some **to** be ready at hand **u**pon occasion, and particularly he placed a great piece of wildfire upon the same pole that **the** mat had been tied to, and set **it on** fire, and that burnt there so long that all the **wild** creatures left us for that time.

However, we began to be weary of such company, and, to **get** rid of them, we set forward again two days sooner **than** we intended. We found now that, though the **desert** did not end, **nor** could we **see any** appearance of it, yet that **the earth** was pretty full of green stuff, of one sort **or** another, so that our cattle had **no** want; and, secondly, that there were several little rivers which **ran** into the lake, and, so long as the country continued low, **we found** water sufficient, which eased us very much **in our carriage,** and we went **on still** sixteen days more **without yet** coming to any **appearance of better** soil.   After **this** we found the **country rise a little,** and by that we **perceived that the** water **would fail us ;** so, for fear of **the worst, we** filled our bladder bottles with water.   **We found** the country rising gradually thus for three days **con-tinually,** when, on the sudden, we perceived, that though we had mounted up insensibly, yet that **we** were on the top of a very high ridge **of** hills, though not such as at first.

When we came to look down on the other side of the hills, we saw, to the great joy of all our hearts, that the desert was at an end ; that the country was clothed with green, abundance of trees, and a large river ; and we made no doubt but that we should find people and cattle also.   And here, by our gunner's account, who kept our computations, **we** had marched **about** four hundred miles over this dismal place of horror, having been four-and-thirty days a-doing of it, and, consequently, were come about eleven hundred miles of our journey.

We would willingly have descended the hills that night, but it was too late.   The next morning we saw everything more plain, and rested ourselves under the shade of some trees, which were now the most re-freshing things imaginable **to us,** who had been scorched above a month without a tree to cover us. We found the country here very pleasant, especially considering that we came from ; and we killed some deer here also, which we found very frequent under the cover of the woods. Also we killed a creature like a goat, whose flesh was very good to eat, but it was no goat. We found also a great number of fowls, like partridge, but something smaller, and were very tame ; so that we lived here very well, but found no people—at least, none that would be seen—no, not for several days' journey ; and, to allay our joy, we were almost every night disturbed with lions and tigers. Elephants we saw none here.

In three days' march we came to a river, which we saw from the hills, and which we called the Golden river ; and we found it ran northward, which was the first stream we had met with that did so. It ran with a very rapid current, and our gunner, pulling out his map, assured me that this was either the river Nile, or ran into the great lake out of which the river Nile was said to take its beginning ; and he brought out his charts and maps, which, by his instruction, I began to understand very well, and told me he would convince me of it, and indeed he seemed to make it so plain to me that I was of the same opinion.

But I did not enter into the gunner's reason for this inquiry—not in the least—till he went on with it further, and stated it thus : If this is the river Nile, why should we **not** build **some more** canoes, and go down this stream, rather than to expose ourselves to any more deserts and scorching sands, in quest **of** the sea, which, when we **are come to, we** shall **be as** much at a loss **how to get home as** we were at Madagascar.

The argument was good had there been no **objections in the** way, **of a** kind which none of **us were** capable of answering; but, upon the whole, it was an undertaking of such a nature that every one of us thought it impracticable, and **that** upon several accounts; and our surgeon, who was himself a good scholar, and a man of reading, though not acquainted with the business of sailing, opposed it, and some of his reasons, I remember, were such as these: first, the length of the way, which both he and **the** gunner allowed, by the course of the water and turnings of the river, would **be** at least four thousand miles; secondly, the innumerable crocodiles **in** the river, which we should never be able to escape; thirdly, the dreadful deserts **in** the way; and, lastly, the approaching rainy season, **in** which the streams of the Nile would **be** so furious, and rise so high, spreading far and **wide** over all the plain country, that we should never be **able** to know when **we were in the** channel **of** the river and when not, **and** should certainly be **cast** away, overset, **or** run aground so **often** that **it would** be impossible **to** proceed by a **river** so excessively dangerous.

This last reason he made so **plain to** us that we began to be sensible of it ourselves; **so that** we agreed to lay that thought aside, and proceed **in our first** course **westwards towards the sea :** but, as if we had been loath to depart, we continued, by way of refreshing **ourselves, to** loiter two days upon this river, in **which** time our black prince, who delighted much **in** wandering up and down, came one evening, and brought us several little bits of something, he knew not what; but he found it felt heavy, and looked well, and showed it to me, as what he thought was some rarity. I took not much notice of it to him, but stepping out and calling the gunner to me, I showed it to him, and told him what I thought, viz. that it was certainly gold : he agreed with me in that, and also in what followed, that we would take the black prince out with us the next day, and make him show us where he found it; that, if there was any quantity to be found, we would tell our company of it ; but, if there was but little, we would keep counsel, and have **it** to ourselves.

But **we** forgot to engage the prince in the secret, who innocently told so much to all **the** rest, as that they guessed what it was, and came to us to see : when we found it was public, we were more concerned **to** prevent their suspecting that we had any design to conceal it, and openly telling our thoughts of it, we called **our** artificer, who agreed presently that it was gold ; so **I** proposed, that we should all go with the prince to the place where **he** found **it,** and, if any quantity was to be had, we **would lie here** some time, and see what we could **make of it.**

Accordingly, we went every man of us, for **no** man **was** willing to be left behind in a discovery of **such** a **nature.** When we came to the place we found **it was** on the west side of the river, not in the main river, but in another small river or stream which came from the west, and ran into the other at that place. We fell to raking in the sand, and washing it in our hands, and we seldom took up a handful of sand but we washed some little round lumps as big as a pin's head, or sometimes as big as a grape-stone, into our hands, and we found, in **two or** three hours' time, that every one had got some, so we agreed to leave off, and go to dinner.

While we were eating, it came into my thoughts, **that** while we worked at this rate in a thing of such nicety and consequence, it was ten to one if the gold, which was the makebate of the world, did not, first or last, **set** us together **by** the ears, to break our good articles and our understanding one among another, and perhaps cause us to part companies, or worse ; I therefore told them that I was indeed the youngest man of the company, but, as they had always allowed **me** to give my opinion in things, and **had** been some- times pleased to follow my advice, so I had something to propose now which I thought would be for all our advantages, **and** I believed they would all like **it** very **well.** I told them we were in a country where we all knew there was a great deal of gold, and that all **the** world sent ships thither to get it : that we did not indeed **know** where it was, **and** so we might get a great **deal, or** a little, we did not know whether ; but I offered it to them to consider, whether it would not be the best way for us, and to preserve the good harmony and friendship that had been always kept among us, and which was so absolutely necessary to our safety, that what we found should be brought together to one common stock, and be equally divided at last, rather than to run the hazard of any difference which might happen among us, from any one's having found more or less than another. I told them that, **if** we were all upon one bottom, we should all apply ourselves heartily to the work ; and, besides that, we might then set our negroes all to work **for** us, and receive equally the fruit of their labour, and of our own, and being all exactly alike sharers, there could be no just **cause** of quarrel or disgust among us.

They all approved the proposal, and every one jointly swore, and gave their hands to one another, **that** they would not conceal the least grain of gold **from** the rest ; and consented that, if any one or more should be found to conceal any, all that he had

should be taken from **him, and divided** among the
rest ; and one thing more was **added to** it by our
gunner, from considerations equally good and **just,**
that, if **any** one of us, by any play, **bet, game, or**
wager, won any money or gold, or the value **of any,**
from another, during our whole voyage, till our **return**
quite to Portugal, he should be obliged by us all **to**
restore it again, on the penalty of being disarmed, and
turned out of the company, and of having no relief
from us on any account whatsoever. This was to
prevent wagering and playing for money, which our
men were apt to do by several games, though they
had neither cards nor dice.

Having made this wholesome agreement, we went
cheerfully to work, and showed our negroes how to
work for us ; and, working up the stream on both
sides, and **in** the bottom of the **river, we** spent about
three weeks' time dabbling in the water ; by which
time, **as** it lay all in our way, we had been gone about
six miles, and not more ; and still the higher we went,
the more gold we found ; till at last, having passed
by the side of a hill, **we** perceived on a sudden that
the gold stopped, **and** that **there** was not a bit taken
up beyond that place : it presently occurred to my
mind, that it must then be from the side of that little
hill that all the gold we found was worked down.

Upon this we went back to the hill, and fell to
work with that. We found the earth loose, and of a

yellowish loamy colour, and in some places a **white** hard kind **of stone,** which, in describing since **to** some **of** our artists, they tell me was the spar which **is** found **by** ore, and surrounds it in the mine.   However, **if it** had been all gold, we had no instrument to force it out ; so we **passed** that : but scratching into the loose earth with our fingers, we came to a surprising place, where **the** earth, for the quantity of two bushels, I believe, **or** thereabouts, crumbled down with little more than touching it, and apparently showed us that there was a great deal of gold in it.   We took it all carefully up, and, washing it in the water, the loamy earth washed away, and left the gold dust free in our hands ; and that which was more remarkable, was, that when this loose earth was all taken away, and we came to the rock or hard stone, there was **not** one grain of gold more to be found.

At night we came all together to see what we had **got ;** and it appeared we had found, in that day's heap of earth, about fifty pound weight of gold dust, and about thirty-four pound more **in** all the rest of our works in the river.

It was a happy kind of disappointment to us, that we found a full stop put to our work ; for, had the quantity of gold been ever so small, yet, had any at **all** come, I do not know when we should have given over ; for, having rummaged this place, and not finding the least grain of gold in any other place, or in any of the earth there, except **in** that **loose** parcel, we went quite back down the small river **again,** working it over and over again, as long **as we could** find any-thing, how small soever; and we did get six or seven pound more the second time. Then we **went** into the **first** river, and tried it up the stream and down **the** stream, on the one side and on the other. **Up** the **stream we** found nothing, no not a grain; down the stream we found very little, not above the quantity of half an ounce in two miles working; so back we came again to the Golden river, as we justly called it, and worked it up the stream and down the stream twice more apiece, and every time we found some gold, and perhaps might have done so if we had stayed there till this time; but the quantity was at last so small, and the work so much the harder, that we agreed by consent to give it over, lest we should **fatigue** ourselves and our negroes so as to be quite unfit for our journey. When we had brought all our purchase together, we had in the whole three pound and a half of gold to a man, share and share alike, according to such a weight and scale as our ingenious cutler made for us to weigh it by, which he did indeed by guess, but which, as he said, he was sure was rather more than less, and so it proved at last; for it was near two ounces more than weight **in** a pound. Besides this, there was seven or eight pounds' weight left, which we agreed to leave in his hands, to work it into such shapes as we thought fit, to give away to such people as we might yet meet with, from whom we might have occasion to buy provisions, or even to buy friendship, or the like; and particularly we gave a pound to our black prince, which he hammered and worked by his own indefatigable hand, and some tools our artificer lent him, into little round bits, as round almost as beads, though not exact in shape, and, drilling holes through them, put them all upon a string, and wore them about his black neck, and they looked very well there I assure you; but he was many months a-doing it. And thus ended our first golden adventure.

We now began to discover what we had not troubled our heads much about before; and that was, that let the country be good or bad that we were in, we could not travel much farther for a considerable time. We had been now five months and upwards in our journey, and the seasons began to change; and nature told us, that, being in a climate that had a winter as well as a summer, though of a different kind from what our country produced, we were to expect a wet season, and such as we should not be able to travel in, as well by reason of the rain itself, as of the floods which it would occasion wherever we should come; and though we had been no strangers to those wet seasons in the island of Madagascar, yet we had not thought much of them since we began our travels ; for, setting out when the sun was about the solstice, that is, when it was at the greatest northern distance from us, we had found the benefit of it in our travels.   But now it drew near us apace, and we found **it** began **to rain** ; upon which we called another general council, in which we debated our present circumstances, and, in particular, whether we should **go** forward, or seek for a proper place upon the bank **of our** Golden river, which had been so lucky to us, **to fix** our camp for the winter.

Upon the whole, it was resolved to abide where we were ; and it was not the least part of our happiness that we did **so, as** shall appear in its place.

Having resolved upon this, our first measures were to set our negroes to work, to make huts or houses for our habitation ; and **this** they did very dexterously, only that we changed the ground where we had at first intended it, thinking, as indeed it happened, that the river might reach it upon any sudden rain.   Our camp was like a little town, in which **our** huts were in the centre, having one large one in **the** centre of them also, into which all **our** particular lodgings opened ; so that none of us went into our apartments but through a public tent, where we all ate and drank together, and kept our councils **and** society ; and our carpenters made us tables, benches, and stools in abundance, **as** many as **we** could make use **of.**

We had no need of chimneys—it was hot enough without fire ; but yet we found ourselves at last obliged to keep a fire every night upon a particular occasion ; for, though we had in all other respects a very pleasant and agreeable situation, yet we were rather worse troubled with the unwelcome visits of wild beasts here than in the wilderness itself; for, as the deer and other gentle creatures came hither for shelter and food, so the lions, and tigers, and leopards, haunted these places continually for prey.

When first we discovered this, we were so uneasy at it that we thought of removing our situation ; but, after many debates about it, we resolved to fortify ourselves in such a manner as not to be in any danger from it, and this our carpenters undertook, who first palisadoed our camp quite round with long stakes (for we had wood enough), which stakes were not stuck in one by another, like pales, but in an irregular manner—a great multitude of them so placed that they took up near two yards in thickness, some higher, some lower, all sharpened at the top, and about a foot asunder ; so that, had any creature jumped at them, unless he had gone clean over, which it was very hard to do, he would be hung upon twenty or thirty spikes.

The entrance into this had larger stakes than the rest, so placed before one another as to make three or four short turnings, which no four-footed beast bigger than a **dog** could possibly come in at ; and that we might not be attacked by any multitude together, and consequently be alarmed in our sleep, as we **had** been, or be obliged to waste our ammunition, **which we** were very chary of, we kept a great **fire every night** without the entrance of our palisado, having a **hut** for our two sentinels to stand **in** free from the rain, just **within the** entrance, and **right** against the fire.

To maintain this fire we cut a prodigious deal of wood, and piled it up in a heap to dry, and, with the green boughs, made a second covering over our huts, so high and thick that it might cast the rain off from the first, and keep us effectually dry.

We had scarce finished all these works, but the rain came on **so** fierce, and **so** continued, that we had little time to stir abroad for food, except indeed that **our** negroes, who wore no clothes, seemed to **make** nothing of **the** rain, though to us Europeans, in those hot climates, nothing is **more** dangerous.

We continued in **this** posture for four months— that **is, from** the middle of June to the middle of October ; **for,** though the rains went off—at least the greatest violence of them—about the equinox, yet, as the sun **was then** just over our heads, **we** resolved **to** stay awhile till it had passed us **a** little to the southward.

During our encampment here we had several

adventures with the ravenous creatures of that country ; and, had not our fire been always kept burning, I question much whether all our fence, though we strengthened it afterwards with twelve or fourteen rows of stakes or more, would have kept us secure. It was always in the night that we had the disturbance of them, and sometimes they came in such multitudes that we thought all the lions and tigers, and leopards and wolves of Africa, were come together to attack us. One night, being clear moonshine, one of our men being upon the watch, told us he verily believed he saw ten thousand wild creatures, of one sort or another, pass by our little camp ; and as soon as ever they saw the fire they sheered off, but were sure to howl or roar, or whatever it was, when they were past.

The music of their voices was very far from being pleasant to us, and sometimes would be so very disturbing, that we could not sleep for it ; and often our sentinels would call us, that were awake, to come and look at them. It was one windy tempestuous night, after a very rainy day, that we were indeed all called up; for such innumerable numbers of devilish creatures came about us, that our watch really thought they would attack us. They would not come on the side where the fire was ; and though we thought ourselves secure everywhere else, yet we all got up, and took to our arms. The moon was near the full, but the air

full of flying clouds, and **a** strange hurricane of wind, to add to the terror of the night ; when, looking on the back part of our camp, I thought **I saw** a creature within our fortification, and so indeed he was, except his **haunches ; for he** had taken a running leap, I suppose, and with all his might had thrown himself **clear over** our palisadoes, except one strong pile, which **stood** higher than the rest, and which **had** caught hold of him, and by his weight he had hanged himself upon it, the spike of the pile running into his hinder-haunch or thigh, on the inside, and by that he hung growling and biting the wood for rage. I snatched up a lance from one of the negroes that stood just by me, and, running to him, struck it three or four times into him, and despatched him ; being unwilling to shoot, because I had a mind **to** have a volley fired among the rest, which I could see standing without, as thick as a drove of bullocks going to **a** fair. I immediately called our people out, and showed them the object of terror which I had seen, and, without any further consultation, fired a full volley among them, most of our pieces being loaded with three slugs or bullets apiece. It made a horrible clatter among them, and in general they all took to their heels, only that we could observe that some walked off with more gravity and majesty than others, being not so much frightened at the noise **and fire ;** and we could perceive that some were left upon the ground struggling **as for life,** but we **durst not** stir out to see what they were.

Indeed they stood so thick, and were so **near us,** that we could not well miss killing or wounding some of them, and we believed they had certainly the smell of us, and **our** victuals we had been killing; for we had killed **a** deer, and three or four of those creatures like goats, **the** day before; and some of the offal had been thrown out behind our camp; and this, we suppose, drew them so much about **us; but we** avoided it for the future.

Though the creatures fled, yet we heard a frightful roaring all night at the place where they stood, which we supposed was from some that were wounded; **and,** as soon **as** day came, we went out to see what execution we had done, and, indeed, it was a strange sight; there were three tigers and **two** wolves quite killed, besides the creature I had killed within our palisado, which seemed to be of an ill-gendered kind, between a tiger **and** a leopard. Besides this, there **was** a noble old lion alive, but with both his fore-legs broken, so that he could not stir away, and he had almost beat himself to death with struggling all night; and we found that this was the wounded soldier that had **roared so** loud, and given us **so** much disturbance. Our surgeon, looking at him, smiled: 'Now,' says he, 'if I could be sure this lion would be as grateful to me as one of his majesty's ancestors was **to** Androcles, **the** Roman slave, I would certainly **set both** his legs **again, and** cure him." I had not **heard the story of** Androcles, so he told it me at large ; but, **as to the** surgeon, we told him he had no way **to know whether the** lion would **be so or** not, but **to cure him first,** and trust to his honour ; **but he** had **no faith ; so, to** despatch him, and put him **out** of **his** torment, he shot him into the head, and killed him, **for** which we called him the king-killer ever after.

Our negroes found **no** less than five of these ravenous creatures wounded and dropt at a distance from our quarters ; whereof, one was a wolf, one a fine spotted young leopard, and the other were creatures that we knew not what to call them.

We had several more **of** these gentlefolks about after **that,** but no such general rendezvous of them as that **was** any more ; but this ill effect it had to us, that **it** frightened the deer and other creatures from our neighbourhood, of whose company we were much more **desirous,** and which were necessary for our subsistence : however, our negroes went out every day a-hunting, as they **called** it, **with** bow and arrow, and they **scarce ever** failed of bringing us home something or other ; **and** particularly we found in this part **of** the country, after the rains had fallen some time, abundance of wildfowl, such as we have in England ; **duck,** teal, widgeon, etc., some geese, and some kinds that we had never seen before, and we frequently killed them. Also we caught a great deal of fresh fish out of the river, so that we wanted no provision ; if we wanted anything, it was salt to eat with our fresh meat, but we had a little left, and we used it sparingly ; for as to our negroes they could not taste it, nor did they care to eat any meat that was seasoned with it.

The weather began now to clear up, the rains were down, and the floods abated, and the sun, which had passed our zenith, was gone to the southward a good way, so we proceeded on our way.

It was the 12th of October, or thereabouts, that we began to set forward ; and, having an easy country to travel in, as well as to supply us with provisions, though still without inhabitants, we made more despatch, travelling sometimes, as we calculated it, twenty or twenty-five miles a day ; nor did we halt anywhere in eleven days' march, one day excepted, which was to make a raft to carry us over a small river, which, having been swelled with the rains, was not yet quite down.

When we were past this river, which by the way ran to the northward too, we found a great row of hills in our way : we saw indeed the country open to the right at a great distance ; but, as we kept true to our course due west, we were not willing to go a great way out of our way only to shun a few hills ; so we advanced ; but we were surprised, when, being not quite come to the top, one of our company, who, with two negroes, was got up before us, cried out, ' The Sea ! the Sea !' and fell a dancing and jumping, as signs of joy.

The gunner and I were most surprised at it, because we had but that morning been calculating that we were then above a thousand miles from the sea-side, and that we could not expect to reach it till another rainy season would be upon us, so that, when our man cried out, ' The Sea,' the gunner was angry, and said he was mad.

But we were both in the greatest surprise imaginable, when, coming to the top of the hill, and, though it was very high, we saw nothing but water, either before us, or to the right hand or the left, being a vast sea, without any bound but the horizon.

He went down the hill full of confusion of thought, not being able to conceive whereabouts we were, or what it must be, seeing by all our charts the sea was yet a vast way off.

It was not above three miles from the hill before we came to the shore, or water-edge of this sea, and there, to our further surprise, we found the water fresh and pleasant to drink ; so that, in short, we knew not what course to take : the sea, as we thought it to be, put a full stop to our journey (I mean westward), for it lay just in the way. Our next question was, which hand to turn to, to the right or the left? but this was soon resolved; for, as we knew not the extent of it, we considered that our way, if it had been the sea really, must be to the north; and, therefore, if we went to the south now, it must be just so much out of our way at last. So, having spent a good part of the day in our surprise at the thing, and consulting what to do, we set forward to the north.

We travelled upon the shore of this sea full twenty-three days before we could come to any resolution about what it was: at the end of which, early one morning, one of our seamen cried out, 'Land!' and it was no false alarm, for we saw plainly the tops of some hills at a very great distance, on the further side of the water, due west; but though this satisfied us that it was not the ocean, but an inland sea or lake, yet we saw no land to the northward, that is to say, no end of it; but were obliged to travel eight days more, and near a hundred miles farther, before we came to the end of it, and then we found this lake or sea ended in a very great river, which ran N. or N. by E., as the other river had done, which I mentioned before.

My friend the gunner, upon examining, said, that he believed that he was mistaken before, and that this was the river Nile, but was still of the mind that we were of before, that we should not think of a voyage into Egypt that way; so we resolved upon crossing this river, which, however, was not so easy as before, the river being **very** rapid, **and** the channel very broad.

It cost us, therefore, **a** week here to get materials **to waft** ourselves and cattle over this **river**; for though here were store of trees, yet there was **none of any** considerable growth, sufficient to make a **canoe.**

During **our** march **on** the edge of this bank **we** met with great fatigue, and therefore travelled fewer miles **in** a day than before, there being such a pro-digious number of little rivers that came down from the hills on the east side, emptying themselves into this gulf, all which waters were pretty high, the rains having been but newly over.

In the last three days of our travel we met with some inhabitants, but we found they lived upon the little hills, and not by the water-side; nor were we a **little put to it for food** in this march, having killed **nothing** for four or five days, but some fish we caught **out of** the lake, **and** that not in such plenty as **we** found **before.**

But, **to** make us some amends, we had no disturb-ance upon all the shore **of this** lake from any wild beasts; **the** only inconveniency of that kind was, that we met an ugly, venomous, deformed **kind** of a snake or serpent in the wet grounds near the lake, that several times pursued us, as if it would attack us;

and, if we struck, or threw anything at it, it would raise itself up, and hiss so loud that it might be heard a great way off; it had a hellish ugly deformed look and voice, and our men would not be persuaded but it was the devil, only that we did not know what business Satan could have there, where there were no people.

It was very remarkable that we had now travelled a thousand miles without meeting with any people, in the heart of the whole continent of Africa, where, to be sure, never man set his foot since the sons of Noah spread themselves over the face of the whole earth. Here also our gunner took an observation with his forestaff, to determine our latitude, and he found now, that, having marched about thirty-three days northward, we were in 6 degrees 22 minutes south latitude.

After having, with great difficulty, got over this river, we came into a strange wild country, that began a little to affright us; for though the country was not a desert of dry scalding sand, as that was we had passed before, yet it was mountainous, barren, and infinitely full of most furious wild beasts, more than any place we had past yet. There was indeed a kind of coarse herbage on the surface, and now and then a few trees or rather shrubs; but people we could see none, and we began to be in great suspense about victuals; for we had not killed a deer a great while, but had lived chiefly upon fish and fowl, always by the water-side, both which **seemed to** fail us now ; and we **were** in the more consternation, because we could not **lay in a stock** here to proceed **upon, as we** did **before, but were** obliged to set out with scarcity, **and** without any certainty of a supply.

We had, however, **no** remedy but patience ; and, having killed some fowls, and dried some fish, **as** much as, with short allowance, we reckoned would last us five days, we resolved to venture, and venture we did ; nor was it without cause that we were apprehensive of the danger, for we travelled the five days and met with neither fish, nor fowl, nor four-footed beast whose flesh was fit to eat ; and we were in a most dreadful apprehension of being famished to death ; on the sixth day we almost fasted, or, as we may say, we ate up all the scraps of what we had left, and at night lay down supperless upon our mats with heavy hearts, being obliged, the eighth day, to kill one of our poor faithful servants, the buffaloes, that carried our baggage ; the flesh of this creature was very good, and so sparingly did we eat of it that it lasted us all three days and a half, and was just spent, and we were upon the point of killing another, when we saw before us a country that promised better, having high trees and a large river in the middle of it.

This encouraged us, and we quickened our march for the river side, though with empty stomachs, and very faint and weak; but, before we came to this river, we had the good hap to meet with some young deer, a thing we had long wished for. In a word, having shot three of them, we came to a full stop to fill our bellies, and never gave the flesh time to cool before we ate it; nay, it was much we could stay to kill it, and had not eaten it alive, for we were, in short, almost famished.

Through all that inhospitable country we saw continually lions, tigers, leopards, civet cats, and abundance of kinds of creatures that we did not understand; we saw no elephants, but every now and then we met with an elephant's tooth lying on the ground, and some of them lying, as it were half buried, by the length of time that they had lain there.

When we came to the shore of this river we found it ran northerly still, as all the rest had done, but with this difference, that, as the course of the other rivers were N. by E. or N.N.E., the course of this lay N.N.W.

On the farther bank of this river we saw some sign of inhabitants, but met with none for the first day; but the next day we came into an inhabited country, the people all negroes, and stark naked, without shame, both men and women.

We made signs of friendship to them, and found them a very frank, civil, and friendly sort of people. They came to our negroes without any suspicion, nor did they give us any reason **to suspect** them of any villainy, as the others had done ; we made signs to them that we were hungry, and immediately some naked women **ran** and fetched us great quantities of roots, **and of** things like pumpkins, which **we** made **no scruple to** eat ; and our artificer showed them **some of** his trinkets that he had made, some of iron, **some of** silver, but none **of** gold : they had so much judgment as to choose those of silver before the iron ; but when we showed them some gold we found they did not value it so much as either of the other.

For some of these things they brought us more provisions, and three living creatures as big as calves, but not of that kind ; neither did we ever see any of them before ; their flesh was very good ; and after **that** they brought us twelve more, and some smaller creatures, like hares ; all which were very welcome **to us,** who were indeed at a very great loss for provisions.

We grew very intimate with these people, and indeed they were the civillest and most friendly people that we met with at all, and mightily pleased with us ; and, which was very particular, they were much easier to be made to understand our meaning than any we had met with before.

At last we began to inquire our way, pointing to **the** west : they made us understand easily that we could not go **that** way, but they pointed to us that we might go north-west, so that we presently understood that there was another lake in our way, which proved to be true; for in two days more we saw it plain, and it held us till we passed the equinoctial line, lying all the way on our left hand, though at a great distance.

Travelling thus northward, our gunner seemed very anxious about our proceedings; for he assured us, and made me sensible of it by the maps which he had been teaching me out of, that when we came into the latitude of six degrees, or thereabouts, north of the line, the land trenched away to the west, to such a length, that we should not come at the sea under a march of above fifteen hundred miles farther westward than the country we desired to go to. I asked him if there were no navigable rivers that we might meet with, which, running into the west ocean, might perhaps carry us down their stream, and then, if it were fifteen hundred miles, or twice fifteen hundred miles, we might do well enough, if we could but get provisions.

Here he showed me the maps again, and that there appeared no river whose stream was of such a length as to do any kindness, till we came perhaps within two or three hundred miles of the shore, except the Rio Grand, as they call it, which lay farther northward from us, at least seven hundred miles; and that then he knew not what kind of country it might carry us through; for he said it was his opinion that the heats on the north of the line, even in the same latitude, were violent, and the country more desolate, barren, and barbarous than those of the south; and that, when we came among the negroes in the north part of Africa, next the sea, especially those who had seen and trafficked with the Europeans, such as Dutch, English, Portuguese, Spaniards, etc., they had most of them been so ill-used at some time or other that they would certainly put all the spite they could upon us in mere revenge.

Upon these considerations, he advised us that, as soon as we had passed this lake, we should proceed W.S.W., that is to say a little inclining to the south, and that in time we should meet with the great river Congo, from whence the coast is called Congo, being a little north of Angola, where we intended at first to go.

I asked him if ever he had been on the coast of Congo? He said, Yes, he had, but was never on shore there. Then I asked him how we should get from thence to the coast where the European ships came, seeing, if the land trenched away west for fifteen hundred miles, we must have all that shore to traverse before we could double the west point of it?

He told me it was ten to one but we should hear of some European ships to take us in, for that they often visited the coast of Congo and Angola, in trade with the negroes ; and that if we could not, yet, if we could but find provisions, we should make our way as well along the seashore as along the river, till we came to the gold coast, which, he said, was not above four or five hundred miles north of Congo, besides the turning of the coast west about three hundred more, that shore being in the latitude of 6 or 7 degrees ; and that there the English, or Dutch, or French, had settlements or factories, perhaps all of them.

I confess I had more mind, all the while he argued, to have gone northward, and shipped ourselves in the Rio Grand, or, as the traders call it, the river Negro, or Niger, for I knew that at last it would bring us down to the Cape de Verd, where we were sure of relief ; whereas at the coast we were going to now we had a prodigious way still to go, either by sea or land, and no certainty which way to get provisions but by force ; but for the present I held my tongue, because it was my tutor's opinion.

But when, according to his desire, we came to turn southward, having passed beyond the second great lake, our men began all to be uneasy, and said we were now out of our way for certain, for that we were going farther from home, and that we were indeed far enough off already.

But we had not marched above twelve days more, eight whereof was taken up in rounding the lake, and four more south-west, in **order** to make for the river Congo, but we **were put to another** full **stop by** entering a country **so** desolate, so frightful, **and so** wild, that we **knew not what to think or do** ; for, besides that it appeared as a terrible and boundless desert, having **neither** woods, trees, rivers, nor inhabitants, so even the place where we **were was** desolate of inhabitants, **nor had** we any way to gather in a stock **of** provisions for the passing of this desert, as we did before at **our entering** the first, unless we had marched **back four days** to the place where we turned the head **of the lake.**

Well, notwithstanding this, we ventured ; for, to men that had passed such wild places as we had done, nothing could seem too desperate **to** undertake : we ventured, I say, and the rather because we **saw** very high mountains in our way at a great distance, and we imagined wherever there were mountains there would be springs and rivers ; where rivers there **would be trees and** grass; where trees and grass there would be cattle ; and where cattle some kind **of** inhabitants.

At last, in consequence of this speculative philosophy, we entered this waste, having a great heap of roots and plants for our bread, such as the Indians gave us, **a very little flesh, or** salt, and but a little water.

We travelled two days towards those hills, and still

they seemed as far off as they did at first, and it was the fifth day before we got to them; indeed, we travelled softly, for it was excessively hot, and we were much about the very equinoctial line— we hardly knew whether to the south or the north of it.

As we had concluded, that where there were hills there would be springs, so it happened; but we were not only surprised, but really frightened, to find the first spring we came to, and which looked admirably clear and beautiful, to be salt as brine. It was a terrible disappointment to us, and put us under melancholy apprehensions at first; but the gunner, who was of a spirit never discouraged, told us we should not be disturbed at that, but be very thankful, for salt was a bait we stood in as much need of as anything, and there was no question but we should find fresh water as well as salt; and here our surgeon stept in to encourage us, and told us that, if we did not know, he would show us a way how to make that salt water fresh, which indeed made us all more cheerful, though we wondered what he meant.

Meantime our men, without bidding, had been seeking about for other springs, and found several; but still they were all salt; from whence we concluded that there was a salt rock or mineral stone in those mountains, and perhaps they might be all of such a substance; but still I wondered by what witchcraft it was that our artist, the surgeon, would make this salt water turn fresh ; and I longed to see the experiment, which was indeed a very odd one ; but he went to work with as much assurance as if he had tried it on the very spot before.

He took two of our large mats, and sewed them together ; and they made a kind of a bag four feet broad, three feet and a half high, and about a foot and a half thick when it was full.

He caused us to fill this bag with dry sand, and tread it down as close as we could, not to burst the mats.   When thus the bag was full within a foot, he sought some other earth, and filled up the rest with it, and still trod all in as hard as he could.   When he had done, he made a hole in the upper earth, about as broad as the crown of a large hat, or something bigger, but not so deep, and bade a negro fill it with water, and still, as it shrunk away, to fill it again, and keep it full.   The bag he had placed at first across two pieces of wood, about a foot from the ground ; and under it he ordered some of our skins to be spread, that would hold water.   In about an hour, and not sooner, the water began to come dropping through the bottom of the bag, and, to our great surprise, was perfectly fresh and sweet ; and this continued for several hours : but in the end the water began to be a little brackish.   When we told him that, ' Well then,' said he, ' turn the sand out and fill it again.' Whether he did this by way of experiment from his own fancy, or whether he had seen it done before, I do not remember.

The next day we mounted the tops of the hills, where the prospect was indeed astonishing; for, as far as the eye could look, south, or west, or north-west, there was nothing to be seen but a vast howling wilderness, with neither tree nor river, nor any green thing. The surface we found, as the part we passed the day before, had a kind of thick moss upon it, of a blackish dead colour, but nothing in it that looked like food, either for man or beast.

Had we been stored with provisions to have entered for ten or twenty days upon this wilderness, as we were formerly, and with fresh water, we had hearts good enough to have ventured, though we had been obliged to come back again; for, if we went north, we did not know but we might meet with the same; but we neither had provisions, neither were we in any place where it was possible to get them. We killed some wild ferine creatures at the foot of these hills: but, except two things, like to nothing that we ever saw before, we met with nothing that was fit to eat. These were creatures that seemed to be between a kind of buffalo and a deer, but indeed resembled neither; for they had no horns, and had great legs like a cow, with a fine head, and the neck like a deer. We killed also, at several times, a tiger, two young lions, and a wolf : but God be thanked, we were not so reduced as to eat carrion.

Upon this terrible prospect I renewed my motion of turning northward, and, making towards the river Niger or Rio Grand, then to turn west towards the English settlements on the gold coast, to which every one most readily consented, only our gunner, who was indeed our best guide, though he happened to be mistaken at this time. He moved that, as our coast was now northward, so we might slant away north-west, that so, by crossing the country, we might perhaps meet with some other river that ran into the Rio Grand northward, or down to the gold coast southward, and so both direct our way and shorten the labour ; as also, because, if any of the country was inhabited and fruitful, we should probably find it upon the shore of the rivers, where alone we could be furnished with provisions.

This was good advice, and too rational not to be taken ; but our present business was what to do to get out of this dreadful place we were in. Behind us was a waste, which had already cost us five days' march, and we had not provisions for five days left to go back again the same way. Before us was nothing but horror, as above : so we resolved, seeing the ridge of the hills we were upon had some appearance of fruitfulness, and that they seemed to lead away to the northward a great way, to keep under the foot of them on the east side, to go on as far as we could, and in the meantime to look diligently **out** for food.

Accordingly, we moved on the next morning, for we had no time to lose ; and to our great comfort **we** came, in our first morning's march, to very good springs **of** fresh water ; and, lest we should have a scarcity again, we filled all our bladder-bottles, and carried it with us. · I should also have observed that our surgeon, who made the **salt water** fresh, took the opportunity of those salt springs, and made us the quantity of three or four pecks of very good **salt.**

In our third march we found an unexpected supply of food, the hills being full of hares ; they were of a kind something different from ours in England, larger, and not so swift of foot, but very good meat. We shot several of them, and the little tame leopard, which I told you we took at the negro town that we plundered, hunted them like a dog, and killed us several every day ; but she would eat nothing of them unless we gave it her, which indeed in our own circumstances was very obliging. We salted them **a** little, and dried them in the sun whole, and carried a strange parcel along with us. I think it was almost three hundred ; for we did not know when we might **find** any more, either of these, or any other food. We continued our course under these hills very comfortably eight or nine days, when we found, to our great satisfaction, the country beyond us began to look with something of a better countenance. As for the west side of the hills, we never examined it till this day, when three of our company, the rest halting for refreshment, mounted the hills again to satisfy their curiosity, but found it all the same; nor could they see any end of it, not even to the north, the way we were going; so the tenth day, finding the hills made a turn, and led, as it were, into the vast desert, we left them, and continued our course north, the country being very tolerably full of woods, some waste, but not tediously long, till we came, by our gunner's observation, into the latitude of 8 degrees 5 minutes, which we were nineteen days in performing.

All this way we found no inhabitants, but abundance of wild ravenous creatures, with which we became so well acquainted now, that really we did not much mind them. We saw lions, and tigers, and leopards, every night and morning in abundance; but, as they seldom came near us, we let them go about their business; if they offered to come near us we made false fire with any gun that was uncharged, and they would walk off as soon as they saw the flash.

We made pretty good shift for food all this way; for sometimes we killed hares, sometimes some fowls, but for my life I cannot give names to any of them, except a kind of partridge, and another that was like our turtle. Now and then we began to **meet** with elephants again **in** great **numbers**; those creatures delighted chiefly in the woody part **of** the country.

This long-continued march fatigued **us very** much, and two of **our** men fell sick, indeed so very sick that we thought they would have died; and one of our negroes died suddenly. Our surgeon said it was an apoplexy, but he wondered at it, he said, for he could never complain of his high feeding. Another of them was very ill, but our surgeon with much ado persuading him, indeed it was almost forcing him, to be **bled,** he recovered.

We halted **here** twelve days for the **sake** of our sick men, and **our** surgeon persuaded **me,** and three **or** four more of **us,** to be bled during the time of rest, which, with other things he gave us, contributed very much to our continued health, in so tedious a march and in so hot a climate.

In this march we pitched our matted tents every night, and they were very comfortable to us, though we had trees and woods to shelter us also in most places. **We** thought it very strange that in all this part of the country we yet met with no inhabitants; but the principal reason, as we found afterwards, was, that we, having kept a western course first, and then a northern course, were gotten too much into the middle of the country, and among the deserts: whereas the inhabitants are principally found among the rivers, lakes, and lowlands, as well to the south-west as to the north.

What little rivulets we found here were so empty of water, that, except some pits, and little more than ordinary pools, there was scarce any water to be seen in them ; and they rather showed that, during the rainy months, they had a channel, than that they had really any running water in them at that time : by which it was easy for us to judge that we had a great way to go ; but this was no discouragement so long as we had but provisions, and some reasonable shelter from the violent heat, which indeed I thought was greater now than when the sun was just over our heads.

Our men being recovered, we set forward again, very well stored with provisions, and water sufficient, and, bending our course a little to the westward of the north, travelled in hopes of some favourable stream which might bear a canoe ; but we found none till after twenty days' travel, including eight days' rest ; for our men being weak, we rested very often, especially when we came to places which were proper for our purposes, where we found cattle, fowl, or anything to kill for food. In those twenty days' march we advanced four degrees to the northward, besides some meridian distance westward, and we met with abundance of elephants' teeth scattered up and down, here and there, in the woody grounds

especially, **some of** which were very large.   **But** they
were no booty to us ; our business was provisions,
and a good passage out of the country ; **and it** had
been much more to our purpose to have found **a**
good fat deer, and to have killed it for our food, than
a hundred ton of elephants' teeth ; and yet, as you
shall presently hear, when we came to begin our passage by water, we once thought to have built a large
canoe, on purpose to have loaded it with ivory ; but
this was when we knew nothing of the rivers, nor
knew anything how dangerous and how difficult a
passage it was that we were likely to have in them,
nor had considered the weight of carriage to lug them
to the rivers where we might embark.

At the end of twenty days' travels, as above, in
the latitude of 3 degrees 16 minutes, we discovered
in a valley, at some distance from us, a pretty tolerable stream, which we thought deserved the name of
a river, and which ran its course N.N.W., which was
just what we wanted.   As we had fixed our thoughts
upon our passage by water, we took this for the place
to make our experiment, and bent our march directly
to the valley.

There was a small thicket of trees just in our way,
which we went by, thinking no harm, when on a
sudden one of **our** negroes **was** very dangerously
wounded with an arrow, shot into his back, slanting
between his shoulders.   This put us to a full stop ;

and three of our men, with two negroes, spreading the wood, for it was but a small one, found a negro with a bow, but no arrow, who would have escaped, but our men that discovered him shot him in revenge of the mischief he had done; so we lost the opportunity of taking him prisoner, which, if we had done, and sent him home with good usage, it might have brought others to us in a friendly manner.

Going a little farther, we came to five negro huts or houses, built after a different manner from any we had seen yet; and at the door of one of them lay seven elephants' teeth, piled up against the wall or side of the hut, as if they had been provided against a market: here were no men, but seven or eight women, and near twenty children: we offered them no uncivility of any kind, but gave them every one a bit of silver beaten out thin, as I observed before, and cut diamond-fashion, or in the shape of a bird; at which the women were overjoyed, and brought out to us several sorts of food, which we did not understand, being cakes of a meal made of roots, which they bake in the sun, and which eat very well. We went a little way farther, and pitched our camp for that night, not doubting but our civility to the women would produce some good effect when their husbands might come home.

Accordingly, the next morning, the women, with eleven men, five young boys, and two good big girls, came to our camp ; before they came quite to us the women called aloud, and made an odd screaming noise, to bring us out; and, accordingly, we came out ; when two of the women, showing us what we had given them, and pointing to the company behind, made such signs as we could easily understand signified friendship. When the men advanced, having bows and arrows, they laid them down on the ground, scraped, and threw sand over their heads, and turned round three times, with their hands laid up upon the tops of their heads. This, it seems, was a solemn vow of friendship. Upon this we beckoned them with our hands to come nearer ; then they sent the boys and girls to us first, which, it seems, was to bring us more cakes of bread, and some green herbs, to eat, which we received, and took the boys up and kissed them, and the little girls too ; then the men came up close to us, and sat them down on the ground, making signs that we should sit down by them, which we did. They said much to one another, but we could not understand them, nor could we find any way to make them understand us ; much less whither we were going, or what we wanted, only that we easily made them understand we wanted victuals : whereupon one of the men casting his eyes about him towards a rising ground that was about half a mile off, started up as if he was frightened, flew to the place where they had laid down their bows and

arrows, snatched up a bow and two arrows, and ran
like a racehorse to the place : when he came there,
he let fly both his arrows, and came back again to us
with the same speed ; we seeing he came with the
bow, but without the arrows, were the more inquisitive,
but the fellow saying nothing to us, beckons to one
of our negroes to come to him, and we bid him go ;
so he led him back to the place, where lay a kind of
a deer, shot with two arrows, but not quite dead ;
and between them they brought it down to us.   This
was for a gift to us, and was very welcome, I assure
you, for our stock was low.   These people were all
stark naked.

The next day there came about a hundred men
and women to us, making the same awkward signals
of friendship, and dancing, and showing themselves
very well pleased, and anything they had they gave
us.   How the man in the wood came to be so
butcherly and rude as to shoot at our men, without
making any breach first, we could not imagine ; for
the people were simple, plain, and inoffensive in all
our other conversation with them.

From hence we went down the bank of the little
river I mentioned, and where I found we should see
whole nations of negroes ; but whether friendly to
us or not, that we could make no judgment of yet.

The river was of no use to us, as to the design of
making canoes, a great while ; and we traversed the

country on the edge of it about five days more, when our carpenters, finding the stream increase, proposed to pitch our tents and fall to work to make canoes ; but after we had begun the work, and cut down two or three trees, and spent five days in the labour, some of our men, wandering farther down the river, brought us word that the stream rather decreased than increased, sinking away into the sands, or drying up by the heat of the sun ; so that the river appeared not able to carry the least canoe that could be any way useful to us : so we were obliged to give over our enterprise and move on.

In our farther prospect this way we marched three days full west, the country on the north side being extraordinary mountainous, and more parched and dry than any we had seen yet ; whereas, in the part which looks due west, we found a pleasant valley, running a great way between two great ridges of mountains. The hills looked frightful, being entirely bare of trees or grass, and even white with the dryness of the sand ; but in the valley we had trees, grass, and some creatures that were fit for food, and some inhabitants.

We passed by some of their huts or houses, and saw people about them ; but they ran up into the hills as soon as they saw us. At the end of this valley we met with a peopled country, and at first it put us to some doubt whether we should go among them or keep up towards the hills northerly; and as our aim was principally, as before, to make our way to the river Niger, we inclined to the latter, pursuing our course by the compass to the N.W. We marched thus without interruption seven days more, when we met with a surprising circumstance, much more desolate and disconsolate than our own, and which, in time to come, will scarce seem credible.

We did not much seek the conversing, or acquainting ourselves with the natives of the country, except where we found the want of them for our provision, or their direction for our way; so that, whereas we found the country here begin to be very populous, especially towards our left hand—that is, to the south—we kept at the more distance northerly, still stretching towards the west.

In this tract we found something or other to kill and eat, which always supplied our necessity, though not so well as we were provided in our first setting out. Being thus, as it were, pushing to avoid the peopled country, we at last came to a very pleasant, agreeable stream of water, not big enough to be called a river, but running to the N.N.W., which was the very course we desired to go.

On the farthest bank of this brook we perceived some huts of negroes, not many, and in a little low spot of ground, some maize, or Indian corn, growing, which intimated presently to us, that there were some inhabitants on that side, less barbarous than those we had met with in other places **where we had been.**

As we went forward, our whole **caravan being in** a body, our negroes, who **were in** the front, **cried out** that they saw **a white man!** We were not much surprised **at first,** it being, as we thought, a mistake of the **fellows,** and asked them what they meant, when one **of** them stept up to me, **and,** pointing **to** a hut **on** the other side of the hill, I was astonished to **see a** white man indeed, **but** stark naked, **very** busy near the door of his hut, and stooping down **to** the ground with something in his hand, **as if he had** been at some work, and, his back **being towards us,** he did not see us.

I gave notice to our negroes to make no **noise,** and waited till some more of our men were come **up,** **to** show the sight to them, that they might be sure **I** was not mistaken, and we were soon satisfied of the truth ; for the man, having heard some noise, started up, and looked full at us, as much surprised, to be sure, as we were, but whether with fear or hope we then knew not.

As he discovered us, so did the rest **of** the inhabitants belonging to the huts about him, and all crowded together, looking at us at a distance : a little bottom, in which **the** brook ran, lying between **us, the** white man, and **all** the rest, as he told us afterwards, not knowing well whether they should stay or run away. However, it presently came into my thoughts that, if there were white men among them, it would be much easier for us to make them understand what we meant, as to peace or war, than we found it with others; so, tying a piece of white rag to the end of a stick, we sent two negroes with it to the bank of the water, carrying the pole up as high as they could. It was presently understood, and two of their men and the white man came to the shore on the other side.

However, as the white man spoke no Portuguese, they could understand nothing of one another but by signs ; but our men made the white man understand that they had white men with them too, at which they said the white man laughed. However, to be short, our men came back, and told us they were all good friends, and in about an hour four of our men, two negroes, and the black prince went to the river side, where the white man came to them.

They had not been half a quarter of an hour there, till a negro came running to me, and told me the white man was Inglese, as he called him : upon which I ran back, eagerly enough you may be sure, with him, and found, as he said, that he was an Englishman, upon which he embraced me very passionately, the tears running down his face. The first surprise of his seeing us was over before we came ; but any one may conceive it by the brief account he gave us afterwards of his very unhappy circumstance, and of so unexpected a deliverance, such as perhaps never happened to any man in the world; for it was a million to one odds that ever he could have been relieved—nothing but an adventure that never was heard or read of before could have suited his case, unless heaven, by some miracle that never was to be expected, had acted for him.

He appeared to be a gentleman, not an ordinary-bred fellow, seaman, or labouring man; this showed itself in his behaviour, in the first moment of our conversing with him, and in spite of all the disadvantages of his miserable circumstances.

He was a middle-aged man, not above thirty-seven or thirty-eight, though his beard was grown exceedingly long, and the hair of his head and face strangely covered him to the middle of his back and breast; he was white, and his skin very fine, though discoloured, and in some places blistered, and covered with a brown blackish substance, scurvy, scaly, and hard, which was the effect of the scorching heat of the sun; he was stark naked, and had been so, as he told us, upwards of two years.

He was so exceedingly transported at our meeting with him that he could scarce enter into any discourse at all with us for that day; and, when he could get away from us for a little, we saw him walking alone, and showing all the most extravagant tokens of an ungovernable joy; and even afterwards he was never without tears in his eyes for several days, upon the least word spoken by us of his circumstances, or by him of his deliverance.

We found his behaviour the most courteous and endearing I ever saw in any man whatever, and most evident tokens of a mannerly well-bred person appeared in all things he did or said; and our people were exceedingly taken with him. He was a scholar and a mathematician; he could not speak Portuguese indeed, but he spoke Latin to our surgeon, French to another of our men, and Italian to a third.

He had no leisure in his thoughts to ask us whence we came, whither we were going, or who we were; but would have it always as an answer to himself, that to be sure, wherever we were a-going, we came from heaven, and were sent on purpose to save him from the most wretched condition that ever man was reduced to.

Our men pitching their camp on the bank of a little river opposite to him, he began to inquire what store of provisions we had, and how we proposed to be supplied; when he found that our store was but small, he said he would talk with the natives, and we should have provisions enough; for he said they were the most courteous, good-natured part of the inhabitants in all that part of the country, as we might suppose by his living so safe among them.

The first things this gentleman did for us were indeed of the greatest consequence to us ; for, first, he perfectly informed us where we were, and which was the properest course for us to steer : secondly, he put us in a way how to furnish ourselves effectually with provisions ; and, thirdly, he was our complete interpreter and peace-maker with all the natives, who now began to be very numerous about us ; and who were a more fierce and politic people than those we had met with before ; not so easily terrified with our arms as those, and not so ignorant as to give their provisions and corn for our little toys, such, as I said before, our artificer made ; but, as they had frequently traded and conversed with the Europeans on the coast, or with other negro nations that had traded and been concerned with them, they were the less ignorant and the less fearful, and consequently nothing was to be had from them but by exchange for such things as they liked.

This I say of the negro natives, which we soon came among ; but as to these poor people that he lived among, they were not much acquainted with things, being at the distance of above three hundred miles from the coast, only that they found elephants' teeth upon the hills to the north, which they took and carried about sixty or seventy miles south, where other trading negroes usually met them, and gave them beads, glass, shells, and cowries for them, such as the English and Dutch, and other traders, furnish them with from Europe.

We now began to be more familiar with our new acquaintance ; and, first, though we made but a sorry figure as to clothes ourselves, having neither shoe, nor stocking, nor glove, nor hat, among us, and but very few shirts, yet as well as we could we clothed him ; and first, our surgeon having scissors and razors, shaved him, and cut his hair ; a hat, as I say, we had not in all our stores, but he supplied himself by making a cap of a piece of a leopard's skin, most artificially.   As for shoes or stockings, he had gone so long without them that he cared not even for the buskins and foot-gloves we wore, which I described above.

As he had been curious to hear the whole story of our travels, and was exceedingly delighted with the relation, so we were no less to know, and pleased with, the account of his circumstance, and the history of his coming to that strange place alone, and in that condition, which we found him in, as above. This account of his would indeed be, in itself, the subject of an agreeable history, and would be as long and as diverting as our own, having in it many strange and extraordinary incidents, but we cannot have room here to launch out into so long a digression : the sum of his history was this.

He had been **a** factor for the English Guinea
company at Sierra Leone, or some other **of** their
settlements which had been taken by the **French,**
where he had been plundered of all **his own** effects,
as well as **of** what was entrusted **to** him by the
company. Whether it was that the company did
not do **him** justice in restoring his circumstances, or
in further employing him, **he** quitted their service, **and**
was employed by those they called separate traders ;
and being afterwards out of employ there also,
traded on his own account ; when, passing unwarily
into one of the company's settlements, he was either
betrayed into the hands of some of the natives, or,
somehow or other, was surprised by them. However,
as they did not kill him, he found means to escape
from them at that time, and fled to another nation
of the natives, who, being enemies to the other,
entertained him friendly, and with them he lived
some time ; but not liking his quarters or his
company he fled again, and several times changed
his landlords ; sometimes was carried by force,
sometimes hurried by fear, as circumstances altered
with him (the variety of which deserves a history by
itself), till at last he had wandered beyond all
possibility of return, and had taken up his abode
where we found him, where he was well received
by the petty king of the tribe he lived with ; and he,
in **return,** instructed him how to value the product

of their labour, and on what terms to trade with those negroes who came up to them for teeth.

As he was naked, and had no clothes, so he was naked of arms for his defence, having neither gun, sword, staff, nor any instrument of war about him, no not to guard himself against the attacks of a wild beast, of which the country was very full. We asked him how he came to be so entirely abandoned of all concern for his safety? He answered, That to him, that had so often wished for death, life was not worth defending; and that, as he was entirely at the mercy of the negroes, they had much the more confidence in him seeing he had no weapons to hurt them. As for wild beasts he was not much concerned about them; for he had scarcely ever gone from his hut; but if he did, the negro king and his men went all armed with bows and arrows, and lances, with which they would kill any of the ravenous creatures, lions as well as others; but that they seldom came abroad in the day; and if the negroes wander anywhere in the night they always build a hut for themselves, and make a fire at the door of it, which is guard enough.

We inquired of him what we should next do towards getting to the seaside: he told us we were about a hundred and twenty English leagues from the coast, where almost all the European settlements and factories were, and which is called the Gold Coast; but that there were so many different nations of negroes in the way that it was ten to one if we were not either fought with continually, or starved for want of provisions : but that there were two other ways to go, which, if he had had any company to go with him, he had often contrived to make his escape by. The one was to travel full west, which, though it was farther to go, yet was not so full of people ; and the people we should find would be so much the civiller to us, or be so much the easier to fight with ; or, that the other way was, if possible, to get to the Rio Grand, and go down the stream in canoes. We told him that was the way we had resolved on before we met with him ; but then he told us there was a prodigious desert to go over, and as prodigious woods to go through, before we came to it, and that both together were at least twenty days' march for us, travel as hard as we could.

We asked him if there were no horses in the country, or asses, or even bullocks or buffaloes, to make use of in such a journey, and we showed him ours, of which we had but three left ; he said no, all the country did not afford anything of that kind.

He told us that in this great wood there were immense numbers of elephants; and, upon the desert, great multitudes of lions, lynxes, tigers, leopards, etc. ; and that it was to that wood, and to that desert, that the negroes went to get elephants' teeth, where they never failed to find a great number.

We inquired still more, and particularly the way to the gold coast, and if there were no rivers to ease us in our carriage ; and told him as to the negroes fighting with us, we were not much concerned at that ; nor were we afraid of starving, for, if they had any victuals among them we would have our share of it ; and, therefore, if he would venture to show us the way we would venture to go ; and as for himself, we told him we would live and die together, there should not a man of us stir from him.

He told us, with all his heart ; if we resolved it, and would venture, we might be assured he would take his fate with us, and he would endeavour to guide us in such a way as we should meet with some friendly savages who would use us well, and perhaps stand by us against some others, who were less tractable ; so, in a word, we all resolved to go full south for the gold coast.

The next morning he came to us again, and being all met in council, as we may call it, he began to talk very seriously with us ; that, since we were now come, after a long journey, to a view of the end of our troubles, and had been so obliging to him as to offer to carry him with us, he had been all night revolving in his mind what he and we all might do to make ourselves some amends for all our sorrows ; and, first, he said, he was to let me know that we were just then in one of the richest parts of the world, though it was really, otherwise, but a desolate, disconsolate wilderness; 'for,' says he, 'there is not a river but runs gold, not a desert but, without ploughing, bears a crop of ivory. What mines of gold, what immense stores of gold those mountains may contain, from whence these rivers come, or the shores which these waters run by, we know not, but may imagine that they must be inconceivably rich, seeing so much is washed down the stream by the water washing the sides of the land, that the quantity suffices all the traders which the European world send thither.' We asked him how far they went for it, seeing the ships only trade upon the coast. He told us that the negroes on the coast search the rivers up for the length of a hundred and fifty or two hundred miles, and would be out a month, or two or three at a time, and always came home sufficiently rewarded; 'but,' says he, 'they never come thus far, and yet hereabouts is as much gold as there.' Upon this he told us that he believed he might have gotten a hundred pounds' weight of gold since he came hither, if he had employed himself to look and work for it, but as he knew not what to do with it, and had long since despaired of being ever delivered from the misery he was in, he had entirely omitted it. 'For what advantage had it been to me,' said he, 'or what richer had I been, if I had a ton of gold dust, and lay and wallowed in it? The richness of it,' said he, 'would not give me one moment's felicity, nor relieve me in the present exigency. Nay,' says he, 'as you all see, it would not buy me clothes to cover me, or a drop of drink to save me from perishing. It is of no value here,' says he; 'there are several people among these huts that would weigh gold against a few glass beads, or a cockle-shell, and give you a handful of gold dust for a handful of cowries.'

N.B.—These are little shells, which our children call blackamoors' teeth.

When he had said this he pulled out a piece of an earthern pot baked hard in the sun : 'Here,' says he, 'is some of the dirt of this country, and if I would, I could have got a great deal more ;' and showing it to us, I believe there was in it between two and three pounds' weight of gold dust, of the same kind and colour with that we had gotten already, as before. After we had looked at it awhile, he told us, smiling, we were his deliverers, and all he had, as well as his life, was ours ; and therefore, as this would be of value to us when we came to our own country, so he desired we would accept of it among us, and that this was the only time that he had repented that he had picked up no more of it.

I spoke for him as his interpreter to my comrades, and in their names thanked him ; but, speaking to them in Portuguese, I desired them to refer the acceptance of his kindness to the next morning ; and so I did, telling him we would further talk of this part in the morning ; so we parted for that time.

When he was gone I found they were all wonderfully affected with his discourse, and with the generosity of his temper, as well as the magnificence of his present, which in another place had been extraordinary. Upon the whole, not to detain you with circumstances, we agreed that, seeing he was now one of our number, and that, as we were a relief to him in carrying him out of the dismal condition he was in, so he was equally a relief to us in being our guide through the rest of the country, our interpreter with the natives, and our director how to manage with the savages, and how to enrich ourselves with the wealth of the country ; that, therefore, we would put his gold among our common stock, and every one should give him as much as would make his up just as much as any single share of our own, and for the future we would take our lot together, taking his solemn engagement to us, as we had before one to another, that we would not conceal the least grain of gold we found one from another.

In the next conference we acquainted him with the adventures of the Golden river, and how we had shared what we got there ; so that every man had a larger stock than he for his share ; that, therefore, instead of taking any from him, we had resolved every one to add a little to him. He appeared very glad that we had met with such good success, but would not take a grain from us, till at last, pressing him very hard, he told us that then he would take it thus : that when we came to get any more he would have so much out of the first as should make him even, and then we should go on as equal adventurers ; and thus we agreed.

He then told us he thought it would not be an unprofitable adventure, if, before we set forward, and after we had got a stock of provisions, we should make a journey north to the edge of the desert he had told us of, from whence our negroes might bring every one a large elephant's tooth, and that he would get some more to assist ; and that, after a certain length of carriage, they might be conveyed by canoes to the coast, where they would yield a very great profit.

I objected against this, on account of our other design we had of getting gold dust ; and that our negroes, who we knew would be faithful to us, would get much more by searching the rivers for gold for us, than by lugging a great tooth of a hundred and fifty pounds' weight, a hundred miles or more, which would be an insufferable labour to them after so hard a journey, and would certainly kill them.

He acquiesced in the justice of this answer, but fain would have had us gone to see the woody part of the hill, and the edge of the desert, that we might see how the elephants' teeth lay scattered up and down there ; but when we told him the story of what **we had** seen before, as is said above, **he said no more.**

We staid here twelve days, during which time the natives were very obliging to us, and brought us fruits, pompions, **and a** root like carrots, though of quite another taste, but not unpleasant neither, and some Guinea fowls, whose names we did not know. In short, they brought us plenty of what they had, **and** we lived very well, and we gave them all such little things as our cutler had made, for he had a whole bag full of them.

On the thirteenth day we set forward, taking our **new** gentleman with us. At parting, the negro king sent two savages with a present to him, of some dried flesh, but I do not remember what it was, and he gave them again three silver birds which our cutler helped him to, which I assure you was a present **for** a king.

We travelled now south, a little west, and here we found the first river for above two thousand miles' march, whose water ran south, all the rest running north or west. We followed this river, which was no bigger than a good large brook in England, **till** it began to increase its water. Every now and then we found our Englishman went down, as it were privately to **the** water, which was to try the sand. At length, after **a** day's march upon this river, he came running up to us with his hands full of sand, and saying, 'Look here.' Upon looking, we found that a good deal of gold lay spangled among the sand of the river. 'Now,' says he, 'I think we may begin to work;' so he divided our negroes into couples, and set them to work, to search and wash the sand and ooze in the bottom of the water, where it was not deep.

In the first day and a quarter our men altogether had gathered a pound and two ounces of gold, or thereabouts; and, as we found the quantity increased the farther we went, we followed it about three days, till another small rivulet joined the first, and then, searching up the stream, we found gold there too; so we pitched our camp in the angle where the rivers joined, and we diverted ourselves, as I may call it, in washing the gold out of the sand of the river, and in getting provisions.

Here we staid thirteen days more, in which time we had many pleasant adventures with the savages, too long to mention here, and some of them too homely to tell of: for some of our men had made something free with their women, which, had not our new guide made peace for us with one of their men, at the price of seven bits of silver, which our artificer had cut out into the shapes of lions and fishes, and birds, and had punched holes to hang them up by (an inestimable treasure!), we must have gone to war with them and all their people.

All the while we were busy washing gold dust out of the rivers, and our negroes the like, our ingenious cutler was hammering and cutting, and he was grown so dexterous by use, that he formed all manner of images. He cut out elephants, tigers, civet cats, ostriches, eagles, cranes, fowls, fishes, and indeed whatever he pleased, in thin plates of hammered gold, for his silver and iron were almost all gone.

At one of the towns of these savage nations we were very friendly received by their king ; and as he was very much taken with our workman's toys, he sold him an elephant cut out of a gold plate as thin as a sixpence at an extravagant rate. He was so much taken with it that he would not be quiet till he had given him almost a handful of gold dust, as they call it. I suppose it might weigh three-quarters of a pound ; the piece of gold that the elephant was made of might be about the weight of a pistole, rather less than more. Our artist was so honest, though the labour and art were all his own, that he brought all the gold, and put it into our common stock ; but we had indeed no manner of reason in the least to be covetous, for, as our new guide told us, we that were strong enough to defend ourselves, and had time enough to stay (for we were none of us in haste), might in time get together what quantity of gold we pleased, even to a hundred pounds' weight a man if we thought fit ; and therefore, he told us, though he

had as much reason to be sick of the country as any
of us, yet, if we thought to turn our march a little to
the south-east, and pitch upon a place proper for our
head-quarters, we might find provisions plenty enough,
and extend ourselves over the country among the
rivers, for two or three years, to the right and left,
and we should soon find the advantage of it.

The proposal, however good as to the profitable
part of it, suited none of us, for we were all more
desirous to get home than to be rich, being tired of
the excessive fatigue of above a year's continual
wandering among deserts and wild beasts.

However, the tongue of our new acquaintance had
a kind of charm in it, and used such arguments, and
had so much the power of persuasion, that there was
no resisting him. He told us it was preposterous
not to take the fruit of all our labours now we were
come to the harvest; that we might see the hazard
the Europeans ran, with ships and men, and at great
expense, to fetch a little gold; and that we that were
in the centre of it to go away empty-handed was un-
accountable; that we were strong enough to fight our
way through whole nations, and might make our
journey afterward to what part of the coast we pleased;
and we should never forgive ourselves when we came
to our own country to see we had five hundred
pistoles in gold, and might as easily have had five
thousand or ten thousand, or what we pleased; that

he was no more covetous than we, but, seeing it was in all our powers to retrieve our misfortunes at once, and make ourselves easy for all our lives, he could not be faithful to us, or grateful for the good we had done him, if he did not let us see the advantage we had in our hands; and he assured us he would make it clear to our own understanding that we might, in two years' time, by good management, and by the help of our negroes, gather every man a hundred pounds' weight of gold, and get together perhaps two hundred tons of teeth; whereas, if once we pushed on to the coast, and separated, we should never be able to see that place again with our eyes, or do any more than sinners did with heaven—wish themselves there, but know they can never come at it.

Our surgeon was the first man that yielded to his reasoning, and after him the gunner; and they two indeed had a great influence over us, but none of the rest had any mind to stay, nor I either, I must confess; for I had no notion of a great deal of money, or what to do with myself, or what to do with it if I had it. I thought I had enough already, and all the thought I had about disposing of it, if I came to Europe, was only how to spend it as fast as I could, buy me some clothes, and go to sea again, to be a drudge for more.

However, he prevailed with us by his good words, at last, to stay but for six months in the country, and then, if we did resolve to go, he would submit : so at length we yielded to that, and he carried us about fifty English miles south-east, where we found several rivulets of water, which seemed to come all from a great ridge of mountains which lay to the north-east, and which, by our calculation, must be the beginning that way of the great waste, which we had been forced northward to avoid.

Here we found the country barren enough ; but yet we had, by his directions, plenty of food ; for the savages round us, upon giving them some of our toys, as I have so often mentioned, brought us in whatever they had ; and here we found some maize, or Indian wheat, which the negro-women planted, as we sow seeds in a garden, and immediately our new providitor ordered some of our negroes to plant it, and it grew up presently, and, by watering it often, we had a crop in less than three months' growth.

As soon as we were settled, and our camp fixed, we fell to the old trade of fishing for gold in the rivers mentioned above, and our English gentleman so well knew how to direct our search, that we scarce ever lost our labour.

One time, having set us to work, he asked if we would give him leave, with four or five negroes, to go out for six or seven days to seek his fortune, and see what he could discover in the country, assuring us whatever he got should be for the public stock.

We all gave him our consent, and lent him a gun; and two of our men desiring to go with him, they took then six negroes with them, and two of our buffaloes that came with us the whole journey; they took about eight days' provision of bread with them, but no flesh, except about as much dried flesh as would serve them two days.

They travelled up to the top of the mountains I mentioned just now, where they saw (as our men afterwards vouched it to be) the same desert which we were so justly terrified at, when we were on the farther side, and which, by our calculation, could not be less than three hundred miles broad, and above six hundred miles in length, without knowing where it ended.

The journal of their travels is too long to enter upon here; they stayed out two and fifty days, when they brought us seventeen pounds, and something more (for we had no exact weight), of gold dust, some of it in much larger pieces than any we found before; besides about fifteen tons of elephants' teeth, which he had, partly by good usage, and partly by bad, obliged the savages of the country to fetch and bring down to him from the mountains, and which he made others bring with him quite down to our camp. Indeed we wondered what was coming to us when we saw him attended with above two hundred negroes; but he soon undeceived us, when he made them all throw down their burthens on a heap, at the entrance of our camp.

Besides this, they brought lions' skins, and five leopards' skins, very large and very fine. He asked our pardon for his long stay, and that he had made no greater a booty, but told us, he had one excursion more to make, which he hoped should turn to a better account.

So, having rested himself, and rewarded the savages that brought the teeth for him, with some bits of silver and iron cut out diamond-fashion, and with two shaped like little dogs, he sent them away mightily pleased.

The second journey he went some more of our men desired to go with him, and they made a troop of ten white men, and ten savages, and the two buffaloes to carry their provisions and ammunition. They took the same course, only not exactly the same track, and they stayed thirty-two days only, in which time they killed no less than fifteen leopards, three lions, and several other creatures, and brought us home four and twenty pounds some ounces of gold dust, and only six elephants' teeth, but they were very great ones.

Our friend the Englishman showed us now that our time was well bestowed ; for in five months, which we had stayed here, we had gathered so much gold dust, that, when we came to share it, we had

five pounds and a quarter to a man, besides what
we had before, and besides six or seven pounds'
weight which we had at several times given to our
artificer to make baubles with; and now we talked
of going forward to the coast to put an end to our
journey; but our guide laughed at us then: 'Nay,
you cannot go now,' says he, 'for the rainy season
begins next month, and there will be no stirring
then.' This we found indeed reasonable, so we
resolved to furnish ourselves with provisions, that
we might not be obliged to go abroad too much in
the rain, and we spread ourselves, some one way,
and some another, as far as we cared to venture,
to get provisions, and our negroes killed us some
deer, which we cured, as well as we could, in the
sun, for we had no salt.

By this time the rainy months were set in, and
we could scarce, for above two months, look out of
our huts. But that was not all, for the rivers were
so swelled with the landfloods, that we scarce knew
the little brooks and rivulets from the great navigable
rivers. This had been a very good opportunity to
have conveyed by water, upon rafts, our elephants'
teeth, of which we had a very great pile; for, as
we always gave the savages some reward for their
labour, the very women would bring us teeth upon
every opportunity, and sometimes a great tooth
carried between two; so that our quantity was

increased to about two and twenty tons of teeth.

As soon as the weather proved fair again, he told us he would not press us to any further stay, since we did not care whether we got any more gold or not : that we were indeed the first men he ever met with in his life that said they had gold enough, and of whom it might be truly said that, when it lay under our feet, we would not stoop to take it up. But since he had made us a promise, he would not break it, nor press us to make any further stay, only he thought he ought to tell us, that now was the time, after the landflood, when the greatest quantity of gold was found ; and that, if we stayed but one month, we should see thousands of savages spread themselves over the whole country to wash the gold out of the sand, for the European ships which would come on the coast ; that they do it then, because the rage of the floods always works down a great deal of gold out of the hills ; and if we took the advantage to be there before them, we did not know what extraordinary things we might find.

This was so forcible, and so well argued, that it appeared in all our faces we were prevailed upon ; so we told him we would all stay ; for, though it was true we were all eager to be gone, yet the evident prospect of so much advantage could not be well resisted—that he was greatly mistaken when he suggested that we did not desire to increase **our** **store of** gold, and in [short] that we were resolved to make the utmost use of the advantage that was in our hands, and would stay as long as any gold was **to be** had, if it was another year.

He could hardly express the joy he was in on this occasion ; and the fair weather coming on, we began, just as he directed, to search about the rivers for more gold. At first we had but little encouragement, and began to be doubtful ; but it was very plain that the reason was, the water was not fully fallen, or the rivers reduced to their usual channel. But in a few days we were fully requited, and found much more gold than at first, and in bigger lumps ; and one of our men washed out of the sand a piece of gold as big as a small nut, which weighed, by our estimation, for we had no small weights, almost an ounce and a half.

This success made us extremely diligent, and in a little more than a month we had altogether gotten near sixty pounds' weight of gold ; but after this, as he told us, we found abundance of the savages, men, women, and children, hunting every river and brook, and even the dry land of the hills, for gold, so that we could do nothing like then, compared to what we **had** done before.

But our artificer found a way **to make other** people find us in **gold without our own labour** ;

for, when these people began to appear, he had a
considerable quantity of his toys, birds, beasts, etc.,
such as before, ready for them, and, the English
gentleman being the interpreter, he brought the
savages to admire them ; so our cutler had trade
enough, and, to be sure, sold his goods at a
monstrous rate, for he would get an ounce of gold,
sometimes two, for a bit of silver, perhaps of the
value of a groat—nay, if it were iron—and if it were
of gold, they would not give the more for it ; and it
was incredible almost to think what a quantity of
gold he got that way.

In a word, to bring this happy journey to a
conclusion, we increased our stock of gold here,
in three months' stay more, to such a degree that,
bringing it all to a common stock, in order to share
it, we divided almost four pounds' weight again to
every man ; and then we set forward for the gold
coast, to see what method we could find out for our
passage into Europe.

There happened several very remarkable incidents
in this part of our journey, as to how we were, or
were not, received friendly by the several nations of
savages through which we passed ; how we delivered
one negro king from captivity who had been a
benefactor to our new guide ; and how our guide,
in gratitude, by our assistance, restored him to his
kingdom, which, perhaps, might contain about three

hundred subjects; how he entertained us; and how he made his subjects go with **our** Englishman, and **fetch** all our elephants' **teeth which we had been** obliged to leave behind **us, and to carry them for** us to the river, **the name of** which I forgot, where **we** made rafts, **and** in eleven days more came down to one of the Dutch settlements on the gold coast, where **we arrived** in perfect health, and to our great satisfaction. As for our cargo of teeth, we sold it to **the** Dutch factory, and received clothes and other necessaries for ourselves and such of our negroes as **we** thought fit **to keep with us**; and it is to be observed that we had four pounds of gunpowder **left** when we ended our journey. The negro prince we made perfectly free, clothed him out of our common stock, and gave him a pound and a half of gold for himself, which he knew very well how to manage; and here **we all** parted after the most friendly manner possible. **Our** Englishman remained in the Dutch factory some time, and, as I heard afterwards, died there of grief; for he having sent a thousand pounds sterling over to England, by the way of Holland, for his refuge at his return to his friends, the **ship** was taken by the French, and the effects all lost.

The rest of my comrades **went away, in a** small **bark, to** the two Portuguese factories, near Gambia, in the latitude of 14 degrees; and I, with two negroes which I kept with me, went away to Cape Coast Castle, where I got passage for England, and arrived there in September ; and thus ended my first harvest of wild oats ; the rest were not sowed to so much advantage.

*(**In** his ' second harvest' Singleton falls into piratical company, and the rest of the book is occupied with **his** experiences thereof. The chief figure of this part—a **figure** in which Defoe's skill in character-drawing re-appears—is a certain Quaker named William Walters, whom the pirates capture, and who very ingeniously, while declining actually to join them, assists them in their plans. He finally converts Singleton (after Defoe's very odd **notions** of conversion), the pair make their way to England with their gains, Singleton marries William's sister, **and** all is well. But this is how William under-stood neutrality.)*

We had one very merry fellow here, a quaker, whose name was William Walters, whom we took out of a sloop bound from Pennsylvania to Barbadoes. He was a surgeon, and they called him doctor ; but he was not employed in the sloop as a surgeon, but was going to Barbadoes to get a birth, as the sailors call it. However, he had all his surgeon's chest on board, and we made him go with us, and take all his implements with him. He was a comic fellow indeed, a man of very good solid sense, and an excellent surgeon; but, what was worth all, very good humoured, and pleasant in his conversation, **and a bold stout fellow too, as any we had among us.**

I found William, **as I** thought, not very averse to **go** along with us, and yet resolved to do it so that it might be apparent **he was** taken away by force; and, to this **purpose, he** comes to me: 'Friend,' says he, 'thou sayest I must go with thee, and it is **not** in my power **to** resist thee, if I would; but I desire thou wilt oblige the master of the sloop which I **am on board,** to certify under his hand, that I was taken away by force, and against my will.' **And this he** said with so much satisfaction in his face, that **I** could not but understand him. 'Ay, ay,' says I, 'whether it be against your will or no, I'll make him **and** all **the men** give you a certificate of it, or I'll take **them** all along with us, and keep them till they do.' So **I** drew up the certificate myself, wherein I wrote that **he was** taken away **by** main force, as a prisoner, by a pirate ship; that they carried away his chest and instruments first, and then bound his hands behind him, and forced him into their boat; and this was signed by the master and all his men.

Accordingly, I fell a swearing at him, and called to my men to tie his hands behind him, and so we put **him into our** boat, **and** carried him away. When I **had him on board, I** called him to me; 'Now, friend,' says I, 'I have brought you away by force, it is true, but I am not of the opinion I have brought you away so much against your will as they imagine : come,' says I, 'you will be a useful man to us, and you shall have very good usage among us.'   So I unbound his hands, and first ordered all things that belonged to him to be restored to him, and our captain gave him a dram.

'Thou hast dealt friendly by me,' says he, 'and I will be plain with thee, whether I came willingly to thee or not.   I shall make myself as useful to thee as I can ; but thou knowest it is not my business to meddle when thou art to fight.'   'No, no,' says the captain, 'but you may meddle a little when we share the money.'   'Those things are useful to furnish a surgeon's chest,' says William, and smiled, 'but I shall be moderate.'

In short, William was a most agreeable companion ; but he had the better of us in this part, that, if we were taken, we were sure to be hanged, and he was sure to escape ; and he knew it well enough : but, in short, he was a sprightly fellow, and fitter to be captain than any of us.   I shall have often an occasion to speak of him in the rest of the story.

Our cruising so long in these seas began now to be so well known, that, not in England only, but in France and Spain, accounts had been made public of our adventures, and many stories told, how we murdered the people in cold blood, tying them back to back and throwing them into the sea : one half of which, however, was not true, though more was done than it is fit to speak of here.

The consequence of this however, was, that several English men of war were sent to the West Indies, and were particularly instructed to cruise in the bay of Mexico, and the gulf of Florida, and among the Bahama islands, if possible, to attack us. We were not so ignorant of things as not to expect this, after so long a stay in that part of the world ; but the first certain account we had of them was at Honduras, when a vessel, coming in from Jamaica, told us that two English men of war were coming directly from Jamaica thither in quest of us. We were indeed as it were embayed, and could not have made the least shift to have got off, if they had come directly to us ; but as it happened, somebody had informed them that we were in the bay of Campeachy, and they went directly thither, by which we were not only free of them, but were so much to the windward of them that they could not make any attempt upon us, though they had known we were there.

We took this advantage, and stood away for Carthagena, and from thence with great difficulty beat it up at a distance from under the shore of St. Martha, till we came to the Dutch island of Curasoe, and from thence to the island of Tobago ; which, as before, was our rendezvous; and it being a deserted, uninhabited island, we at the same time made use of it for a retreat: here the captain of the brigantine died, and Captain Harris, at that time my lieutenant, took the command of the brigantine.

Here we came to a resolution to go away to the coast of Brazil, and from thence to the Cape of Good Hope, and so for the East Indies: but Captain Harris, as I have said, being now captain of the brigantine, alleged that his ship was too small for so long a voyage; but that, if Captain Wilmot would consent, he would take the hazard of another cruise, and he would follow us in the first ship he could take: so we appointed our rendezvous to be at Madagascar, which was done by my recommendation of the place, and the plenty of provisions to be had there.

Accordingly he went away from us in an evil hour; for, instead of taking a ship to follow us, he was taken, as I heard afterwards, by an English man-of-war, and being laid in irons, died of mere grief and anger before he came to England. His lieutenant, I have heard, was afterwards executed in England for a pirate, and this was the end of the man who first brought me into this unhappy trade.

We parted from Tobago three days after, bending our course for the coast of Brazil, but had not been at sea above twenty-four hours when we were separated by a terrible storm, which held three days, with very little abatement or intermission. In this juncture Captain Wilmot happened unluckily to be on board my ship, very much to his mortification; for we not only lost sight of his ship, but never saw her more till we came to Madagascar, where she was cast away. In short, after having in this tempest lost our fore-top-mast, we were forced to put back to the isle of Tobago for shelter, and to repair our damage, which brought us all very near our destruction.

We were no sooner on shore here, and all very busy looking out for a piece of timber for a top-mast, but we perceived, standing in for the shore, an English man-of-war of thirty-six guns: it was a great surprise to us indeed, because we were disabled so much; but to our great good fortune, we lay pretty snug and close among the high rocks, and the man-of-war did not see us, but stood off again upon his cruise: so we only observed which way she went, and at night, leaving our work, resolved to stand off to sea, steering the contrary way from that which we observed she went; and this we found had the desired success, for we saw him no more. We had gotten an old mizen top-mast on board, which made us a jury fore-top-mast for the present; and so we stood away for the isle of Trinidad, where, though there were Spaniards on shore, yet we landed some men with our boat, and cut a very good piece of fir to make us a new top-mast, which we got fitted up effectually ; and also we got some cattle here to eke out our provisions ; and, calling a council of war among ourselves, we resolved to quit those seas for the present, and steer away for the coast of Brazil.

The first thing we attempted here was only getting fresh water : but we learnt that there lay the Portuguese fleet at the bay of All Saints, bound for Lisbon, ready to sail, and only waiting for a fair wind. This made us lie by, wishing to see them put to sea, and, accordingly, as they were with or without convoy, to attack or avoid them.

It sprung up a fresh gale in the evening, at S.W. by W., which, being fair for the Portugal fleet, and the weather pleasant and agreeable, we heard the signal given to unmoor, and, running in under the island of Si——, we hauled our main-sail and fore-sail up in the brails, lowered the top-sail upon the cap, and clewed them up, that we might lie as snug as we could, expecting their coming out, and the next morning saw the whole fleet come out accordingly, but not at all to our satisfaction, for they consisted of twenty-six sail, and most of them ships of force as well as burthen, both merchantmen and men-of-war ; so, seeing there was no meddling, we lay still where we were also, till the fleet was out of sight, and then stood off and on, in hopes of meeting with further purchase.

It was not long before we saw a sail, and immediately gave her chase; but she proved an excellent sailor, and, standing out to sea, we saw plainly she trusted to her heels—that is to say, to her sails. However, as we were a clean ship, we gained upon her, though slowly, and, had we had a day before us, we should certainly have come up with her; but it grew dark apace, and in that case we knew we should lose sight of her.

Our merry quaker, perceiving us to crowd still after her in the dark, wherein we could not see which way she went, came very drily to me: 'Friend Singleton,' says he, 'dost thee know what we are doing?' Says I, 'Yes, why we are chasing yon ship, are we not?' 'And how dost thou know that?' says he, very gravely still. 'Nay, that's true,' says I again, 'we cannot be sure.' 'Yes, friend,' says he, 'I think we may be sure that we are running away from her—not chasing her. I am afraid,' adds he, 'thou art turned quaker, and hast resolved not to use the hand of power, or art a coward, and art flying from thy enemy.'

'What do you mean?' says I (I think I swore at him); 'what do ye sneer at now? you have always one dry rub or another to give us.'

'Nay,' says he, 'it is plain enough the ship stood off to sea due east, on purpose to lose us, and thou mayest be sure her business does not lie that way;

for what should she do at the coast of Africa in this latitude, which should be as far south as Congo or Angola? But as soon as it is dark, that we shall lose sight of her, she will tack, and stand away west again for the Brazil coast, and for the bay, where, thou knowest, she was going before; and are we not then running away from her? I am greatly in hopes, friend,' says the dry gibing creature, 'thou wilt turn quaker, for I see thou art not for fighting.'

'Very well, William,' says I, 'then I shall make an excellent pirate.' However, William was in the right, and I apprehended what he meant immediately; and Captain Wilmot, who lay very sick in his cabin, over-hearing us, understood him as well as I, and called out to me that William was right, and it was our best way to change our course, and stand away for the bay, where it was ten to one but we should snap her in the morning.

Accordingly, we went about ship, got our larboard tacks on board, set the top-gallant sails, and crowded for the bay of All Saints, where we came to an anchor, early in the morning, just out of gunshot of the forts. We furled our sails with rope-yarns, that we might haul home the sheets without going up to loose them, and, lowering our main and fore yards, looked just as if we had lain there a good while.

In two hours after we saw our game standing in for the bay with all the sail she could make, and she came innocently into our very mouths, for we lay still till we saw her **almost within gunshot, when our** fore-mast geers **being** stretched **fore and aft, we first ran** up our yards, and then hauled home the **top-sail** sheets ; the rope-yarns that furled them giving way of themselves, **the** sails were set in a few minutes ; **at** the same time slipping our cable, we came upon **her** before she could get **under** way upon the other tack. They **were so** surprised that they made little or **no** resistance, but struck after the first broadside.

We were considering **what to** do with her, **when** William came to me : ' Hark thee, friend,' says **he,** ' thou hast made a fine piece of work of it now, hast thou not ? To borrow thy neighbour's ship here **just at** thy neighbour's door, and never **ask** him leave. **Now,** dost thou not think there are some men-of-war in the port ? Thou hast given them the alarm suffi-ciently ; thou wilt have them upon **thy** back before night, depend upon **it, to** ask thee wherefore **thou** didst so.'

' Truly, William,' said I, ' for aught **I** know that may be true. What, then, shall we **do next ?'** Says he, ' Thou hast but two things to do, either to **go in** and take all the rest, **or** else get thee gone **before they** come out and **take** thee ; for **I** see they **are** hoisting a top-mast to yon great ship, **in order to put to sea** immediately, and they won't **be long before** they come to talk with thee ; and **what wilt thou say**

to them when they ask thee **why** thou borrowest their
ship without leave?'

As William **said, so it was : we** could **see** by our
glasses they were **all in a hurry,** manning **and** fitting
some **sloops they had** there, and a large man-of-war,
and it was plain they would soon be with us ; **but** we
were not at a loss what to do. We found the ship
we **had** taken was loaden with nothing considerable
for **our** purpose, except some cocoa, some sugar, and
twenty barrels of flour; the rest of her loading was
hides ; **so we** took out all we thought for our turn,
and, among the rest, all her ammunition, great shot,
and small arms, **and** turned her off; we also took a
cable and three anchors she had, which were for our
purpose, and some **of her** sails. **She had** enough
left just to carry her into port, and that was all.

Having done this, we stood on **upon the** Brazil
coast, southward, till we came **to the** mouth of the
river Janeiro : but, as we had two days the wind
blowing hard at S.E. and S.S.E., we were obliged to
come to an anchor under a little island and wait **for**
a wind. **In** this time, the Portuguese had, it seems,
given notice over land to the governor there, that a
pirate was **upon the coast; so** that, when we came in
view of the port, **we** saw two men-of-war riding just
without the bar, whereof one we found was getting
under sail with all possible speed, having slipt her
cable, on purpose **to** speak with us ; the other was

not so forward, but was preparing to follow; in less than an hour they stood both fair after us, with all the sail they could make.

Had not the night come on, William's words had been made good; they would certainly have asked us the question what we did there? for we found the foremost ship gained upon us, especially upon one tack; for we plied away from them to windward; but in the dark losing sight of them, we resolved to change our course, and stand away directly to sea, not doubting but we should lose them in the night.

Whether the Portuguese commander guessed we would do so or no, I know not; but in the morning, when the daylight appeared, instead of having lost him, we found him in chase of us, about a league astern; only, to our great good fortune, we could see but one of the two; however, this one was a great ship, carried six and forty guns, and an admirable sailor, as appeared by her outsailing us; for our ship was an excellent sailor too, as I have said before.

When I found this, I easily saw there was no remedy, but we must engage; and, as we knew we could expect no quarter from those scoundrels the Portuguese, a nation I had an original aversion to, I let Captain Wilmot know how it was. The captain, sick as he was, jumped up in the cabin, and would be led out upon the deck (for he was very weak) to see how it was. 'Well,' says he, 'we'll fight them.'

Our men were all in good heart before; but, to see the captain so brisk, who had lain ill of a calenture ten or eleven days, gave them double courage, and they went all hands to work to make a clear ship and be ready. William the quaker comes to me with a kind of smile: 'Friend,' says he, 'what does yon ship follow us for?' 'Why,' says I, 'to fight us, you may be sure.' 'Well,' says he, 'and will she come up with us, dost thou think?' 'Yes,' said I, 'you see she will.' 'Why, then, friend,' says the dry wretch, 'why dost thou run from her still, when thou seest she will overtake thee? will it be better for us to be overtaken farther off than here?' 'Much at one for that,' says I; 'why, what would you have us do?' 'Do!' says he, 'let us not give the poor man more trouble than needs must; let us stay for him, and hear what he has to say to us.' 'He will talk to us in powder and ball,' said I. 'Very well, then,' says he, 'if that be his country language we must talk to him in the same, must we not? or else how shall he understand us?' 'Very well, William,' says I, 'we understand you.' And the captain, as ill as he was, called to me, 'William's right again,' says he, 'as good here as a league farther.' So he gave a word of command, 'Haul up the mainsail; we'll shorten sail for him.'

Accordingly we shortened sail; and, as we expected her upon our lee-side, we being then upon our starboard tack, brought eighteen of our guns to the larboard side, resolving **to** give him a broadside that should warm him ; it was about **half an hour before** he came up with us, all which time we luffed up, **that we** might keep **the** wind of him, by which he **was** obliged to run up under our lee, as we designed him ; when we got him upon our quarter we edged down, and received **the** fire of five or six of his guns ; by this time **you** may be sure all **our** hands were at their quarters, so we clapped our helm hard a-weather, let go **the** lee-braces of the main top-sail, and laid it a-back, and so our ship fell athwart the Portuguese **ship's** hawse ; then we immediately poured in our broadside, raking them fore and aft, and killed **them** a great many men.

The Portuguese, we could see, were in the utmost confusion ; and, not being aware of our design, their ship having fresh way, ran their bowsprit into the fore part of our main shrouds, as that **they** could not easily get clear of us, and so we lay locked after that manner ; **the** enemy could not bring above two **or** three guns, besides their small arms, to bear upon us, while we played our whole broadside upon him.

In the middle of the heat of this fight, as I was **very** busy upon the quarter-deck, the captain calls to **me**, for he never stirred from us, ' What the devil is friend William a-doing yonder ? ' says the captain, ' has **he any** business upon deck ? ' I stept forward, and there was friend William, with two or three stout fellows, lashing the ship's **bowsprit fast** to our mainmast, **for fear** they **should get away from** us ; and every now **and then** he pulled **a bottle** out of his pocket, **and gave** the men a dram to encourage them. The **shot flew** about **his ears as** thick as may be **supposed in** such an action, where the Portuguese, **to give them** their due, fought very briskly, believing at **first they were sure of** their game, and trusting **to their** superiority ; but there was William, as composed, and **in as** perfect tranquillity as to danger, as if **he** had been over a bowl of punch, only very busy securing **the** matter, that a ship of **forty-six guns** should not run away from a ship of eight-and-twenty.

This work **was too** hot **to** hold long ; our men behaved bravely ; our gunner, a gallant man, shouted below, pouring in **his** shot at such a rate that the Portuguese began to slacken their fire ; we had dismounted several **of** their guns by firing in at their forecastle, and raking them, as I said, fore and aft ; **and presently** comes William up to me : 'Friend,' says **he,** very calmly, 'what dost thou mean ? **Why dost thou not** visit thy neighbour in the ship, the door being open for thee ?' I understood him immediately, for our guns had so torn **their hull** that we had beat two **port-holes** into one, and the bulkhead of their steerage was split to pieces, so that they **could** not retire to their close quarters ; I then gave the word immediately to board **them.** Our second lieutenant, with about thirty men, entered in an instant over the forecastle, followed by some more, with the boatswain, and cutting in pieces about twenty-five men that they found upon the deck, and then, throwing some grenadoes into the steerage, they entered there also ; upon which the Portuguese cried quarter presently, and we mastered the ship, contrary indeed to our own expectation ; for we would have compounded with them if they would have sheered off, but laying them athwart the hawse at first, and following our fire furiously, without giving them any time to get clear of us, and work their ship ; by this means, though they had six-and-forty guns, they were not able to point them forward, as I said above, for we beat them immediately from their guns in the forecastle, and killed them abundance of men between decks, so that, when we entered, they had hardly found men enough to fight us hand to hand upon their deck.

The surprise of joy, to hear the Portuguese cry quarter, and see their ancient struck, was so great to our captain, who, as I have said, was reduced very weak with a high fever, that it gave him new life. Nature conquered the distemper, and the fever abated that very night ; so that in two or three days he was sensibly better, his strength began to come, and he was able to give his orders effectually in everything that was material, and in about ten days was entirely well, and about the ship.

In the meantime I took possession of the Portuguese man-of-war; and Captain Wilmot made me, or rather I made myself, captain of her for the present. About thirty of their seamen took service with us, some of whom were French, some Genoese; and we set the rest on shore the next day, on a little island on the coast of Brazil, except some wounded men, who were not in a condition to be removed, and whom we were bound to keep on board; but we had an occasion afterwards to dispose of them at the Cape, where, at their own request, we set them on shore.

Captain Wilmot, as soon as the ship was taken, and the prisoners stowed, was for standing in for the river Janeiro again, not doubting that we should meet with the other man-of-war, who, not having been able to find us, and having lost the company of her comrade, would certainly be returned, and might be surprised by the ship we had taken, if we carried Portuguese colours; and our men were all for it.

But our friend William gave us better counsel; for he came to me; 'Friend,' says he, 'I understand the captain is for sailing back to the Rio Janeiro, in hopes to meet with the other ship that was in chase of thee yesterday. Is it true, dost thou intend it?' 'Why, yes,' says I, 'William, pray why not?' 'Nay,' says he, 'thou mayest do so if thou wilt.' 'Well, I know that too, William,' said I; 'but the captain is a man who will be ruled by reason; what have you

to say to it?' 'Why,' says William, gravely, 'I only
ask what is thy business, and the business of all the
people thou hast with thee? Is it not to get money?'
'Yes, William, it is so, in our honest way.' 'And
wouldst thou,' says he, 'rather have money without
fighting, or fighting without money? I mean, which
wouldst thou have by choice, suppose it to be left to
thee?' 'O William,' says I, 'the first of the two, to
be sure.' 'Why then,' says he, 'what great gain hast
thou made of the prize thou hast taken now, though
it has cost thee the lives of thirteen of thy men,
besides some hurt? It is true thou hast got the
ship and some prisoners; but thou wouldst have had
twice the booty in a merchant ship, with not one
quarter of the fighting; and how dost thou know
either what force, or what number of men, may be in
the other ship, and what loss thou mayest suffer, and
what gain it shall be to thee if thou take her? I
think indeed thou mayest much better let her alone.'
  'Why, William, it is true,' said I, 'and I'll go tell
the captain what your opinion is, and bring you word
what he says.' Accordingly I went to the captain,
and told him William's reasons; and the captain was
of his mind—that our business was indeed fighting
when we could not help it, but that our main affair
was money, and that with as few blows as we could.
So that adventure was laid aside, and we stood along-
shore again south for the river de la Plata, expecting

some purchase thereabouts ; especially we had our eyes upon some **of the** Spanish ships from Buenos Ayres, **which are** generally very rich in silver, and one **such prize would** have done our business. We plied about here, in the latitude **of near 22** degrees south, for near a month, and nothing **offered** ; and **here we began** to consult what we should do next, **for we had come to no** resolution yet. Indeed, **my** design was always for **the** Cape de Bona Speranza, **and so to the** East Indies. I had heard some flaming stories of Captain Avery, **and** the fine things he had done in the Indies, which **were doubled** and doubled, even ten thousandfold : and from taking a great prize **in the bay of** Bengal, where **he took a** lady, said to be the Great Mogul's daughter, with a great quantity of **jewels about her, we had** a story told us that he took a Mogul ship, **so the** foolish sailors called it, loaden with diamonds.

I would fain have had friend William's advice— whither we should **go** ; but he always put it off with **some quaking** quibble or other. In short, he did **not care** for directing us neither. Whether he made a piece of conscience of it, or whether he **did** not care to venture having it come against him afterwards, or no, this **I know** not ; but we concluded at last without him.

*　.　　　*　　　*　　　*　　　*

At last, our old never-failing friend, William, helped

us out again, as he had often done at a dead-lift. His proposal was this, that he should go as master of the ship, and about twenty men, such as we could best trust, and attempt to trade privately, upon the coast of Brazil, with the planters, not at the principal ports, because that would not be admitted.

We all agreed to this, and appointed to go away ourselves towards the Rio de la Plata, where we had thought of going before, and to wait for him, not there, but at Port St. Pedro, as the Spaniards call it, lying at the mouth of the river which they call Rio Grande, and where the Spaniards had a small fort and a few people, but we believe there was nobody in it.

Here we took up our station, cruising off and on, to see if we could meet any ships going to, or coming from, Buenos Ayres, or the Rio de la Plata ; but we met with nothing worth notice. However, we employed ourselves in things necessary for our going off to sea ; for we filled all our water-casks, and got some fish for our present use, to spare as much as possible our ship's stores.

William, in the meantime, went away to the north, and made the land about the Cape of St. Thomas ; and, betwixt that and the isles of Tuberon, he found means to trade with the planters for all his negroes, as well the women as the men, and at a very good price too ; for William, who spoke Portuguese pretty well, told them a fair story enough, that the ship was in scarcity of provisions, that they were driven a great way out of their way, and indeed, as we say, out of their knowledge, and that they must go up to the northward as far as Jamaica, or sell there upon the coast. This was a very plausible tale, and was easily believed; and, if you observe the manner of the negroes' sailing, and what happened in their voyage, was every word of it true.

By this method, and being true to one another, William past for what he was; I mean for a very honest fellow, and, by the assistance of one planter, who sent to some of his neighbour planters, and managed the trade among themselves, he got a quick market; for in less than five weeks William sold all his negroes, and at last sold the ship itself, and shipped himself and his twenty men, with two negro boys whom he had left, in a sloop, one of those which the planters used to send on board for the negroes. With this sloop, Captain William, as we then called him, came away, and found us at Port St. Pedro, in the latitude of 32 degrees 30 minutes south.

Nothing was more surprising to us than to see a sloop come along the coast, carrying Portuguese colours, and come in directly to us, after we were assured he had discovered both our ships. We fired a gun, upon her nearer approach, to bring her to an anchor, but immediately she fired five guns by way of salute, and spread her English ancient : then we began to guess it was friend William, but wondered what was the meaning of his being in a sloop, whereas we sent him away in a ship of near three hundred tons ; but he soon let us into the whole history of his management, with which we had a great deal of reason to be very well satisfied. As soon as he had brought the sloop to an anchor he came aboard of my ship, and there he gave us an account how he began to trade, by the help of a Portuguese planter, who lived near the sea-side ; how he went on shore, and went up to the first house he could see, and asked the man of the house to sell him some hogs, pretending at first he only stood in upon the coast to take in fresh water, and buy some provisions ; and the man not only sold him seven fat hogs, but invited him in, and gave him, and five men he had met with, a very good dinner ; and he invited the planter on board his ship, and, in return for his kindness, gave him a negro girl.

This so obliged the planter, that the next morning he sent him on board, in a great luggage-boat, a cow and two sheep, with a chest of sweetmeats, and some sugar, and a great bag of tobacco, and invited Captain William on shore again : that, after this, they grew from one kindness to another ; that they began to talk about trading for some negroes ; and William, pretending it **was to do him service,** consented to sell him **thirty** negroes **for his** private use in his plantation, for which **he gave** William ready money in **gold, at the rate of five and** thirty moidores per head ; **but the planter was** obliged to use great **caution in** the bringing them on shore : for which **purpose, he** made William weigh and stand out **to sea, and put** in again, about fifty miles farther **north, where, at** a little creek, he took the negroes **on shore** at another plantation, belonging to a friend **of** his, whom, it seems, he could trust.

This remove brought William into **a** further intimacy, not only with the first planter, but also with his friends, who desired to have some of the negroes also ; **so** that, from one to another, they bought so many, till one overgrown planter took **a** hundred negroes, **which was** all William **had left,** and sharing them with another planter, that other **planter** chaffered **with** William for ship and **all,** giving him in exchange a very clean, large, well-**built sloop of near** sixty tons, very well furnished, **carrying six guns ;** but we made her afterwards carry **twelve guns.** William had three hundred moidores in gold, besides the sloop, in payment for the ship ; and **with this** money he stored the sloop **as** full as she could hold with provisions, especially bread, some pork, and about sixty hogs alive : among the rest, William got **eighty** barrels of good gunpowder, which was very much for our purpose; and all the provisions which were in the French ship he took out also.

This was a very agreeable account to us, especially when we saw that William had received in gold coined, or by weight, and some Spanish silver, sixty thousand pieces of eight, besides a new sloop, and a vast quantity of provisions.

We were very glad of the sloop in particular, and began to consult what we should do, whether we had not best turn off our great Portuguese ship, and stick to our first ship and the sloop, seeing we had scarce men enough for all three, and that the biggest ship was thought too big for our business; however, another dispute, which was now decided, brought the first to a conclusion. The first dispute was, whither we should go? My comrade, as I called him now, that is to say, he that was my captain before we took this Portuguese man-of-war, was for going to the South Seas, and coasting up the west side of America, where we could not fail of making several good prizes upon the Spaniards; and that then, if occasion required, we might come home by the South Seas to the East Indies, and so go round the globe, as others had done before us.

But my head lay another way; I had been in the East Indies, and had entertained a notion, ever since that, that if we went thither we could not fail of making good work of it, and that we might have a safe retreat, and good beef to victual our ship, among my old friends the natives of Zanguebar, on the coast of Mozambique, or the island of St. Laurence: I say, my thoughts lay this way; and I read so many lectures to them all, of the advantages they would certainly make of their strength, by the prizes they would take in the gulf of Mocha, or the Red Sea, and on the coast of Malabar, or the bay of Bengal, that I amazed them.

With these arguments I prevailed on them, and we all resolved to steer away S.E. for the Cape of Good Hope; and, in consequence of this resolution, we concluded to keep the sloop, and sail with all three, not doubting, as I assured them, but we should find men there to make up the number wanting, and, if not, we might cast any of them off when we pleased.

We could not do less than make our friend William captain of the sloop, which, with such good management, he had brought us. He told us, though with much good manners, he would not command her as a frigate, but, if we would give her to him for his share of the Guinea ship, which we came very honestly by, he would keep us company as a victualler, if we commanded him, as long as he was under the same force that took him away.

We understood him, so we gave him the sloop, but upon condition **that he should** not go from us, and should be entirely under command : however, William was not so easy as before ; and indeed, **as** we afterwards wanted the sloop to cruise for purchase, and a right thorough-paced pirate in her, so I was in such pain for William that I could not be without him, for he was my privy-councillor and companion upon all occasions ; so **I** put a Scotsman, a bold enterprising gallant fellow, into her, named Gordon, and made her **carry twelve** guns, and four petereroes, though, indeed, we wanted men, for we were none of us manned in proportion to our force.

(And this was the way William made Singleton leave off piracy, deserting his men.)

'Wilt **thou** give me leave,' says William, 'to talk plainly with thee upon thy present circumstances, and thy future prospect of living ; and wilt thou promise, on thy word, to take nothing ill of me ?'

'With all my heart,' said I, 'William ; I have always found your advice good ; and your designs have not only been well laid, but your counsel has been very lucky to us ; and therefore **say what you will**, I promise you I will not take **it ill**'

'But that is not all my demand,' says William ; 'if thou **dost** not like **what** I am going to propose to thee, thou shalt promise me not to make it public among the men.'

'I will not, William,' says I, 'upon my word;' and swore to him too very heartily.

'Why then,' says William, 'I have but one thing more to article with thee about, and that is, that thou wilt consent, that, if thou dost not approve of it for thyself, thou wilt yet consent that I shall put so much of it in practice as relates to myself and my new comrade doctor, so that it be in nothing to thy detriment and loss.'

'In anything,' says I, 'William, but leaving me, I will; but I cannot part with you upon any terms whatever.'

'Well,' says William, 'I am not designing to part from thee, unless it is thy own doing; but assure me in all these points, and I will tell my mind freely.'

So I promised him everything he desired of me, in the most solemn manner possible, and so seriously and frankly withal, that William made no scruple to open his mind to me.

'Why then, in the first place,' says William, 'shall I ask thee if thou dost not think thou and all thy men are rich enough, and have really gotten as much wealth together (by whatsoever way it has been gotten, that is not the question), as ye all know what to do with?'

'Why, truly, William,' said I, 'thou art pretty right; I think we have had pretty good luck.'

'Well then,' says William, 'I would ask, whether, if thou hast gotten enough, thou hast any thought of leaving off this trade; for most people leave off trading when they are satisfied with getting, and are rich enough; for nobody trades for the sake of trading; much less do any men rob for the sake of thieving.'

'Well, William,' says I, 'now I perceive what it is thou art driving at: I warrant you,' says I, 'you begin to hanker after home.'

'Why, truly,' says William, 'thou hast said it, and so I hope thou dost too. It is natural for most men that are abroad to desire to come home again at last, especially when they are grown rich, and when they are (as thou ownest thyself to be) rich enough, and so rich, as they know not what to do with more, if they had it.'

'Well, William,' said I, 'but now you think you have laid your preliminary at first so home, that I should have nothing to say; that is, that when I had got money enough, it would be natural to think of going home; but you have not explained what you mean by home; and there you and I shall differ. Why, man, I am at home; here is my habitation; I never had any other in my lifetime: I was a kind of a charity-school boy; so that I can have no desire of going anywhere for being rich or poor, for I have nowhere to go.'

'Why,' says William, looking a little confused, 'art not thou an Englishman?'

'Yes,' says I, 'I think so; you see I speak English: but I came out of England a child, and never was in it but once since I was a man; and then I was cheated and imposed upon, and used so ill that I care not if I never see it more.'

'Why, hast thou no relations or friends there?' says he: 'no acquaintance? none that thou hast any kindness, or any remains of respect for?'

'Not I, William,' said I; 'not one, more than I have in the court of the Great Mogul.'

'Nor any kindness for the country where thou wast born?' says William.

'Not I, any more than for the island of Madagascar, nor so much neither; for that has been a fortunate island to me more than once, as thou knowest, William,' said I.

William was quite stunned at my discourse, and held his peace; and I said to him, 'Go on, William; what hast thou to say further? for I hear you have some project in your head,' says I; 'come, let's have it out.'

'Nay,' says William, 'thou hast put me to silence, and all I had to say is overthrown; all my projects are come to nothing, and gone.'

'Well, but, William,' said I, 'let me hear what they were; for though it is so that what I have to aim at does not look your way, and though I have no relation, no friend, no acquaintance in England, yet I do not say I like this roving, cruising life so well as never to give it over; let me hear if thou canst propose to me anything beyond it.'

'Certainly, friend,' says William, very gravely, 'there is something beyond it;' and lifting up his hands, he seemed very much affected, and I thought I saw tears standing in his eyes; but I, that was too hardened a wretch to be moved with these things, laughed at him. 'What!' says I, 'you mean death, I warrant you; don't you? that is beyond this trade. Why, when it comes, it comes; then we are all provided for.'

'Aye,' says William, 'that is true; but it would be better that some things were thought on before that came.'

'Thought on!' says I; 'what signifies thinking of it? To think of death, is to die; and to be always thinking of it, is to be all one's life long a-dying: it is time enough to think of it when it comes.'

You will easily believe I was well qualified for a pirate, that could talk thus; but let me leave it upon record, for the remark of other hardened rogues like myself. My conscience gave me a pang that I had never felt before, when I said—'What signifies thinking of it?' and told me I should one day think of these words with a sad heart; but the time of my reflection was not yet come; so I went on.

Says William, very seriously, 'I must tell thee, friend, I am sorry to hear thee talk so; they that never think of dying often die without thinking of it.'

I carried on the jesting way a while further, and said—'Prithee do not talk of dying; how do we know we shall ever die?' and began to laugh.

'I need not answer thee to that,' says William; 'it is not my place to reprove thee who art commander over me here; but I had rather thou wouldst talk otherwise of death; it is a coarse thing.'

'Say anything to me, William,' said I, 'I will take it kindly.' I began now to be very much moved at his discourse.

Says William (tears running down his face), 'It is because men live as if they were never to die, that so many die before they know how to live; but it was not death that I meant, when I said,—That there was something to be thought of beyond this way of living.'

'Why, William,' said I, 'what was that?'

'It was repentance,' says he.

'Why,' says I, 'did you ever know a pirate repent?'

At this he started a little, and returned,—'At the

gallows I have known one repent, **and I hope** thou wilt be the second.'

He spoke **this** very affectionately, with **an appear**ance of concern for me.

'Well, William,' says **I**, 'I thank you, and I am not so senseless of these things, perhaps, as I make myself **seem to** be ; but come, let me hear your proposal.'

'My proposal,' says William, 'is for thy good, as well as my own. We may put an end to this kind of life, and repent ; and I think the fairest occasion offers for both, at this very time, that ever did, or ever will, or indeed can happen again.'

'Look you, William,' says **I**, 'let me have **your** proposal for putting an end to our present way **of** living first, for that is the case before us, and you and I will talk of the other afterward. I am not so insensible,' said I, 'as you may **think** me to be ; but let us get out of this hellish condition we are in first.'

'Nay,' says William, 'thou art in the right there ; we must never talk of repenting while we continue pirates.'

'Well,' says I, '**William**, that is what I meant ; for if we must not reform, as well as be **sorry for** what is done, I have **no** notion what repentance **means** : indeed, at best I know little **of the** matter ; but the nature of the **thing** seems to tell me, that the first step we have to take is to break off this wretched course ; and I'll begin there with you, with all my heart.'

I could see by his countenance that William was thoroughly pleased with the offer ; and if he had tears in his eyes before, he had more now ; but it was from a quite different passion ; for he was so swallowed up with joy he could not speak.

'Come, William,' says I, 'thou showest me plain enough thou hast an honest meaning.   Dost thou think it is practicable for us to put an end to our unhappy way of living here, and get off?'

'Yes,' says he, 'I think it is very practicable for me ; whether it is for thee or no, that will depend upon thyself.'

'Well,' says I, 'I give you my word, that as I have commanded you all along, from the time I first took you on board, so you shall command me from this hour, and everything you direct me I'll do.'

'Wilt thou leave it all to me?   Dost thou say this freely ?'

'Yes, William,' says I, 'freely ; and I'll perform it faithfully.'

'Why then,' says William, 'my scheme is this :— We are now at the mouth of the gulf of Persia ; we have sold so much of our cargo here at Surat, that we have money enough : send me away for Bassora with the sloop, loaden with the China goods we have on board, which will make another good cargo, and I'll warrant thee I'll **find means, among the English and** the Dutch merchants there, to lodge a quantity of goods and money also as **a merchant, so** as we will be able to have recourse to it again upon any occasion ; and when **I come** home we will contrive the rest ; and **in** the meantime do you bring the ship's **crew** to take a resolution to go to Madagascar as soon as I return.'

I told him I thought he need not go so far as Bassora, but might run into Gombaroon, or to Ormus, and pretend the same business.

' No,' says he, ' **I cannot act** with the same freedom there, because the Company's factory are there, and I **may** be laid hold of there, on pretence of interloping.'

' Well, but,' said I, ' you may go to Ormus then ; **for** I am loath to part with you so long as to go to the bottom of the Persian Gulf.' He returned, that I should leave it to him to do as he should see cause.

(They levant accordingly, and make much money as merchants ; but Singleton's conscience grows troublesome.)

It was during my being here, for here we stayed near two months, that I grew very thoughtful about **my** circumstances ; not as to the danger, neither indeed were we in any, but were entirely concealed and unsuspected ; but I really began to have other thoughts of myself, and of the world, than ever I had before.

William had struck so deep into my unthinking temper, with hinting to me that there was something beyond all this; that the present time was the time of enjoyment, but that the time of account approached; that the work that remained was gentler than the labour past, viz. repentance, and that it was high time to think of it : I say these, and such thoughts as these, engrossed my hours, and, in a word, I grew very sad.

As to the wealth I had, which was immensely great, it was all like dirt under my feet ; I had no value for it, no peace in the possession of it, no great concern about me for the leaving of it.

William had perceived my thoughts to be troubled, and my mind heavy and oppressed for some time ; and one evening, in one of our cool walks, I began with him about the leaving our effects.   William was a wise and wary man ; and indeed all the prudentials of my conduct had for a long time been owing to his advice, and so now all the methods for preserving our effects, and even ourselves, lay upon him ; and he had been telling me of some of the measures he had been taking for our making homeward, and for the security of our wealth, when I took him very short. ' Why, William,' says I, ' dost thou think we shall ever be able to reach Europe with all this cargo that we have about us?'

'Aye,' says William, 'without doubt, as well as other merchants with theirs, as long as it is not publicly known what quantity or of what value our cargo consists.'

'Why, William,' says I, smiling, 'do you think that, if there is a God above, as you have so long been telling me there is, and that we must give an account to Him; I say, do you think, if He be a righteous judge, He will let us escape thus with the plunder, as we may call it, of so many innocent people, nay, I might say nations, and not call us to an account for it before we can get to Europe, where we pretend to enjoy it?'

William appeared struck and surprised at the question, and made no answer for a great while; and I repeated the question, adding that it was not to be expected.

After a little pause, says William, 'Thou hast started a very weighty question, and I can make no positive answer to it; but I will state it thus: first, it is time that, if we consider the justice of God, we have no reason to expect any protection; but as the ordinary ways of Providence are out of the common road of human affairs, so we may hope for mercy still upon our repentance, and we know not how good He may be to us; so we are to act as if we rather depended upon the last, I mean the merciful part, than claimed the first, which must produce nothing but judgment and vengeance.'

'But hark ye, William,' says I, 'the nature of repentance, as you hinted once to me, included reformation; and we can never reform; how then can we repent?'

'Why can we never reform?' says William.

'Because,' said I, 'we cannot restore what we have taken away by rapine and spoil.'

'It is true,' says William, 'we can never do that; for we can never come to the knowledge of the owners.'

'But what then must be done with our wealth,' said I, 'the effects of plunder and rapine? If we keep it, we continue to be robbers and thieves; and if we quit it, we cannot do justice with it, for we cannot restore it to the right owners.'

'Nay,' says William, 'the answer to it is short. To quit what we have, and do it here, is to throw it away to those who have no claim to it, and to divest ourselves of it, but to do no right with it; whereas we ought to keep it carefully together, with a resolution to do what right with it we are able; and who knows what opportunity Providence may put into our hands, to do justice, at least, to some of those we have injured; so we ought, at least, to leave it to Him, and go on. As it is, without doubt, our present business is to go to some place of **safety,** where we may wait His will.'

This resolution **of** William was very satisfying **to** me indeed, as, the truth is, all he **said, and at all** times, was solid and good ; and had not William **thus,** as it were, quieted my mind, I think, verily, I was so alarmed at the just reason I had to expect vengeance from Heaven upon me for my ill-gotten wealth, that I should have run away from it as the devil's goods, that **I** had nothing to do with, that did not belong to me, and that I had no right to keep, and was **in** certain danger of being destroyed for.

However, William settled my mind to more prudent steps than these, and I concluded that I ought, **how**ever, to proceed to a place of safety, and leave the **event to** God Almighty's mercy ; but this **I must** leave upon record, that I **had,** from this time, no joy of the wealth I had got ; I looked upon it as stolen, and so indeed the greatest part of it was ; I looked upon it as a hoard of other men's goods, which I had robbed the innocent owners of, and which **I** ought, in a word, to be hanged for here, and damned for hereafter ; and now, indeed, I began sincerely **to** hate myself **for** a dog ; a wretch, that had been a thief, and a murderer ; a wretch, that was in a condi**tion** which nobody was ever in ; for I had robbed, and though I had the wealth by me, yet it was impossible I should ever make any restitution ; and upon this account it ran in my head that I could never repent, for that repentance could not be sincere without restitution, and therefore must of necessity be damned; there was no room for me to escape; I went about with my heart full of these thoughts, little better than a distracted fellow; in short, running headlong into the most dreadful despair, and pre-meditating nothing but how to rid myself out of the world; and, indeed, the devil, if such things are of the devil's immediate doing, followed his work very close with me; and nothing lay upon my mind for several days but to shoot myself into the head with my pistol.

I was all this while in a vagrant life, among infidels, Turks, pagans, and such sort of people; I had no minister, no Christian to converse with, but poor William; he was my ghostly father, or confessor; and he was all the comfort I had. As for my knowledge of religion, you have heard my history; you may suppose I had not much; and, as for the word of God, I don't remember that I ever read a chapter in the Bible in my lifetime; I was little Bob at Busselton, and went to school to learn my Testament.

However, it pleased God to make William the quaker everything to me. Upon this occasion I took him out one evening, as usual, and hurried him away into the fields with me, in more haste than ordinary; and there, in short, I told him the perplexity of my mind, and under what terrible temptations of the devil I had been ; that I must shoot myself, for I could not support the weight and terror that was upon me.

'Shoot yourself!' says William ; 'why, what will that do for you ?'

'Why,' says I, 'it will put an end to a miserable life.'

'Well,' says William, 'are you satisfied the next will be better ?'

'No, no,' says I, 'much worse, to be sure.'

'Why then,' says he, 'shooting yourself is the devil's motion, no doubt; for it is the devil of a reason, that, because thou art in an ill case, therefore thou must put thyself into a worse.'

This shocked my reason indeed. 'Well but,' says I, 'there is no bearing the miserable condition I am in.'

'Very well,' says William ; 'but it seems there is some bearing a worse condition ; and so you will shoot yourself, that you may be past remedy ?'

'I am past remedy already,' says I.

'How do you know that ?' says he.

'I am satisfied of it,' said I.

'Well,' says he, 'but you are not sure ; so you will shoot yourself to make it certain ; for, though on this side death you cannot be sure you will be damned at all, yet the moment you step on the other side of time you are sure of it ; for when it is done, it is not

to be said then that you will be, but that you are
damned.'

'Well, but,' says William, as if he had been between
jest and earnest, 'pray, what didst thou dream of last
night?'

'Why,' said I, 'I had frightful dreams all night;
and, particularly, I dreamed that the devil came for
me, and asked me what my name was? and I told
him. Then he asked me what trade I was?
"Trade!" says I; "I am a thief, a rogue, by my
calling; I am a pirate, and a murderer, and ought to
be hanged." "Ay, ay," says the devil, "so you do;
and you are the man I looked for, and therefore
come along with me;" at which, I was most horribly
frightened, and cried out, so that it waked me; and
I have been in horrible agony ever since.'

'Very well,' says William; 'come, give me the
pistol thou talkedst of just now.'

'Why,' says I, 'what will you do with it?'

'Do with it!' says William, 'why, thou needest
not shoot thyself; I shall be obliged to do it for thee:
why, thou wilt destroy us all.'

'What do you mean, William?' said I.

'Mean!' said he; 'nay, what didst thou mean, to
cry out aloud in thy sleep, I am a thief, a pirate, a
murderer, and ought to be hanged? Why, thou wilt
ruin us all; 'twas well the Dutchman did not understand English. In short, I must shoot thee, to save

my own life: come, come,' says he, 'give me thy pistol.'

I confess this terrified me again another way; and I began to be sensible, that, if anybody had been near me to understand English, I had been undone. The thought of shooting myself forsook me from that time; and I turned to William; 'You disorder me extremely, William,' said I; 'why I am never safe, nor is it safe to keep me company; What shall I do? I shall betray you all.'

'Come, come, friend Bob,' says he, 'I'll put an end to it all, if you will take my advice.'

'How's that?' said I.

'Why, only,' says he, 'that the next time thou talkest with the devil, thou wilt talk a little softlier, or we shall be all undone, and you too.'

This frightened me, I must confess, and allayed a great deal of the trouble of mind I was in; but William, after he had done jesting with me, entered upon a very long and serious discourse with me about the nature of my circumstances, and about repentance; that it ought to be attended, indeed, with a deep abhorrence of the crime that I had to charge myself with; but that to despair of God's mercy was no part of repentance, but putting myself into the condition of the devil; indeed, that I must apply myself with a sincere humble confession of my crime, to ask pardon of God, whom I had offended, and cast myself upon His mercy, resolving to be willing to make restitution, if ever it should please God to put it in my power, even to the utmost of what I had in the world; and this, he told me, was the method which he had resolved upon himself; and in this, he told me, he had found comfort.

I had a great deal of satisfaction in William's discourse, and it quieted me very much; but William was very anxious ever after about my talking in my sleep, and took care to lie with me always himself, and to keep me from lodging in any house where so much as a word of English was understood.

(*For William, as will be seen, understood how to make the best of both worlds.*)

II.—'MOLL FLANDERS'

(*In my judgment* Moll Flanders *is not only the most remarkable of Defoe's minor novels, but the most remarkable example of pure realism in literature.* To *read any one of* M. Zola's *much-talked-of books, and then* to return to *this, is to see the difference between talent* misled by theory *and genius conducted by* art. *The book* is of course *not wholly edifying, containing as* it *does the history of* a woman *who allows herself to be led astray by vanity and cupidity quite as much as by passion in early youth ; and who afterwards for more than forty years lives the life of an adventuress, ending (or all but ending, for there is a final rehabilitation)* as a common thief. *But the* nature of it is astonishing, and the art more *astonishing* still. *The author made some apology for the crudity* of the scenes ; and this *crudity, being of course more strongly apparent now, makes selection a little difficult.* But the two *following passages* are still *fairly representative.* The *separation of* them from *the story* does *no* harm, for *there is hardly any plot, though there is a certain* con-catenation *of episode.*

In the earlier part of the book the heroine has married, lost *her first husband* (the brother *of* her first lover), *and being relieved of her children by* the *family,* is *left to herself in* London, *a young* widow of *four-and-twenty, with some* money, *no* principles, and *a* distinct inclination to make the most of herself. *She* passes thence through divers hands, and when this extract opens is already in middle age, but still handsome. She has been persuaded by a more artful adventuress, whom she met at Bath, to go to Lancashire ; she does so, and is introduced to the woman's brother, with a curious result of ' cross-biting.')

Well, I went with my friend as I **called her,** into Lancashire ; all **the** way we went she caressed **me with the** utmost appearance of a sincere undissembled affection ; treated me, except my coach-hire, all the way ; and her brother brought **a** gentleman's coach to Warrington to receive us, and **we** were carried from thence to Liverpool with **as much ceremony as** I could desire.

We were also entertained at a merchant's house in Liverpool three or four days very handsomely ; I **forbear** to tell **his** name, because of what followed ; **then** she told me she would carry **me** to an uncle's house of hers where we should be nobly entertained ; and her uncle, as she called him, sent a coach and four horses for us, and we were carried near forty miles I know not whither.

We came however to a gentleman's seat, where was a numerous family, a large park, extraordinary company indeed, and where she was called cousin ; I told her if she had resolved to bring me into such company as this, she should have let me have furnished myself with better clothes ; the ladies took notice of that, and told me very genteelly they did not value people in their own country so much by their clothes as they did in London ; that their cousin had fully informed them of my quality, and that I did not want clothes to set me off ; in short, they entertained me not like what I was, but like what they thought I had been, namely, a widow lady of a great fortune.

The first discovery I made here was, that the family were all Roman Catholics, and the cousin too ; however, nobody in the world could behave better to me, and I had all the civility shown that I could have had if I had been of their opinion. The truth is, I had not so much principle of any kind, as to be nice in point of religion ; and I presently learned to speak favourably of the Romish church ; particularly I told them I saw little but the prejudice of education in all the differences that were among Christians about religion, and if it had so happened that my father had been a Roman Catholic, I doubted not but I should have been as well pleased with their religion as my own.

This obliged them in the highest degree, and as I was besieged day and night with good company, and pleasant discourse, so I had two or three old ladies that lay at me upon the subject of religion too; I was so complaisant that I made no scruple to be present at their mass, and to conform to all their gestures as they showed me the pattern, but I would not come too cheap; so that I only in the main encouraged them to expect that I would turn Roman Catholic if I was instructed in the Catholic doctrine, as they called it; and so the matter rested.

I stayed here about six weeks; and then my conductor led me back to a country village, about six miles from Liverpool, where her brother, as she called him, came to visit me in his own chariot, with two footmen in a good livery; and the next thing was to make love to me. As it happened to me, one would think I could not have been cheated, and indeed I thought so myself, having a safe card at home, which I resolved not to quit unless I could mend myself very much. However, in all appearance this brother was a match worth my listening to, and the least his estate was valued at was £1000 a year, but the sister said it was worth £1500 a year, and lay most of it in Ireland.

I that was a great fortune, and passed for such, was above being asked how much my estate was; and my false friend taking it upon a foolish hearsay, had raised it from £500 to £5000, and by the time she came into the country she called it £15,000. The Irishman, for such I understood him to be, was stark mad at this bait: in short, he courted me, made me presents, and run in debt like a madman for the expenses of his courtship: he had, to give him his due, the appearance of an extraordinary fine gentleman; he was tall, well-shaped, and had an extraordinary address; talked as naturally of his park and his stables, of his horses, his game-keepers, his woods, his tenants, and his servants, as if he had been in a mansion-house, and I had seen them all about me.

He never so much as asked me about my fortune or estate; but assured me that when we came to Dublin he would jointure me in £600 a year in good land; and that he would enter into a deed of settlement, or contract here, for the performance of it.

This was such language indeed as I had not been used to, and I was here beaten out of all my measures; I had a she-devil in my bosom, every hour telling me how great her brother lived: one time she would come for my orders, how I would have my coach painted, and how lined; and another time what clothes my page should wear: in short, my eyes were dazzled, I had now lost my power of saying no, and to cut the story short, I consented to be married; but to be more private, we were carried farther into the country, and married by a priest, which I was assured would marry us as effectually as a Church of England parson.

But the glittering show of a great estate and of fine things which the deceived creature that was now my deceiver represented every hour to my imagination, hurried me away, and gave me no time to think of London, or of anything there, much less of the obligation I had to a person of infinitely more real merit than what was now before me.

But the thing was done, I was now in the arms of my new spouse, who appeared still the same as before; great even to magnificence, and nothing less than a thousand pounds a year could support the ordinary equipage he appeared in.

After we had been married about a month he began to talk of my going to West-chester in order to embark for Ireland. However, he did not hurry me, for we stayed near three weeks longer, and then he sent to Chester for a coach to meet us at the Black Rock, as they call it, over against Liverpool. Thither we went in a fine boat they call a pinnace, with six oars; his servants, and horses, and baggage going in a ferry-boat. He made his excuse to me that he had no acquaintance at Chester, but he would go before and get some handsome apartments for me at a private house; I asked him how long we should stay at Chester? he said, not at all, **any longer than** one night or two, but he would **immediately hire a coach** to go to Holyhead; then I told him he should by no means give himself the trouble to get private lodgings for one night or two, for that Chester being a great place, I made no doubt but there would be very good inns, and accommodation enough; so we lodged at an inn not far from the cathedral; I forgot what sign it was at.

Here my spouse, talking of my going to Ireland, **asked me** if I had no affairs to settle at London before we went off; I told him no, not of any great consequence, but what might be done as well by letter from Dublin: 'Madam,' says he very respectfully, 'I suppose the greatest part of your estate, which my sister tells me is most of it in money in the Bank of England, lies secure enough, but in case it required transferring, or any way altering its property, it might be necessary to go up to London, and settle these things before we went over.'

I seemed to look strange at it, and told him I knew not what he meant; that I had no effects **in** the Bank of England that I knew of; and I hope he could not say that I had ever told him I had. 'No,' he said, 'I had not told him so, but his sister had said the greatest part of my estate lay there; and I **only** mentioned it, my dear,' said he, 'that if there was **any** occasion to settle it, or order anything about it, we might not be obliged to the hazard and trouble of another voyage **back again ;** ' **for, he added,** that he did not care to **venture me too much upon the** sea.

I was surprised at **this talk, and** began to consider what **the meaning of** it must **be !** and **it** presently **occurred to me** that my friend, who called **him** brother, had represented me in colours which **were** not my due ; and I thought that I would know the **bottom of** it before I went out of England, and before I should put myself into I know not whose hands, in a strange country.

Upon this I called **his sister into my** chamber the next morning, and letting her know the discourse her brother and I had been upon, I conjured her to tell me what she had said to him, and upon what footing it was that she had made this marriage ? She owned that she had told him that I was a great fortune, and said that she was told so at London : ' Told so,' says I **warmly,** ' did I ever tell you so ?' 'No,' she said, 'it **was true I never did** tell her so, but I had said several times **that what I had** was in my **own** disposal.' 'I did so,' returned I very quick, 'but I never told you I had anything called a fortune ; no, that I had £100 or the **value of** £100 in the world : and how did it consist with my being a fortune,' said I, '**that I should come** here into the north of England **with** you, only upon the account of living cheap ?' At these words, **which I** spoke warm and high, **my** husband came into the room, and I desired him to come in and sit down, for I had something of moment to say before them both, which it was absolutely necessary he should hear.

He looked a little disturbed at the assurance with which I seemed to speak it, and came and sat down by me, having first shut the door; upon which I began, for I was very much provoked, and turning myself to him, 'I am afraid,' says I, 'my dear' (for I spoke with kindness on his side), 'that you have a very great abuse put upon you, and an injury done you never to be repaired in your marrying me, which, however, as I have had no hand in it, I desire I may be fairly acquitted of it, and that the blame may lie where it ought and nowhere else, for I wash my hands of every part of it.' 'What injury can be done me, my dear,' says he, 'in marrying you? I hope it is to my honour and advantage every way.' 'I will soon explain it to you,' says I, 'and I fear there will be no reason to think yourself well used, but I will convince you, my dear,' says I again, 'that I have had no hand in it.'

He looked now scared and wild, and began, I believed, to suspect what followed; however, looking towards me, and saying only, 'Go on,' he sat silent, as if to hear what I had more to say; so I went on: 'I asked you last night,' said I, speaking to him, 'if ever I made any boast to you of my estate, or ever told you I had any estate in the Bank of England, or anywhere else, and you owned I had not, as is most true; and I desire you will tell me here, before your sister, if ever I gave you any reason from me to think so, or that ever we had any discourse about it;' and he owned again I had not; **but said, I** had **appeared** always as a woman of fortune, and he de-**pended on** it that I was so, and hoped he was not **de-ceived.** 'I am not inquiring whether you have been de-ceived,' said I, 'I fear you have, and I too; but I am clearing myself from being concerned in deceiving you.

'I have been now asking your sister if ever I told her of **any fortune or estate** I had, or gave her any particulars of it; and she **owns I** never did: "And pray, madam," said I, "be so just to me, to charge me if you can, **if ever I** pretended to you **that I** had an estate; and why if I had, should I ever come down into this country with you on purpose to spare that little I had, and live cheap?"' She could not deny one word, but said she had been told in London that **I had** a very great fortune, **and** that it lay in the Bank of England.

'And now, dear sir,' said I, turning myself to my new spouse again, 'be so just to me as to tell me **who** has abused both you and me so much, as to make you believe I was a fortune, and prompt you to court me to this marriage?' He could not speak a word, but pointed to her; and after some more pause, flew out in the most furious passion that **ever I** saw a man **in my life**; cursing her, and calling her all the ——

and hard names he could think of; and that she had ruined him, declaring that she had told him I had £15,000, and that she was to have £500 of him for procuring this match for him: he then added, directing his speech to me, that she was none of his sister, but had been his —— for two years before; that she had had £100 of him in part of this bargain, and that he was utterly undone if things were as I said; and in his raving he swore he would let her heart's blood out immediately, which frightened her and me too. She cried, said she had been told so in the house where I lodged: but this aggravated him more than before, that she should put so far upon him, and run things such a length upon no other authority than a hearsay; and then turning to me again, said very honestly, he was afraid we were both undone; 'for to be plain, my dear, I have no estate,' says he; 'what little I had, this devil has made me run out in putting me into this equipage.' She took the opportunity of his being earnest in talking with me, and got out of the room, and I never saw her more.

I was confounded now as much as he, and knew not what to say: I thought many ways that I had the worst of it, but his saying he was undone, and that he had no estate neither, put me into a mere distraction. 'Why,' says I to him, 'this has been a hellish juggle, for we are married here upon the foot of a double fraud; you are undone by the disappointment it seems, and if I had had a fortune I had been cheated too, for you say you have nothing.'

'You would indeed have been cheated, my dear,' says he, 'but you would not have been undone, for £15,000 would have maintained us both very handsomely in this country; and I had resolved to have dedicated every groat of it to you; I would not have wronged you of a shilling, and the rest I would have made up in my affection to you, and tenderness of you as long as I lived.'

This was very honest indeed, and I really believe he spoke as he intended, and that he was a man that was as well qualified to make me happy, as to his temper and behaviour, as any man ever was; but his having no estate, and being run into debt on this ridiculous account in the country, made all the prospect dismal and dreadful, and I knew not what to say, or what to think.

I told him it was very unhappy, that so much love, and so much good nature as I discovered in him, should be thus precipitated into misery; that I saw nothing before us but ruin, for as to me, it was my unhappiness, that what little I had was not able to relieve us a week, and with that I pulled out a bank-bill of £20 and eleven guineas, which I told him I had saved out of my little income; and that by the account that creature had given me of the way of living in that country, I expected it would maintain me three or four years; that if it was taken from me, I was left destitute, and he knew what the condition of a woman must be, if she had **no money in her** pocket; however, I told him, if **he** would take it, there it was.

He told me with great concern, and I thought I saw tears in his eyes, that he would not touch it, that he abhorred the thoughts of stripping me and making me miserable; that he had fifty guineas left, which was all **he** had in the world, and he pulled it out and threw it down on the table, bidding me take it, though he were to starve for want of it.

I returned, with the same concern for him, that I could not bear to hear him talk so; that, on the contrary, if he could propose any probable method of living I would do anything that became me, and that I would live as narrow as he could desire.

He begged of me to talk no more at that rate, for it would make him distracted; he said he was bred a gentleman, though he was reduced to a low fortune, and that there was but one way left which he could think of, **and** that would not do, unless I could answer him one question, which however he said he would not press me to; I told him I would answer it honestly; whether it would be to his satisfaction or **no** that I could not tell.

'Why then, my dear, tell me plainly,' says he, 'will **the** little you have keep us together in any figure, or **in any** station or place, or will it not?'

It was my happiness **that** I had **not** discovered

myself, or my circumstances, at all; no, not so much as my name; and **seeing there** was nothing to be expected **from him,** however good-humoured, and however honest he seemed **to** be, but to live on what I **knew** would soon be wasted, I resolved **to** conceal **everything** but the bank-bill, and eleven guineas, **and** I **would have** been very glad **to** have lost that, **and have** been set down where he took me up. I **had** indeed another bank-bill about me of £30, which **was the** whole **of what I** brought with me, as well **to** subsist on in the **country, as not** knowing what might offer; because this creature, the go-between that had thus betrayed us **both,** had made me **believe** strange things of marrying **to** my advantage, and I was not willing to be without money, whatever might happen. This bill I concealed, and that made me the freer of the rest, in consideration of his circumstances, for I **really** pitied him heartily.

But to return to this question, I told him I **never willingly** deceived him, and I never would. I was very **sorry** to tell him that the little I had would **not** subsist **us:** that **it** was not sufficient to subsist **me** alone in the south country, and that this was the reason that **made me** put myself into the hands of that woman who called him brother, she having assured me that I might board very handsomely at a town called Manchester, where I had not yet been, for about £6 a year, and my whole **income** not being above £15 a year, I thought I might live easy upon it, and wait for better things.

He shook his head, and remained silent, and a very melancholy evening we had ; however we supped together, and abode together that night, and when we had almost supped he looked a little better, and more cheerful, and called for a bottle of wine ; 'Come, my dear,' says he, 'though the case is bad, it is to no purpose to be dejected ; Come, be as easy as you can, I will endeavour to find out some way or other to live ; if you can but subsist yourself, that is better than nothing, I must try the world again ; a man ought to think like a man ; to be discouraged, is to yield to the misfortune.' With this he filled a glass, and drank to me, holding my hand all the while the wine went down, and protesting his main concern was for me.

It was really a true gallant spirit he was of, and it was the more grievous to me. 'Tis something of relief even to be undone by a man of honour, rather than by a scoundrel ; but here the greatest disappointment was on his side, for he had really spent a great deal of money, and it was very remarkable on what poor terms she proceeded ; first, the baseness of the creature herself is to be observed, who for the getting £100 herself, could be content to let him spend three or four more, though perhaps it was all he had in the world, and more than all ; when she had not the least ground more than a little tea-table chat, to say that I had any estate, or was a fortune, or the like. It is true the design of deluding a woman of a fortune, if I had been so, was base enough; the putting the face of great things upon poor circumstances was a fraud, and bad enough; but the case a little differed too, and that in his favour, for he was not a rake that made a trade to delude women, and as some have done, get six or seven fortunes after one another, and then rifle and run away from them; but he was already a gentleman, unfortunate and low, but had lived well; and though if I had had a fortune, I should have been enraged at the slut for betraying me, yet really for the man, a fortune would not have been ill bestowed on him, for he was a lovely person indeed, of generous principles, good sense, and of abundance of good humour.

We had a great deal of close conversation that night, for we neither of us slept much; he was as penitent, for having put all those cheats upon me, as if it had been felony, and that he was going to execution; he offered me again every shilling of the money he had about him, and said he would go into the army and seek for more.

I asked him why he would be so unkind to carry me into Ireland, when I might suppose he could not have subsisted me there? He took me in his arms; 'My dear,' said he, 'I never designed to go to Ireland at all, much less to have carried you thither; but came hither to be out of the observation of the people, who had heard what I pretended to, and that nobody might ask me for money before I was furnished to supply them.'

'But, where then,' said I, 'were we to have gone next?'

'Why, my dear,' said he, 'I'll confess the whole scheme to you, as I had laid it; I purposed here to ask you something about your estate, as you see I did, and when you, as I expected you would, had entered into some account of the particulars, I would have made an excuse to have put off our voyage to Ireland for some time, and so have gone for London.

'Then, my dear,' says he, 'I resolved to have confessed all the circumstances of my own affairs to you, and let you know I had indeed made use of these artifices to obtain your consent to marry me, but had now nothing to do but to ask your pardon, and to tell you how abundantly I would endeavour to make you forget what was past, by the felicity of the days to come.'

'Truly,' said I to him, 'I find you would soon have conquered me ; and it is my affliction now, that I am not in a condition to let you see how easily I should have been reconciled to you, and have passed by all the tricks you had put upon me, in recompense of so much good humour ; 'but, my dear,' said I, 'what can we do now? we are both undone, and what better are we for our being reconciled, seeing we have nothing to live on?'

We proposed a great many things, but nothing could offer, where there was nothing to begin with. He begged me at last to talk no more of it, for, he said, I would break his heart; so we talked of other things a little, till at last he took a husband's leave of me, and so went to sleep.

He rose before me in the morning, and indeed having lain awake almost all night, I was very sleepy, and lay till near eleven o'clock, in this time he took his horses, and three servants, and all his linen and baggage, and away he went, leaving a short but moving letter for me on the table, as follows:

'My dear,—I am a dog; I have abused you; but I have been drawn in to do it by a base creature, contrary to my principle, and the general practice of my life. Forgive me, my dear! I ask you pardon with the greatest sincerity; I am the most miserable of men, in having deluded you: I have been so happy to possess you, and am now so wretched as to be forced to fly from you. Forgive me, my dear; once more I say, forgive me! I am not able to see you ruined by me, and myself unable to support you. Our marriage is nothing; I shall never be able to see you again; I here discharge you from it; if you can marry to your advantage do not decline it on my account; I here swear to you on my faith, and on the word of a man of honour, I will never disturb your repose if I should know of it, which however is not likely: on the other hand, if you should not marry, and if good fortune should befall me, it shall be all yours wherever you are.

'I have put some of the stock of money I have left into your pocket; take places for yourself and your maid in the stage coach, and go for London; I hope it will bear your charges thither, without breaking into your own. Again I sincerely ask your pardon, and will do so as often as I shall ever think of you.— Adieu, my dear, for ever! I am yours most affectionately, J. E.'

Nothing that ever befell me in my life sunk so deep into my heart as this farewell: I reproached him a thousand times in my thoughts for leaving me, for I would have gone with him through the world, if I had begged my bread. I felt in my pocket, and there I found ten guineas, his gold watch, and two little rings, one a small diamond ring, worth only about £6, and the other a plain gold ring.

I sat down and looked upon these things two hours together, and scarce spoke a word, till my maid interrupted me, by telling me my dinner was ready: I ate but little, and after dinner I fell into a violent fit of crying, every now and then calling him by his name, which was James; 'O Jemmy!' said I, 'come back, come back, I'll give you all I have; I'll beg,

I'll starve with you.' And thus I ran raving about the room several times, and then sat down between whiles, and then walked about again, called upon him to come back, and then cried again; and thus I passed the afternoon, till about seven o'clock, when it was near dusk in the evening, being August, when to my unspeakable surprise he comes back into the inn, and comes directly up into my chamber.

I was in the greatest confusion imaginable, and so was he too : I could not imagine what should be the occasion of it; and began to be at odds with myself whether to be glad or sorry; but my affection biassed all the rest, and it was impossible to conceal my joy, which was too great for smiles, for it burst out into tears. He was no sooner entered the room, but he ran to me and took me in his arms, holding me fast, and almost stopping my breath with his kisses, but spoke not a word; at length I began. 'My dear,' said I, 'how could you go away from me ?' to which he gave no answer, for it was impossible for him to speak.

When our ecstasies were a little over, he told me he was gone above fifteen miles, but it was not in his power to go any farther, without coming back to see me again, and to take his leave of me once more.

I told him how I had passed my time, and how loud I had called him to come back again; he told me he heard me very plain upon Delamere Forest, at a place about twelve miles off. I smiled. 'Nay,' says he, 'do not think I am in jest, for if ever I heard your voice in my life, I heard you call me aloud, and sometimes I thought I saw you running after me.' 'Why,' said I, 'what did I say?' for I had not named the words to him. 'You called aloud,' says he, 'and said, "O Jemmy! O Jemmy! come back, come back."'

I laughed at him. 'My dear,' says he, 'do not laugh, for depend upon it, I heard your voice as plain as you hear mine now; if you please, I'll go before a magistrate and make oath of it;' I then began to be amazed and surprised, and indeed frighted, and told him what I had really done, and how I had called after him, as above. When we had amused ourselves awhile about this, I said to him, 'Well, you shall go away from me no more, I'll go all over the world with you rather.' He told me, it would be a very difficult thing for him to leave me, but since it must be, he hoped I would make it as easy to me as I could; but as for him, it would be his destruction, that he foresaw.

However, he told me that he had considered he had left me to travel to London alone, which was a long journey; and that as he might as well go that way as any way else, he was resolved to see me hither, or near it; and if he did go away then without taking his leave, I should not take it ill of him; and this he made me promise.

He told me how he had dismissed his three servants, sold their horses, and sent the fellows away to seek their fortunes, and all in a little time, at a town on the road, I know not where ; 'and,' says he, 'it cost me some tears all alone by myself, to think how much happier they were than their master, for they could go to the next gentleman's house to see for a service, whereas,' said he, 'I knew not whither to go, or what to do with myself.'

I told him I was so completely miserable in parting with him, that I could not be worse ; and that now he was come again, I would not go from him, if he would take me with him, let him go whither he would. And in the meantime I agreed that we would go together to London ; but I could not be brought to consent he should go away at last, and not take his leave of me ; but told him jesting, that if he did, I would call him back again as loud as I did before. Then I pulled out his watch, and gave it him back, and his two rings, and his ten guineas ; but he would not take them, which made me very much suspect that he resolved to go off upon the road, and leave me.

The truth is, the circumstances he was in, the passionate expressions of his letter, the kind gentlemanly treatment I had from him in all the affair, with the concern he showed for me in it, his manner of parting with that large share which he gave me of his little stock left, all these had joined to make such impressions on me, that I could not bear the thoughts of parting with him.

Two days after this we quitted Chester, I in the stage-coach, and he on horseback ; **I** ˙dismissed **my** maid at Chester ; he **was** very much against my **being** without a maid, but she being hired in the **country** (keeping no servant at London), I told him it would have been barbarous to have taken the poor wench, and have **turned** her away as soon as I came to town ; and it would also have been a needless charge on the road ; so I satisfied him, and he was easy on that score

He came with me as far as Dunstable, within **thirty** miles of London, and then he told me fate and **his** own misfortunes obliged him to leave me, and that it was not convenient for him to go **to** London, for reasons which **it was of no** value to me to know, and I saw him preparing to go. The stage-coach we **were** in did not usually stop at Dunstable, **but** I desiring it for a quarter of an hour, they were content **to** stand at an inn-door a while, and we went into the house.

Being in the inn, I told him I had but one favour more to **ask** him, and that was, that since he could not go any farther, he would give me leave to stay **a** week or two **in** the town with him, that we might **in** that time think of something to prevent such a ruin-**ous** thing to us both, as a final separation would be ; **and** that I had something of moment to offer to him, **which** perhaps he might find practicable to our advantage.

This was too reasonable a proposal to be denied, so he called the landlady of the house, and told her his wife was taken ill, and so ill that she could not think of going any farther in a stage-coach, which had tired her almost to death, and asked if she could not get us a lodging for two or three days in a private house where I might rest me a little, for the journey had been too much for me? The landlady, a good sort of a woman, well-bred, and very obliging, came immediately to see me; told me, she had two or three very good rooms in a part of the house quite out of the noise, and if I saw them she did not doubt but I would like them, and I should have one of her maids, that should do nothing else but wait on me; this was so very kind, that I could not but accept of it; so I went to look on the rooms, and liked them very well, and indeed they were extraordinarily furnished, and very pleasant lodgings; so we paid the stage-coach, took out our baggage, and resolved to stay here awhile.

Here I told him I would live with him now till all my money was spent, but would not let him spend a shilling of his own: we had some kind squabble about that, but I told him it was the last time I was like to enjoy his company, and I desired that he would let me be master in that thing only, and he should govern in everything else; so he acquiesced.

Here one evening, taking a walk into the fields, I

told him I would now make the proposal to him I had told him of; accordingly I related to him how I had lived in Virginia, that I had a mother, I believed was alive there still, though my husband was dead some years; I told him that had not my effects miscarried, which by the way I magnified pretty much, I might have been fortune good enough to him to have kept us from being parted in this manner. Then I entered into the manner of people's settling in those countries, how they had a quantity of land given them by the constitution of the place; and if not, that it might be purchased at so easy a rate that it was not worth naming.

I then gave him a full and distinct account of the nature of planting, how with carrying over but two or three hundred pounds' value in English goods, with some servants and tools, a man of application would presently lay a foundation for a family, and in a few years would raise an estate.

I let him into the nature of the product of the earth, how the ground was cured and prepared, and what the usual increase of it was; and demonstrated to him, that in a very few years, with such a beginning, we should be as certain of being rich as we were now certain of being poor.

He was surprised at my discourse; for we made it the whole subject of our conversation for near a week together, in which time I laid it down in black and white, as we say, that it was morally impossible, with a supposition of any reasonable good conduct, but that we must thrive there and do very well.

Then I told him what measures I would take to raise such a sum as £300 or thereabouts; and I argued with him how good a method it would be to put an end to our misfortunes, and restore our circumstances in the world, to what we had both expected; and I added, that after seven years we might be in a posture to leave our plantation in good hands, and come over again and receive the income of it, and live here and enjoy it; and I gave him examples of some that had done so, and lived now in very good figure in London.

In short, I pressed him so to it, that he almost agreed to it, but still something or other broke it off; till at last he turned the tables, and began to talk almost to the same purpose of Ireland.

He told me that a man that could confine himself to a country life, and that could but find stock to enter upon any land, should have farms there for £50 a year, as good as were let here for £200 a year; that the produce was such, and so rich the land, that if much was not laid up, we were sure to live as handsomely upon it as a gentleman of £3000 a year could do in England; and that he had laid a scheme to leave me in London, and go over and try; and if he found he could lay a handsome foundation of living, suitable to the respect he had for me, as he doubted not he should do, he would come over and fetch me.

I was dreadfully afraid that upon such a proposal he would have taken me at my word, viz. to turn my little income into money, and let him carry it over into Ireland and try his experiment with it; but he was too just to desire it, or to have accepted it if I had offered it; and he anticipated me in that, for he added, that he would go and try his fortune that way, and if he found he could do anything at it to live, then by adding mine to it when I went over, we should live like ourselves; but that he would not hazard a shilling of mine till he had made the experiment with a little, and he assured me that if he found nothing to be done in Ireland he would then come to me and join in my project for Virginia.

He was so earnest upon his project being to be tried first that I could not withstand him; however he promised to let me hear from him in a very little time after his arriving there, to let me know whether his prospect answered his design; that, if there was not a probability of success, I might take the occasion to prepare for our other voyage, and then, he assured me, he would go with me to America with all his heart.

I could bring him to nothing further than this, and which entertained us near a month, during which

I enjoyed his company, which was the most entertaining that ever I met with in my life before. In this time he let me into part of the story of his own life, which was indeed surprising, and full of an infinite variety, sufficient to fill up a much brighter history for its adventures and incidents, than any I ever saw in print; but I shall have occasion to say more of him hereafter.

We parted at last, though with the utmost reluctance on my side; and indeed he took his leave very unwillingly too, but necessity obliged him, for his reasons were very good, why he would not come to London, as I understood more fully afterwards.

(This husband turns out to be a noted highwayman, for which and other reasons the easy-going heroine indulges herself with yet another, whom she has already held in play. She is happy enough with him, but he dies; and her circumstances being very much embarrassed, she has recourse to an old harridan who has before obliged her in awkward straits, and with whose connivance she at last takes to shop-lifting. We begin after her husband's death.)

I lived two years in this dismal condition, wasting that little I had, weeping continually over my dismal circumstances, and as it were only bleeding to death, without the least hope or prospect of help; and now

I had cried so long, and so often, that tears were exhausted, and I began to be desperate, for I grew poor apace.

For a little relief, I had put off my house and took lodgings; and as I was reducing my living, so I sold off most of my goods, which put a little money in my pocket, and I lived near a year upon that, spending very sparingly, and eking things out to the utmost; but still when I looked before me, my heart would sink within me at the inevitable approach of misery and want. O let none read this part without seriously reflecting on the circumstances of a desolate state, and how they would grapple with want of friends and want of bread; it will certainly make them think not of sparing what they have only, but of looking up to heaven for support, and of the wise man's prayer, 'Give me not poverty, lest I steal.'

Let them remember that a time of distress is a time of dreadful temptation, and all the strength to resist is taken away; poverty presses, the soul is made desperate by distress, and what can be done? It was one evening, when being brought, as I may say, to the last gasp, I think I may truly say I was distracted and raving, when prompted by I know not what spirit, and as it were doing I did not know what, or why, I dressed me (for I had still pretty good clothes), and went out: I am very sure I had no manner of design in my head when I went out;

I neither knew, or considered where to go, or on what business; but as the devil carried me out, and laid his bait for me, so he brought me to be sure to the place, for I knew not whither I was going or what I did.

Wandering thus about, I knew not whither, I passed by an apothecary's shop in Leadenhall-street, where I saw lie on a stool just before the counter a little bundle wrapt in a white cloth; beyond it stood a maidservant with her back to it, looking up towards the top of the shop, where the apothecary's apprentice, as I suppose, was standing upon the counter, with his back also to the door, and a candle in his hand, looking and reaching up to the upper shelf, for something he wanted, so that both were engaged, and nobody else in the shop.

This was the bait; and the devil who laid the snare, prompted me, as if he had spoke, for I remember, and shall never forget it, 'twas like a voice spoken over my shoulder, ' Take the bundle ; be quick; do it this moment.' It was no sooner said but I stepped into the shop, and with my back to the wench, as if I had stood up for a cart that was going by, I put my hand behind me and took the bundle, and went off with it, the maid or fellow not perceiving me, or any one else.

It is impossible to express the horror of my soul all the while I did it. When I went away I had no heart to run, or scarce to mend my pace: I crossed the street indeed, and went down the first turning I came to, and I think it was a street that went through into Fenchurch-street; from thence I crossed and turned through so many ways and turnings, that I could never tell which way it was, nor where I went; I felt not the ground I stept on, and the farther I was out of danger the faster I went till, tired and out of breath, I was forced to sit down on a little bench at a door, and then found I was got into Thames-street, near Billingsgate: I rested me a little and went on; my blood was all in a fire, my heart beat as if I was in a sudden fright: in short, I was under such a surprise that I knew not whither I was agoing, or what to do.

After I had tired myself thus with walking a long way about, and so eagerly, I began to consider, and make home to my lodging, where I came about nine o'clock at night.

What the bundle was made up for, or on what occasion laid where I found it, I knew not, but when I came to open it, I found there was a suit of child-bed-linen in it, very good, and almost new, the lace very fine; there was a silver porringer of a pint, a small silver mug, and six spoons, with some other linen, a good smock, and three silk handkerchiefs, and in the mug a paper, 18s. 6d. in money.

All the while I was opening these things I was

under such **dreadful** impressions of fear, and in such terror of mind, though I **was** perfectly safe, that I cannot express **the manner of it**; I sat me down, and cried most vehemently; 'Lord,' said I, 'what am I now? a thief! why, I shall be taken next time, and be carried to Newgate, and be tried for my life!' and with that I cried again a long time, and I am sure, as poor as I was, if I had durst for fear, I would certainly have carried the things back again; but that went off after a while. Well, I went to bed for that night, but slept little, the horror of the **fact** was upon my mind, and I knew not what I said or did all night, and all the next day. Then I was impatient to hear some news of the loss; and would fain know how it was, whether they were a poor body's goods, or a rich; 'perhaps,' said I, 'it may be some poor widow like me, that had packed up these goods to go and sell them for a little bread for herself and a poor child, and are now starving and breaking their hearts, for want of that little they would have fetched;' and this thought tormented **me worse** than all the rest, for three or four days.

But my own distresses silenced all these reflections, and the prospect of my own starving, which grew every day more frightful to me, hardened my heart by degrees. It was then particularly heavy upon my mind, that I had been reformed, and had, as I hoped, repented of all my past wickedness; that I had lived a sober, grave, retired life for several years, but now I should be driven by the dreadful necessity of my circumstances to the gates of destruction, soul and body; and two or three times I fell upon my knees, praying to God, as well as I could, for deliverance; but I cannot but say my prayers had no hope in them: I knew not what to do, it was all fear without, and dark within; and I reflected on my past life as not repented of, that heaven was now beginning to punish me, and would make me as miserable as I had been wicked.

Had I gone on here I had perhaps been a true penitent; but I had an evil counsellor within, and he was continually prompting me to relieve myself by the worst means; so one evening he tempted me again by the same wicked impulse that had said, 'Take that bundle,' to go out again and seek for what might happen.

I went out now by daylight, and wandered about I knew not whither, and in search of I knew not what, when the devil put a snare in my way of a dreadful nature indeed, and such a one as I have never had before or since. Going through Aldersgate-street, there was a pretty little child had been at a dancing-school, and was agoing home all alone; and my prompter, like a true devil, set me upon this innocent creature. I talked to it, and it prattled to me again, and I took it by the hand and led it along

till I came **to a** paved alley that goes into Bartholomew-close, and **I led it in there** ; the child said, that
was not **its way home** ; **I said,** 'Yes, my dear,' it is,
I'll show **you the way home ;'** the child **had a** little
necklace **on of** gold beads, and I had my eye upon
that, and in the dark of the alley I stooped, pretending to mend the child's clog that was loose, and took
off her necklace and the child never felt it, and **so
led the** child **on again.**   Here, I say, the devil **put**
me upon killing the child in the dark alley, that it
might not cry, but the very thought frighted me so
that I was ready **to drop down ; but** I turned the
child about and bade it go back **again, for** that was
not its way home ; **the** child said, so she would, and
I went through **into** Bartholomew-close, and then
turned round to another passage that goes into Long-
lane, so away into Charterhouse-yard, and out **into**
St. John's-street ; then crossing into Smithfield, went
down Chick-lane, and into Field-lane, to Holborn-
bridge, when mixing with the crowd of people usually
passing there, it was not possible to have been found
out ; and thus I made my second sally into the world.

The thoughts of this booty put out all the thoughts
of the first, and the reflections I had made wore quickly
off ; poverty hardened my heart, and my own necessities made me regardless of anything.   The last
affair left no great concern upon me, **for as** I did the
poor child no harm, I only thought **I had** given the

parents a just reproof for their negligence, in leaving the poor lamb to come home by itself, and it would teach them to take more care another time.

This string of beads was worth about £12 or £14. I suppose it might have been formerly the mother's, for it was too big for the child's wear, but that, perhaps, the vanity of the mother to have her child look fine at the dancing-school, had made her let the child wear it, and no doubt the child had a maid sent to take care of it, but she, like a careless jade, was taken up perhaps with some fellow that had met her, and so the poor baby wandered till it fell into my hands.

However, I did the child no harm; I did not so much as fright it, for I had a great many tender thoughts about me yet, and did nothing but what, as I may say, mere necessity drove me to.

I had a great many adventures after this, but I was young in the business, and did not know how to manage, otherwise than as the devil put things into my head; and indeed he was seldom backward to me. One adventure I had which was very lucky to me; I was going through Lombard-street, in the dusk of the evening, just by the end of Three King-court, when on a sudden comes a fellow running by me as swift as lightning, and throws a bundle that was in his hand just behind me, as I stood up against the corner of the house at the turning into the alley; just as he threw it in, he said, 'God bless you, mistress, let it lie there a little,' and away he runs : after him comes two more, and **immediately a** young fellow without his hat, crying, 'Stop **thief**;' they pursued **the** two last fellows **so close that they** were forced **to** drop what **they had** got, **and** one **of** them was taken into the **bargain** ; the other got off free.

I stood stockstill all this while, till they came **back** dragging the poor fellow they had taken, and lugging the things they had found, extremely well satisfied that they had recovered the booty, and taken the thief; and thus they passed by me, for I looked only **like one who stood** up while the crowd was gone.

Once or twice I asked what **was** the matter, but **the** people **neglected** answering **me, and I** was not **very** importunate ; **but** after the crowd was wholly passed, I took my opportunity to turn about and take up what was behind me and walk away : this indeed I did with less disturbance than I had done formerly, for these things I did not steal, but they were stolen **to my** hand. I got safe to my lodgings with this **cargo, which** was **a piece** of fine black lustering silk, and **a piece of velvet**; the latter **was** but part **of a** piece **of about** eleven yards ; the former **was a** whole piece of **near** fifty yards ; it seems it was a mercer's shop that they had rifled ; I say rifled, because the **goods** were so considerable that they had lost ; for **the** goods that they recovered were pretty many, and I believe came to about six or seven several pieces of silk : how they came to get so many I could not tell ; but as I had only robbed the thief, I made no scruple at taking these goods, and being very glad of them too.

I had pretty good luck thus far, and I made several adventures more, though with but small purchase, yet with good success, but I went in daily dread that some mischief would befall me, and that I should certainly come to be hanged at last. The impression this made on me was too strong to be slighted, and it kept me from making attempts, that for aught I knew, might have been very safely performed ; but one thing I cannot omit, which was a bait to me many a day. I walked frequently out into the villages round the town to see if nothing would fall in my way there ; and going by a house near Stepney, I saw on the window-board two rings, one a small diamond ring, and the other a plain gold ring, to be sure laid there by some thoughtless lady, that had more money than forecast, perhaps only till she washed her hands.

I walked several times by the window to observe if I could see whether there was anybody in the room or no, and I could see nobody, but still I was not sure ; it came presently into my thoughts to rap at the glass, as if I wanted to speak with somebody, and if anybody was there they would be sure to come to the window, and then I would tell them to remove those rings, for that I had seen two suspicious fellows take notice of them. This was a ready thought; I rapped once or twice, and nobody came, when I thrust hard against the square of glass, and broke it with little noise, and took out the two rings, and walked away; the diamond ring was worth about £3, and the other about 9s.

I was now at a loss for a market for my goods, and especially for my two pieces of silk. I was very loath to dispose of them for a trifle, as the poor unhappy thieves in general do, who after they have ventured their lives for perhaps a thing of value, are forced to sell it for a song when they have done; but I was resolved I would not do thus, whatever shift I made; however, I did not well know what course to take. At last I resolved to go to my old governess, and acquaint myself with her again; I had punctually supplied the £5 a year to her for my little boy as long as I was able; but at last was obliged to put a stop to it. However, I had written a letter to her, wherein I had told her that my circumstances were reduced; that I had lost my husband, and that I was not able to do it any longer, and begged the poor child might not suffer too much for its mother's misfortunes.

I now made her a visit, and I found that she drove something of the old trade still, but that she was not in such flourishing circumstances as before; for she had been sued by a certain gentleman, who had had his daughter stolen from him, and who it seems she had helped to convey away; and it was very narrowly that she escaped the gallows. The expense also had ravaged her, so that her house was but meanly furnished, and she was not in such repute for her practice as before; however, she stood upon her legs, as they say, and as she was a bustling woman, and had some stock left, she was turned pawnbroker, and lived pretty well.

She received me very civilly, and with her usual obliging manner told me she would not have the less respect for me for my being reduced; that she had taken care my boy was very well looked after, though I could not pay for him, and that the woman that had him was easy, so that I needed not to trouble myself about him, till I might be better able to do it effectually.

I told her I had not much money left, but that I had some things that were money's worth, if she could tell me how I might turn them into money. She asked what it was I had? I pulled out the string of gold beads, and told her it was one of my husband's presents to me; then I showed her the two parcels of silk which I told her I had from Ireland, and brought up to town with me: and the little diamond ring. As to the small parcel of plate and spoons, I had found means to dispose of them myself before; and as for the childbed-linen I had, she offered me to take it herself, believing it to have been my own. She told me that she was turned pawnbroker, and that she would sell those things for me as pawned to her, and so she sent presently for proper agents that bought them, being in her hands, without any scruple, and gave good prices too.

I now began to think this necessary woman might help me a little in my low condition to some business; for I would gladly have turned my hand to any honest employment if I could have got it ; but honest business did not come within her reach. If I had been younger, perhaps she might have helped me, but my thoughts were off of that kind of livelihood, as being quite out of the way after fifty, which was my case, and so I told her.

She invited me at last to come and be at her house till I could find something to do, and it should cost me very little, and this I gladly accepted of ; and now living a little easier, I entered into some measures to have my little son by my last husband taken off ; and this she made easy too, reserving a payment only of £5 a year, if I could pay it. This was such a help to me, that for a good while I left off the wicked trade that I had so newly taken up ; and gladly I would have got work, but that was very hard to do for one that had no acquaintance.

However, at last I got some quilting work for ladies' beds, petticoats, and the like ; and this I liked very well, and worked very hard, and with this I began to live; but the diligent devil who resolved I should continue in his service, continually prompted me to go out and take a walk, that is to say, to see if anything would offer in the old way.

One evening I blindly obeyed his summons, and fetched a long circuit through the streets, but met with no purchase; but not content with that, I went out the next evening too, when going by an alehouse I saw the door of a little room open, next the very street, and on the table a silver tankard, things much in use in public-houses at that time; it seems some company had been drinking there, and the careless boys had forgot to take it away.

I went into the box frankly, and setting the silver tankard on the corner of the bench, I sat down before it, and knocked with my foot; a boy came presently, and I bade him fetch me a pint of warm ale, for it was cold weather; the boy ran, and I heard him go down the cellar to draw the ale; while the boy was gone, another boy came, and cried, ' D'ye call?' I spoke with a melancholy air, and said, ' No, the boy is gone for a pint of ale for me.'

While I sat here, I heard the woman in the bar say, ' Are they all gone in the five?' which was the box I sat in, and the boy said, ' Yes.' ' Who fetched the tankard away?' says the woman. ' I did,' says another boy, ' that's it,' pointing it seems to another tankard, which he had fetched from another box by mistake; or else it must be that the rogue forgot that he had not brought it in, which certainly he had not.

I heard all this much to my satisfaction, for I found plainly that the tankard was not missed, and yet they concluded it was fetched away: so I drank my ale, called to pay, and as I went away, I said, 'Take care of your plate, child,' meaning a silver pint mug which he brought me to drink in: the boy said, 'Yes, madam, very welcome,' and away I came.

I came home to my governess, and now I thought it was a time to try her, that if I might be put to the necessity of being exposed she might offer me some assistance. When I had been at home some time, and had an opportunity of talking to her, I told her I had a secret of the greatest consequence in the world to commit to her, if she had respect enough for me to keep it a secret: she told me she had kept one of my secrets faithfully; why should I doubt her keeping another? I told her the strangest thing in the world had befallen me, even without any design; and so told her the whole story of the tankard. 'And have you brought it away with you, my dear?' says she. 'To be sure I have,' says I, and showed it her. 'But what shall I do now?' says I, 'must not I carry it again?'

'Carry it again!' says she; 'ay, if you want to go

to Newgate.' 'Why,' says I, 'they can't be so base to stop me, when I carry it to them again?' 'You don't know those sort of people, child,' says she; 'they'll not only carry you to Newgate, but hang you too, without any regard to the honesty of returning it; or bring in an account of all the other tankards as they have lost, for you to pay for.' 'What must I do then?' says I. 'Nay,' says she, 'as you have played the cunning part and stole it, you must e'en keep it, there's no going back now; besides, child,' says she, 'don't you want it more than they do? I wish you could light of such a bargain once a week.'

This gave me a new notion of my governess, and that, since she was turned pawnbroker, she had a sort of people about her that were none of the honest ones that I had met with there before.

I had not been long there but I discovered it more plainly than before, for every now and then I saw hilts of swords, spoons, forks, tankards, and all such kind of ware brought in, not to be pawned, but to be sold downright; and she bought them all without asking any questions, but had good bargains, as I found by her discourse.

I found also that in following this trade she always melted down the plate she bought, that it might not be challenged; and she came to me and told me one morning that she was going to melt, and if I would, she would put my tankard in, that it might not be seen by anybody; I told her with all my heart; so she weighed it, and allowed me the full value in silver again; but I found she did not do so to the rest of her customers.

Some time after this, as I was at work, and very melancholy, she begins to ask me what the matter was? I told her my heart was very heavy, I had little work and nothing to live on, and knew not what course to take. She laughed, and told me I must go out again and try my fortune; it might be that I might meet with another piece of plate. 'O, mother!' says I, 'that is a trade that I have no skill in, and if I should be taken I am undone at once.' Says she, 'I could help you to a schoolmistress, that shall make you as dexterous as herself;' I trembled at that proposal, for hitherto I had had no confederates nor any acquaintance among that tribe. But she conquered all my modesty, and all my fears; and in a little time, by the help of this confederate, I grew as impudent a thief, and as dexterous, as ever Moll Cutpurse was, though, if fame does not belie her, not half so handsome.

The comrade she helped me to, dealt in three sorts of craft; viz. shoplifting, stealing of shop-books and pocket-books, and taking off gold watches from the ladies' sides; and this last she did so dexterously that no woman ever arrived to the perfection of that art, like her. I liked the first and the last of these things very well, and I attended her some time in the practice, just as a deputy attends a midwife, without any pay.

At length she put me to practice. She had shown me her art, and I had several times unhooked a watch from her own side with great dexterity; at last she showed me a prize, and this was a young lady with child, who had a charming watch. The thing was to be done as she came out of the church; she goes on one side of the lady, and pretends, just as she came to the steps, to fall, and fell against the lady with so much violence as put her into a great fright, and both cried out terribly: in the very moment that she jostled the lady, I had hold of the watch, and holding it the right way, the start she gave drew the hook out and she never felt it; I made off immediately, and left my schoolmistress to come out of her fright gradually, and the lady too; and presently the watch was missed; 'Ay,' says my comrade, 'then it was those rogues that thrust me down, I warrant ye; I wonder the gentlewoman did not miss her watch before, then we might have taken them.'

She humoured the thing so well that nobody suspected her, and I was got home a full hour before her. This was my first adventure in company; the watch was indeed a very fine one, and had many trinkets about it, and my governess allowed us £20 for it, of which I had half. And thus I was entered a complete thief, hardened to a pitch above all the reflections of conscience or modesty, and to a degree which I never thought possible in me.

Thus the devil, who began, by the help of an irresistible poverty, to push me into this wickedness, brought me to a height beyond the common rate, even when my necessities were not so terrifying; for I had now got into a little vein of work, and as I was not at a loss to handle my needle, it was very probable I might have got my bread honestly enough.

I must say, that if such a prospect of work had presented itself at first, when I began to feel the approach of my miserable circumstances; I say, had such a prospect of getting bread by working presented itself then, I had never fallen into this wicked trade, or into such a wicked gang as I was now embarked with; but practice had hardened me, and I grew audacious to the last degree; and the more so, because I had carried it on so long, and had never been taken; for in a word, my new partner in wickedness and I went on together so long, without being ever detected, that we not only grew bold, but we grew rich, and we had at one time one-and-twenty gold watches in our hands.

I remember that one day being a little more serious than ordinary, and finding I had so good a stock beforehand, as I had, for I had near £200 in money for my share; it came strongly into my mind, no doubt from some kind spirit, if such there be, that as at first poverty excited me, and my distresses drove me to these dreadful shifts, so seeing those distresses were now relieved, and I could also get something towards a maintenance by working, and had so good a bank to support me, why should I not now leave off, while I was well; that I could not expect to go always free; and if I was once surprised, I was undone.

This was doubtless the happy minute, when, if I had hearkened to the blessed hint, from whatsoever hand it came, I had still a cast for an easy life. But my fate was otherwise determined; the busy devil that drew me in, had too fast hold of me to let me go back; but as poverty brought me in, so avarice kept me in, till there was no going back; as to the arguments which my reason dictated for persuading me to lay down, avarice stept in and said, 'Go on, you have had very good luck, go on till you have gotten four or five hundred pounds, and then you shall leave off, and then you may live easy without working at all.'

Thus I that was once in the devil's clutches, was held fast there as with a charm, and had no power to go without the circle, till I was ingulfed in labyrinths of trouble too great to get out at all.

However, these thoughts left some impression upon me, and made me act with some more caution than before, and more than my directors used for themselves. My comrade, as I called her (she should have been called my teacher), with another of her scholars, was the first in the misfortune; for happening to be upon the hunt for purchase, they made an attempt upon a linen-draper in Cheapside, but were snapped by a hawk-eyed journeyman, and seized with two pieces of cambric, which were taken also upon them.

This was enough to lodge them both in Newgate, where they had the misfortune to have some of their former sins brought to remembrance; two other indictments being brought against them, and the facts being proved upon them, they were both condemned to die;　　*　　　*　　　*　　　*　　　*
　　　*　　　*　　　*　　　*　　　*　　　*

I went frequently to see them, and condole with them, expecting that it would be my turn next; but the place gave me so much horror, reflecting that it was the place of my unhappy birth, and of my mother's misfortunes, that I could not bear it, so I left off going to see them.

And O! could I but have taken warning by their disasters, I had been happy still, for I was yet free, and had nothing brought against me; but it could not be, my measure was not yet filled up.

My comrade, having the brand of an old offender, was executed; the young offender was spared, having obtained a reprieve; but lay starving a long while in prison, till at last she got her name into what they call a circuit pardon, and so came off.

This terrible example of my comrade frighted me heartily, and for a good while I made no excursions; but one night, in the neighbourhood of my governess's house, they cried, 'Fire;' my governess looked out, for we were all up, and cried immediately that such a gentlewoman's house was all of a light fire a-top, and so indeed it was. Here she gives me a jog; 'Now, child,' says she, 'there is a rare opportunity, the fire being so near that you may go to it before the street is blocked up with the crowd.' She presently gave me my cue; 'Go, child,' says she, 'to the house, and run in and tell the lady, or anybody you see, that you come to help them, and that you came from such a gentlewoman; that is, one of her acquaintance farther up the street.'

Away I went, and, coming to the house, I found them all in confusion, you may be sure; I ran in, and finding one of the maids, 'Alas! sweetheart,' said I, 'how came this dismal accident? where is your mistress? is she safe? and where are the children? I come from Madam —— to help you.' Away runs the maid; 'Madam, madam,' says she, screaming as loud as she could yell, 'here is a gentlewoman come from Madam —— to help us.' The poor woman, half out of her wits, with a bundle under her arm, and two little children, comes towards me ; 'Madam,' says I, 'let me carry the poor children to Madam ——, she desires you to send them ; she'll take care of the poor lambs ;' and so I takes one of them out of her hand, and she lifts the t'other up into my arms : 'Ay do, for God's sake,' says she, 'carry them ; O thank her for her kindness.   'Have you anything else to secure, madam ?' says I ; 'she will take care of it.'   'O dear !' says she, 'God bless her, take this bundle of plate and carry it to her too ; O she is a good woman ; O, we are utterly ruined, undone !'   And away she runs from me out of her wits, and the maids after her, and away comes I with the two children and the bundle.

I was no sooner got into the street, but I saw another woman come to me ; 'O !' says she, 'mistress,' in a piteous tone, 'you will let fall the child ; come, come, this is a sad time, let me help you ;' and immediately lays hold of my bundle to carry it for me. 'No,' says I, 'if you will help me, take the child by the hand, and lead it for me but to the upper end of the street ; I'll go with you and satisfy you for your pains.'

She could not avoid going, after what I said, but the creature, in short, was one of the same business with me, and wanted nothing but the bundle ; however, she went with me to the door, for she could not help it ; when we were come there I whispered

her, 'Go, child,' said I, 'I understand your trade, you
may meet with purchase enough.'

She understood me and walked off; I thundered
at the door with the children, and as the people were
raised before by the noise of the fire, I was soon let
in, and I said, 'Is madam awake? pray tell her Mrs.
—— desires the favour of her to take the two
children in; poor lady, she will be undone, their
house is all of a flame.' They took the children in
very civilly, pitied the family in distress, and away
came I with my bundle. One of the maids asked
me if I was not to leave the bundle too; I said, 'No,
sweetheart, 'tis to go to another place, it does not
belong to them.'

I was a great way out of the hurry now, and so I
went on and brought the bundle of plate, which was
very considerable, straight home, to my old governess;
she told me she would not look into it, but bade me
go again and look for more.

She gave me the like cue to the gentlewoman of
the next house to that which was on fire, and I did
my endeavour to go, but by this time the alarm of
fire was so great, and so many engines playing, and
the street so thronged with people, that I could not
get near the house, whatever I could do; so I came
back again to my governess's, and taking the bundle
up into my chamber I began to examine it. It is
with horror that I tell what a treasure I found there;

'tis enough to say, that besides most of the family plate, which was considerable, I found a gold chain, an old-fashioned thing, the locket of which was broken, so that I suppose it had not been used some years, but the gold was not the worse for that; also a little box of burying rings, the lady's wedding-ring, and some broken bits of old lockets of gold, a gold watch, and a purse with about £24 value in old pieces of gold coin, and several other things of value.

This was the greatest and the worst prize that ever I was concerned in; for indeed, though, as I have said above, I was hardened now beyond the power of all reflection in other cases, yet it really touched me to the very soul, when I looked into this treasure; to think of the poor disconsolate gentlewoman who had lost so much besides; and who would think to be sure that she had saved her plate and best things; how she would be surprised when she should find that she had been deceived, and that the person that took her children and her goods, had come, as was pretended, from the gentlewoman in next street, but that the children had been put upon her without her own knowledge.

I say, I confess the inhumanity of this action moved me very much, and made me relent exceedingly, and tears stood in my eyes upon that subject; but with all my sense of its being cruel and inhuman, I could never find in my heart to make any restitution. The reflection wore off, and I quickly forgot the circumstances that attended it.

Nor was this all; for though by this job I was become considerably richer than before, yet the resolution I had formerly taken of leaving off this horrid trade when I had gotten a little more; and the avarice had such success, that I had no more thoughts of coming to a timely alteration of life, though without it I could expect no safety, no tranquillity in the possession of what I had gained; a little more, and a little more, was the case still.

(*She escapes continually, but is caught at last.*)

I am drawing now towards a new variety of life. Upon my return, being hardened by a long race of crime, and success unparalleled, I had, as I have said, no thoughts of laying down a trade which, if I was to judge by the example of others, must however end at last in misery and sorrow.

It was on the Christmas-day following, in the evening, that, to finish a long train of wickedness, I went abroad to see what might offer in my way; when, going by a working silversmith's in Foster-lane, I saw a tempting bait indeed, and not to be resisted by one of my occupation; for the shop had nobody in it, and a great deal of loose plate lay in the window, and at the seat of the man, who I suppose worked at one side of the shop.

I went boldly in, and was just going to lay my hand upon a piece of plate, and might have done it, and carried it clear off, for any care that the men who belonged to the shop had taken of it; but an officious fellow in a house on the other side of the way, seeing me go in, and that there was nobody in the shop, comes running over the street, and without asking me what I was, or who, seizes upon me, and cries out for the people of the house.

I had not touched anything in the shop, and seeing a glimpse of somebody running over, I had so much presence of mind as to knock very hard with my foot on the floor of the house, and was just calling out too, when the fellow laid hands on me.

However, as I had always most courage when I was in most danger, so when he laid hands on me I stood very high upon it, that I came in to buy half a dozen of silver spoons; and to my good fortune, it was a silversmith's that sold plate, as well as worked plate for other shops. The fellow laughed at that part, and put such a value upon the service that he had done his neighbour, that he would have it be that I came not to buy, but to steal; and raising a great crowd, I said to the master of the shop, who by this time was fetched home from some neighbouring place, that it was in vain to make a noise, and enter into talk there of the case; the fellow had insisted that I came to steal, and he must prove it, and I desired we

might go before a magistrate without any more words ;
for I began to see I should be too hard for the man
that had seized me.

The master and mistress of the shop were really
not so violent as the man from t'other side of the
way ; and the man said, 'Mistress, you might come
into the shop with a good design for aught I know,
but it seemed a dangerous thing for you to come into
such a shop as mine is, when you see nobody there ;
and I cannot do so little justice to my neighbour, who
was so kind, as not to acknowledge he had reason on
his side ; though upon the whole I do not find you
attempted to take anything, and I really know not
what to do in it.' I pressed him to go before a
magistrate with me, and if anything could be proved
on me, that was like a design, I should willingly submit, but if not, I expected reparation.

Just while we were in this debate, and a crowd of
people gathered about the door, came by Sir T. B.,
an alderman of the city, and justice of the peace, and
the goldsmith hearing of it, entreated his worship to
come in and decide the case.

Give the goldsmith his due, he told his story with
a great deal of justice and moderation, and the fellow
that had come over, and seized upon me, told his
with as much heat, and foolish passion, which did me
good still. It came then to my turn to speak, and I
told his worship that I was a stranger in London,

being newly come out of the north ; that I lodged in
such a place, that I was passing this street, and went
into a goldsmith's shop to buy half a dozen of spoons.
By great good luck I had an old silver spoon in my
pocket, which I pulled out, and told him I had carried
that spoon to match it with half a dozen of new ones,
that it might match some I had in the country.

That seeing nobody in the shop, I knocked with
my foot very hard to make the people hear, and had
also called aloud with my voice : 'tis true, there was
loose plate in the shop, but that nobody could say I
had touched any of it ; that a fellow came running
into the shop out of the street, and laid hands on me
in a furious manner, in the very moment while I was
calling for the people of the house ; that if he had
really had a mind to have done his neighbour any
service he should have stood at a distance, and
silently watched to see whether I had touched anything, or no, and then have taken me in the fact.
'That is very true,' says Mr. Alderman, and turning
to the fellow that stopt me, he asked him if it was
true that I knocked with my foot ? He said yes, I
had knocked, but that might be because of his coming. 'Nay,' says the alderman, taking him short,
'now you contradict yourself, for just now you said
she was in the shop with her back to you, and did
not see you till you came upon her.' Now it was
true that my back was partly to the street, but yet as

my business was of a kind that required me to have eyes every way, so I really had a glance of him running over, as I said before, though he did not perceive it.

After a full hearing, the alderman gave it as his opinion that his neighbour was under a mistake, and that I was innocent, and the goldsmith acquiesced in it too, and his wife, and so I was dismissed ; but as I was going to depart, Mr. Alderman said, 'But hold, madam, if you were designing to buy spoons, I hope you will not let my friend here lose his customer by the mistake.' I readily answered, 'No, sir, I'll buy the spoons still, if he can match my odd spoon, which I brought for a pattern,' and the goldsmith showed me some of the very same fashion ; so he weighed the spoons, and they came to 35s., so I pulls out my purse to pay him, in which I had near twenty guineas, for I never went without such a sum about me, whatever might happen, and I found it of use at other times as well as now.

When Mr. Alderman saw my money, he said, 'Well, madam, now I am satisfied you were wronged, and it was for this reason that I moved you should buy the spoons, and stayed till you had bought them, for if you had not had money to pay for them I should have suspected that you did not come into the shop to buy, for the sort of people who come upon those designs that you have been charged with, are seldom troubled with much gold in their pockets, as I see you are.'

I smiled, and told his worship, that then I owed something of his favour to my money, but I hoped he saw reason also in the justice he had done me before. He said, yes, he had, but this had confirmed his opinion, and he was fully satisfied now of my having been injured. So I came well off from an affair in which I was at the very brink of destruction.

It was but three days after this, that not at all made cautious by my former danger, as I used to be, and still pursuing the art which I had so long been employed in, I ventured into a house where I saw the doors open, and furnished myself as I thought verily without being perceived, with two pieces of flowered silks, such as they call brocaded silk, very rich. It was not a mercer's shop, nor a warehouse of a mercer, but looked like a private dwelling-house, and was, it seems, inhabited by a man that sold goods for a weaver to the mercers, like a broker or factor.

That I may make short of the black part of this story, I was attacked by two wenches that came open-mouthed at me just as I was going out at the door, and one of them pulled me back into the room, while the other shut the door upon me. I would have given them good words, but there was no room for it; two fiery dragons could not have been more furious; they tore my clothes, bullied and roared, as if they would have murdered me; the mistress of the house came next, and then the master, and all outrageous.

I gave the master very good words, told him the door was open, and things were a temptation to me, that I was poor and distressed, and poverty was what many could not resist, and begged him, with tears, to have pity on me. The mistress of the house was moved with compassion, and inclined to have let me go, and had almost persuaded her husband to it also, but the saucy wenches were run even before they were sent, and had fetched a constable, and then the master said he could not go back, I must go before a justice; and, answered his wife, that he might come into trouble himself if he should let me go.

The sight of a constable indeed struck me, and I thought I should have sunk into the ground; I fell into faintings, and indeed the people themselves thought I would have died, when the woman argued again for me, and entreated her husband, seeing they had lost nothing, to let me go. I offered him to pay for the two pieces, whatever the value was, though I had not got them, and argued that as he had his goods, and had really lost nothing, it would be cruel to pursue me to death, and have my blood for the bare attempt of taking them. I put the constable in mind too that I had broke no doors, nor carried anything away; and when I came to the justice, and pleaded there that I had neither broken anything to

get in, nor carried anything out, the justice was inclined to have released **me** ; but the **first** saucy jade
that stopped me, affirming **that** I was going out with
the **goods,** but that **she** stopped me **and** pulled me
back, the justice upon that point committed me, and
I was carried to Newgate, that horrid place ! My
very blood chills at the mention of its name ; the
place where so many of my comrades had been locked
up, and from whence they went to the fatal tree ; the
place where my mother suffered so deeply, where **I
was** brought into the world, and from whence I expected no redemption, but by an infamous death : to
conclude, the place that had so long expected me,
and which with so much art and success I had so long
avoided.

I was now fixed indeed ; 'tis impossible to describe
the terror of my mind, when I was first brought **in,
and** when I looked round upon all the horrors of that
dismal place : I looked on myself as lost, and that I
had nothing to think of but of going out of the world,
and that with the utmost infamy ; the hellish noise,
the roaring, swearing and clamour, the stench and
nastiness, and all the dreadful afflicting things that I
saw there, joined to make the place seem an emblem
of hell itself, and a kind of an entrance into it.

Now I reproached myself with the many hints I
had had, as I have mentioned above, from my own
reason, from the sense of my good circumstances, and

of the many dangers I had escaped, to leave off while I was well, and how I had withstood them all, and hardened my thoughts against all fear ; it seemed to me that I was hurried on by an inevitable fate to this day of misery, and that now I was to expiate all my offences at the gallows ; that I was now to give satisfaction to justice with my blood, and that I was to come to the last hour of my life and of my wickedness together. These things poured themselves in upon my thoughts in a confused manner, and left me overwhelmed with melancholy and despair.

Then I repented heartily of all my life past, but that repentance yielded me no satisfaction, no peace, no, not in the least, because, as I said to myself, it was repenting after the power of farther sinning was taken away. I seemed not to mourn that I had committed such crimes, and for the fact, as it was an offence against God and my neighbour ; but that I was to be punished for it ; I was a penitent as I thought, not that I had sinned, but that I was to suffer, and this took away all the comfort of my repentance in my own thoughts.

I got no sleep for several nights or days after I came into that wretched place, and glad I would have been for some time to have died there, though I did not consider dying as it ought to be considered neither ; indeed nothing could be filled with more horror to my imagination than the very place, nothing was more **odious to me than** the company that was there. O! **if I had but** been sent **to** any place in the world, and not to Newgate, I should have thought **myself happy.**

In the next place, how did the hardened wretches **that were there** before me triumph over me! What! Mrs. Flanders come to Newgate at last? What, **Mrs.** Mary, Mrs. Molly, and after that plain Moll Flanders! **They** thought the devil had helped me, they said, **that** I had reigned so long; they expected me there many **years** ago, they said, and was **I come** at last? Then they flouted me with dejection, welcomed me **to** the place, wished me joy, bid me have a good heart, not be cast down, things might not be so bad as I feared, **and the like; then called for** brandy, and drank to me; but put it all up to my score, for they told **me** I was but **just** come to the college, as they **called** it, and sure I had money in my pocket, though they had none.

I asked one of this crew how long she had been there. She said four months. I asked her how the place **looked to her** when she first came into it? 'Just as **it** did now to me,' says she, 'dreadful and frightful;' that she thought she was in **hell**; 'and I believe so still,' adds **she,** 'but it is natural to me now, I don't disturb myself about it.' 'I suppose,' says I, 'you are in no danger of what is to follow.' 'Nay,' says she, 'you are mistaken there I am sure, for I am under

sentence,   *   *   *   *
    *   *   *   *   and I expect to be called down next session.' This 'calling **down**' is calling down to their former judgment,   *
    *   *   *   *   *
    *   *   *   'Well,' says I, **'and are** you thus easy?' 'Ay,' says she, 'I can't help myself, what signifies being sad? if I am hanged there's an end **of me.'** And away she turned dancing, and sings as she goes, the following piece of Newgate wit :

> ' If I swing by the string,
> I shall hear the bell ring [1]
> And then **there's an end of** poor Jenny.'

I mention this because **it would be** worth the observation of any prisoner, who shall hereafter fall into the same misfortune, and come to that dreadful place of Newgate, how time, necessity, and conversing with the wretches that are there, familiarises the place to them ; how at last they become reconciled to that which at first was the greatest dread upon their spirits in the world, and are as impudently cheerful and merry in their misery as they were when out of it.

I cannot say, as some do, **this devil is not so black** as he is painted ; for indeed no **colours can** represent **that place to** the life ; nor any **soul conceive** aright of

---

[1] **The bell** at St. Sepulchre's, which tolls upon execution-day.

it, but those who have been sufferers there. But how hell should become **by** degrees **so** natural, and not only tolerable, but even agreeable, **is** a thing unintelligible, **but by those who** have experienced it, as I have.

The same night that **I was sent to** Newgate **I sent the** news of it to my old governess, who was surprised at it you may be sure, and spent the night almost as ill out of Newgate as I did in it.

The next morning she came to see me; she did **what** she could to comfort me, but she saw that was **to no** purpose; however, as she said, **to sink** under **the** weight was but to increase the weight; she immediately applied herself to all the proper methods to prevent the effects of it, which we feared, and first she found out the two fiery jades that had surprised me; she tampered with them, persuaded them, offered them money, and, in a word, tried all imaginable ways to prevent a prosecution; she offered one of the wenches £100 to go away from her mistress, and not to appear against me; but she was so resolute, that though she was but a servant-maid at £3 **a year** wages, or thereabouts, she refused it, and would have refused, as my governess said she believed, if she had offered her £500. Then she attacked the other maid; she was not so hard-hearted as the other, and sometimes seemed inclined to be merciful; but the first wench kept her up, and would not so much as let my governess talk with her, but threatened to have her up for tampering with the evidence.

Then she applied to the master, that is to say, the man whose goods had been stolen, and particularly to his wife, who was inclined at first to have some compassion for me; she found the woman the same still, but the man alleged he was bound to prosecute, and that he should forfeit his recognisance.

My governess offered to find friends that should get his recognisance off the file, as they call it, and that he should not suffer; but it was not possible to convince him that he could be safe any way in the world but by appearing against me; so I was to have three witnesses of fact against me, the master and his two maids; that is to say, I was as certain to be cast for my life as I was that I was alive, and I had nothing to do but to think of dying. I had but a sad foundation to build upon for that, as I said before, for all my repentance appeared to me to be only the effect of my fear of death, not a sincere regret for the wicked life that I had lived, and which had brought this misery upon me, or for the offending my Creator, who was now suddenly to be my judge.

. I lived many days here under the utmost horror; I had death as it were in view, and thought of nothing night or day, but of gibbets and halters, evil spirits and devils; it is not to be expressed how I was harassed, between the dreadful apprehensions of death, and the terror of my conscience reproaching me with my past horrible life.

The ordinary of Newgate came to me, and talked a little in his way, but all his divinity run upon confessing my crime, as he called it (though he knew not what I was in for), making a full discovery, and the like, without which he told me God would never forgive me ; and he said so little to the purpose that I had no manner of consolation from him ; and then to observe the poor creature preaching confession and repentance to me in the morning, and find him drunk with brandy by noon, this had something in it so shocking, that I began to nauseate the man, and his work too by degrees, for the sake of the man ; so that I desired him to trouble me no more.

I know not how it was, but by the indefatigable application of my diligent governess I had no bill preferred against me the first session, I mean to the grand jury, at Guildhall ; so I had another month or five weeks before me, and without doubt this ought to have been accepted by me as so much time given me for reflection upon what was past, and preparation for what was to come ; I ought to have esteemed it as a space given me for repentance, and have employed it as such ; but it was not in me. I was sorry, as before, for being in Newgate, but had few signs of repentance about me.

On the contrary, like the water in the hollows of

mountains, which petrifies and turns into stone whatever they are suffered to drop upon ; so the continual conversing with such a crew of hell-hounds had the same common operation upon me as upon other people ; I degenerated into stone, I turned first stupid and senseless, and then brutish and thoughtless, and at last raving mad as any of them ; in short, I became as naturally pleased and easy with the place, as if indeed I had been born there.

It is scarce possible to imagine that our natures should be capable of so much degeneracy, as to make that pleasant and agreeable, that in itself is the most complete misery. Here was a circumstance, that I think it is scarce possible to mention a worse ; I was as exquisitely miserable as it was possible for any one to be, that had life and health, and money to help them as I had.

I had a weight of guilt upon me, enough to sink any creature who had the least power of reflection left, and had any sense upon them of the happiness of this life, or the misery of another ; I had at first some remorse indeed, but no repentance ; I had now neither remorse or repentance. I had a crime charged on me, the punishment of which was death ; the proof so evident, that there was no room for me, so much as to plead Not guilty ; I had the name of an old offender, so that I had nothing to expect but death, neither had I myself any thoughts of escaping, and yet a certain strange lethargy of soul possessed me ; I had no trouble, no apprehensions, no sorrow about me ; **the** first surprise was gone ; **I was,** I may well say, **I know not** how ; my senses, **my** reason, nay, my conscience, **were** all asleep ; my course of **life for forty** years had been a horrid complication of wickedness, whoredom, adultery, incest, lying, theft, and, in a word, everything but murder and treason had been my practice, from the age of eighteen, or thereabouts, to threescore ; and now I was ingulfed in the misery of punishment, **and** had **an** infamous death at the door, and yet I had no sense of my condition, no thought of heaven or hell, at least **that** went any further than a bare flying touch, like the stitch or pain **that gives a** hint and goes off; I neither had a heart to ask God's mercy, or indeed to think of it. And in **this I think I** have given a brief description **of the** completest misery on earth.

(*In Newgate she meets her highwayman husband, is condemned to death but reprieved, and is with him sent to America, where she has in early life unwittingly married her brother. She comes to terms with her family there, becomes prosperous, and dies in the odour of sanctity. But the interest ceases with her reprieve.*)

III.—'MEMOIRS OF A CAVALIER'

(These Memoirs *rank second to (or may even be bracketed with)* Moll Flanders *among Defoe's inventions other than* Robinson Crusoe, *supposing that they **are** inventions, or rather (for the facts are exactly enough drawn from Clarendon and other sources) workings up of public material. If they are anything else, it is practically incomprehensible that they should not have been claimed. They are purely descriptive, and have little or no interest of character, though an early scene with an Italian courtezan (not in the modern taste) **has** remarkable merits. The first passage I take shall be the passage of the Lech, for the Cavalier, like Captain Dalgetty, serves the great Gustavus.)*

Tilly was now joined with the Duke of Bavaria, and might together make about twenty-two thousand men; and in order to keep the Swedes out of the country of Bavaria, had planted themselves along the banks of the river Lech, which runs on the edge of the duke's territories; and having fortified the other side of the river, and planted his cannon for several miles, at all the convenient places on the river, resolved to dispute the king's passage.

I shall be the longer in relating this account of the Lech, being esteemed in those days as great an action as any battle or siege of that age, and particularly famous for the disaster of the gallant old general Tilly; and for that I can be more particular in it than other accounts, having been an eye-witness to every part of it.

The king being truly informed of the disposition of the Bavarian army, was once of the mind to have left the banks of the Lech, have repassed the Danube, and so setting down before Ingolstat, the duke's capital city, by the taking that strong town, to have made his entrance into Bavaria and the conquest of such a fortress, one entire action; but the strength of the place, and the difficulty of maintaining his army in an enemy's country, while Tilly was so strong in the field, diverted him from that design; he therefore concluded that Tilly was first to be beaten out of the country, and then the siege of Ingolstat would be easier.

Whereupon the king resolved to go and view the situation of the enemy. His majesty went out the 2nd of April with a strong party of horse, which I had the honour to command; we marched as near as we could to the banks of the river, not to be too much exposed to the enemy's cannon, and having gained a little height, where the whole course of the river might be seen, the king halted, and commanded to draw up. The king alighted, and calling me ¡to him, examined every reach and turning of the river by his glass, but finding the river run a long and almost a straight course, he could find no place which he liked, but at last turning himself north, and looking down the stream, he found the river fetching a long reach, double short upon itself, making a round and very narrow point. 'There's a point will do our business,' says the king, 'and, if the ground be good, I'll pass there, let Tilly do his worst.'

He immediately ordered a small party of horse to view the ground, and to bring him word particularly how high the bank was on each side and at the point; 'and he shall have fifty dollars,' says the king, 'that will bring me word how deep the water is.' I asked his majesty leave to let me go, which he would by no means allow of; but as the party was drawing out, a serjeant of dragoons told the king, if he pleased to let him go disguised as a boor, he would bring him an account of everything he desired. The king liked the motion well enough, and the fellow being very well acquainted with the country, puts on a plough-man's habit, and went away immediately with a long pole upon his shoulder; the horse lay all this while in the woods, **and the king stood** undiscerned by the enemy on the little hill aforesaid. The dragoon with his long **pole comes down** boldly to **the** bank of the river, and calling **to** the sentinels which Tilly had **placed on** the other bank, talked with them, asked **them** if they could not help him over the river, and pretended he wanted to come to them. At last being **come to the** point, where, as I said, the river makes **a** short **turn,** he stands parleying with them a great while, and sometimes pretending to wade over, he puts his long pole into the water, then finding it pretty shallow, he pulls off his hose and goes in, still thrusting his pole in before him, till being gotten up to his middle, he could reach beyond him, where it was too deep, and so shaking his head, comes back again. The soldiers on the other side laughing at him, asked him **if he** could swim? He said no. 'Why you fool you,' says one of the sentinels, 'the channel of the river is twenty feet deep.' 'How do **you** know that?' says the dragoon. 'Why our **engineer,' says** he, 'measured it yesterday.' This **was what** he wanted, but not yet fully satisfied ; 'Ay but,' **says he,** 'may be it may not be very broad, and if one of **you** would wade in to meet me till I could reach you with my pole, I'd give him half a ducat to pull me over.' The innocent way of his discourse so deluded the soldiers, that one of them immediately strips and goes in **up to** the shoulders, and our dragoon goes in on this side to meet him ; but the stream took the other soldier away, and he being a good swimmer, came swimming over to this side. The dragoon was then in a great deal of pain for fear of being discovered, and was once going to kill the fellow, and make off ; but at last resolved to carry on the humour, and having entertained the fellow with a tale of a tub, about the Swedes stealing his oats, the fellow being cold, wanted to be gone, and as he was willing to be rid of him, pretended to be very sorry he could not get over the river, and so makes off.

By this, however, he learned both the depth and breadth of the channel, the bottom and nature of both shores, and everything the king wanted to know. We could see him from the hill by our glasses very plain, and could see the soldier naked with him ; says the king, 'He will certainly be discovered and knocked on the head from the other side : he is a fool,' says the king, ' if he does not kill the fellow and run off ; ' but when the dragoon told his tale, the king was extremely well satisfied with him, gave him one hundred dollars, and made him a quarter-master to a troop of cuirassiers.

The king having further examined the dragoon, he gave him a very distinct account of the shore and ground on this side, which he found to be higher than the enemy's by ten or twelve foot, and a hard gravel.

Hereupon the king **resolves to pass** there, and in order to it, gives himself particular directions for such a bridge **as I believe never army passed a** river on before **nor since.**

His bridge was only loose planks laid upon large trestles, **in the same** homely manner as I have seen bricklayers raise a low scaffold to build a brick wall; **the** trestles were made higher than one another **to** answer **to** the river, as it became deeper or shallower, and [it] was all framed and fitted before any appear- **ance** was made of attempting to pass.

When all was ready, the king brings his army down to the bank of the river, and plants **his** cannon as the enemy had **done,** some here and some there, to amuse them.

At night, April 4th, the king commanded about two thousand men to march to the point, and to throw up a trench on either side, and quite round **it,** with a battery of six pieces of cannon at each end, besides three small mounts, one at the point and one of each side, which had each of them two pieces upon them. **This** work was begun so briskly, and so well **carried on, the** king firing all the night from the other parts of the river, that by daylight all the batteries at the new work were mounted, the trench lined with **two** thousand musketeers, and all the utensils of the bridge lay ready to be put together.

Now the imperialists discovered the **design,** but it

was too late to hinder it. The musketeers in the great trench, and the five new batteries, made such continual fire, that the other bank which, as before, lay twelve feet below them, was too hot for the imperialists; whereupon Tilly, to be provided for the king, at his coming over, falls to work in a wood right against the point, and raises a great battery for twenty pieces of cannon, with a breastwork, or line, as near the river as he could, to cover his men, thinking that when the king had built his bridge, he might easily beat it down with his cannon.

But the king had doubly prevented him, first, by laying his bridge so low that none of Tilly's shot could hurt it; for the bridge lay not above half a foot above the water's edge, by which means the king, who in that showed himself an excellent engineer, had secured it from any batteries to be made within the land, and the angle of the bank secured it from the remoter batteries on the other side, and the continual fire of the cannon and small shot beat the imperialists from their station just against it, they having no works to cover them.

And in the second place, to secure his passage, he sent over about two hundred men, and after that two hundred more, who had orders to cast up a large ravelin on the other bank, just where he designed to land his bridge; this was done with such expedition too, that it was finished before night, and in condition to receive all the shot of Tilly's great battery, and effectually covered his bridge.   While this was doing, the king on his side lays over his bridge.   Both sides wrought hard all day and all night, as if the spade, not the sword, had been to decide the controversy, and that he had got the victory whose trenches and batteries were first ready.   In the meanwhile the cannon and musket bullets flew like hail, and made the service so hot, that both sides had enough to do to make their men stand to their work ; the king in the hottest of it, animated his men by his presence, and Tilly, to give him his due, did the same ; for the execution was so great, and so many officers killed, General Attringer wounded, and two serjeant-majors killed, that at last Tilly himself was obliged to expose himself, and to come up to the very face of our line to encourage his men, and give his necessary orders.

And here, about one o'clock, much about the time that the king's bridge and works were finished, and just as they said he had ordered to fall on upon our ravelin with three thousand foot, was the brave old Tilly slain with a musket bullet in the thigh.   He was carried off to Ingolstat, and lived some days after, but died of that wound the same day as the king had his horse shot under him at the siege of that town.

We made no question of passing the river here, having brought everything so forward, and with such extraordinary success ; but we should have found it a very hot piece of work if Tilly had lived one day more ; and, if I may give my opinion of it, having seen Tilly's battery and breastwork, in the face of which we must have passed the river, I must say, that whenever we had marched, if Tilly had fallen in with his horse and foot, placed in that trench, the whole army would have passed as much danger as in the face of a strong town in the storming a counter-scarp. The king himself, when he saw with what judgment Tilly had prepared his works, and what danger he must have run, would often say, that day's success was every way equal to the victory of Leipsic.

Tilly being hurt and carried off, as if the soul of the army had been lost, they began to draw off; the Duke of Bavaria took horse, and rid away as if he had fled out of battle for his life.

The other generals, with a little more caution, as well as courage, drew off by degrees, sending their cannon and baggage away first, and leaving some to continue firing on the bank of the river to conceal their retreat. The river preventing any intelligence, we knew nothing of the disaster befallen them ; and the king, who looked for blows, having finished his bridge and ravelin, ordered to run a line of palisadoes, to take in more ground on the bank of the river, to cover the first troops he should send over ; this being finished the same night, the king sends over a party of his guards to relieve the men who were in the ravelin, and commanded **six** hundred musketeers to man the new line out of the Scots' brigade.

Early in **the morning,** a small **party of** Scots, com-**manded by one** Captain Forbes, of my Lord Rea's regiment, were sent out to learn something of the enemy, the king observing they had not fired all night ; and while this party were abroad, the **army** stood **in** battalia, and my old friend, Sir John Hepburn, whom of all men the king most depended upon for any desperate service, was ordered to pass the bridge with his brigade, and to draw up without the line, with command to advance as he found the horse, who were to second him, came over.

Sir John being passed without the trench, meets Captain Forbes with some prisoners, and the good news **of** the enemy's retreat. He sends him directly **to the** king, who was by this time at the head of his **army,** in full battalia, ready to follow his vanguard, expecting a hot day's work of it. Sir John sends messenger after messenger to the king, entreating him to give him orders to advance ; **but the** king would not suffer him ; for he was ever upon his guard, **and would** not venture a surprise ; so the army continued on this side the Lech all day and the next night. In the morning the king sent for me, and ordered me to draw out three hundred horse, and a colonel with six hundred horse, and a colonel with eight hundred dragoons, and ordered us to enter

the wood by three ways, but so as to be able to relieve
one another; and then ordered Sir John Hepburn,
with his brigade, to advance to the edge of the **wood**,
to secure our **retreat; and** at the same time commanded another **brigade** of foot to pass the bridge, **if**
need were, **to second Sir John** Hepburn, so warily
did this **prudent** general proceed.

We advanced with our horse into the Bavarian
camp, **which we** found **forsaken**; the plunder of it
was inconsiderable, for the exceeding caution the king
had used gave them time to carry off all their bag-
gage; we followed them three or four miles, and
returned to our camp.

I confess I was most diverted that day with view-
ing the works which Tilly had cast up, and must **own**
again, that **had he** not been taken **off, we had met**
with as desperate a piece of work **as ever** was
attempted. The next day the rest of the cavalry
came up to us, commanded by Gustavus Horn, and
the king and the whole army followed; we advanced
through the heart of Bavaria, took Rain at the first
summons, and several other small towns, and sat
down before Ausburg.

Ausburg, though a protestant city, had **a popish**
Bavarian garrison in **it of** above five thousand men,
commanded by a Függer, a great family in Bavaria.
The governor had posted several little parties, as out-
scouts, **at** the distance **of** two miles **and a half, or**

three miles, from the town. The king, at his coming
up to this town, sends me with my little troop, and
three companies of dragoons, to beat in these out-
scouts. The first party I light on was not above
sixteen men, who had made a small barricado across
the road, and stood resolutely upon their guard. I
commanded the dragoons to alight, and open the
barricado, which, while they resolutely performed, the
sixteen men gave them two volleys of their muskets,
and through the enclosures made their retreat to a
turnpike about a quarter of a mile farther. We
passed their first traverse, and coming up to the
turnpike I found it defended by two hundred
musketeers. I prepared to attack them, sending
word to the king how strong the enemy was, and
desired some foot to be sent to me. My dragoons
fell on, and though the enemy made a very hot fire,
had beat them from this post before two hundred
foot, which the king had sent me, had come up.
Being joined with the foot, I followed the enemy,
who retreated fighting, till they came under the cannon of a strong redoubt, where they drew up, and I
could see another body of foot of about three hundred
join them out of the works; upon which I halted,
and considering I was in view of the town, and a
great way from the army, I faced about, and began to
march off; as we marched I found the enemy followed,
but kept at a distance, as if they only designed to

observe me. I had not marched far, but I heard a volley of small **shot,** answered by **two or** three more, which I presently apprehended to be at the turnpike, where I had left **a** small guard of twenty-six **men,** with a lieutenant. Immediately I detached one hundred dragoons to relieve my men, and secure my retreat, following myself as fast as the foot could march. **The** lieutenant sent me back word the post was taken by the enemy, and my men cut off; upon this I doubled my pace, and when I came up I found **it as** the lieutenant said; for the post was taken and manned with three hundred musketeers, and three troops of horse; **by** this time also I found the party in my rear made up towards me, so that I was like to **be** charged, **in** a narrow place, both **in** front and **rear.**

I saw there was **no** remedy but with **all** my **force** to fall upon that party before me, **and** so to break through before those from the town could come up with me; wherefore, commanding my dragoons to alight, I ordered them to fall on upon the foot; their horse were drawn up in an enclosed field on one side of the road, a great ditch securing the other side, so that they thought, if I charged the foot in front, they would fall upon my flank, while those behind would charge **my** rear; and indeed had the other come in time, they had cut **me off.** My dragoons made three fair charges on their foot, but were received with so much resolution, and so brisk a fire, that they were beaten off, and sixteen **men** killed. Seeing them so rudely handled, and **the** horse ready to fall in, I relieved **them with** one hundred musketeers, and they renewed the attack at the same time with my troop **of horse** ; flanked on both wings with fifty musketeers, I faced their horse, but did not offer to charge them ; the case grew now desperate, and the enemy behind were just at my heels, with near six hundred men. The captain who commanded the musketeers, who flanked my horse, came up to me; says he, 'If we do not force this pass all will be lost; if you will draw out your troop and twenty of my foot, and fall in, I'll engage to keep off the horse with the rest.' 'With all my heart,' says I.

Immediately I wheeled off my troop, and a small party **of** the musketeers followed me, and fell in with the dragoons and foot, who seeing the danger too, as well as **I,** fought like madmen ; the foot at the turn-pike were not able to hinder our breaking through, so we made our way out, killing about one hundred and fifty of them, and put the rest into confusion.

But now was I in as great a difficulty as before, how to fetch off my brave captain of foot, for they charged home upon him. He defended himself with extraordinary gallantry, having the benefit of a piece **of a** hedge to cover him ; but he lost half his men, **and was** just upon the point of being defeated, when the king, informed by a soldier that escaped from the turnpike, one of twenty-six, had sent a party of six hundred dragoons to bring me off. These came upon the spur, and joined with me just as I had broke through the turnpike; the enemy's foot rallied behind their horse, and by this time their other party was come in, but seeing our relief, they drew off together.

I lost above a hundred men in these skirmishes, and killed them about one hundred and eighty; we secured the turnpike, and placed a company of foot there, with a hundred dragoons, and came back well beaten to the army. The king, to prevent such uncertain skirmishes, advanced the next day in view of the town, and, according to his custom, sits down with his whole army within cannon-shot of their walls.

The king won this great city by force of words; for by two or three messages and letters to and from the citizens, the town was gained, the garrison not daring to defend them against their wills. His majesty made his public entrance into the city on the 14th of April, and, receiving the compliments of the citizens, advanced immediately to Ingolstat, which is accounted, and really is, the strongest town in all these parts.

The town had a very strong garrison in it, and the Duke of Bavaria lay intrenched with his army under the walls of it, on the other side of the river. The king, who **never** loved long sieges, having viewed the town, **and brought his army** within musket-shot of it, called **a council of war,** where it **was** the king's **opinion,** in short, that **the town** would **lose** him more than **it was** worth, and therefore he resolved to raise **his siege.**

Here the king going **to view** the town, had his horse shot with a cannon-bullet from the works, which tumbled the king and his horse over one another, that everybody thought he had been killed, but he received no hurt at all; that very minute, as near as could be learnt, General Tilly died in the town, of the shot he received on the bank of the Lech as aforesaid.

*(**The** second piece must of necessity be the famous retreat from Marston Moor, which good judges have pronounced to be, if it be the invented work of a civilian of letters, the most extraordinary thing of the kind ever done.)*

I had but **very coarse** treatment in this fight; for returning with the prince from the pursuit of the right wing, and finding all lost, I halted, with some other officers, to consider what to do; at first we were for making our retreat in a body, and might have done so well enough, if we had known what had happened before we saw ourselves in the middle of the enemy;

for **Sir** Thomas Fairfax, who **had got together** his
scattered troops, and joined by some of the left wing,
knowing who we were, **charged us with great fury.**
It was not a time to think of anything but getting
away, or dying upon the spot; **the prince** kept on **in**
the front, and Sir Thomas Fairfax, by this charge, cut
off about three regiments of us from our body, but
bending **his main** strength at the prince, left us, as it
were, behind him, in the middle of the field of battle.
We took this for the only opportunity we could have
to get off, and joining together, we made across the
place of battle in as good order as we could, with our
carbines presented.   In this posture we passed by
several bodies of the enemy's foot, who stood with
their pikes charged to keep us off; but **they had** no
occasion, for we had no design to meddle with them,
but to get from them.   Thus we made a swift march,
and thought ourselves pretty secure; but our work
was not done yet, for, on a sudden, we saw ourselves
under a necessity of fighting our way through a great
body of Manchester's horse, who came galloping upon
us over the moor.   They had, as we suppose, been
pursuing some of our broken troops which were fled
before, and seeing us, they gave us a home charge.
We received them as well as we could, but pushed to
get through them, which at last we did with a considerable loss to them.   However, we lost so many men,
either killed or separated from us (for all could not

follow the same **way), that** of our three regiments we could not **be above four** hundred horse together when we got **quite clear, and these were mixt** men, some of one troop and regiment, some of another.   Not that I **believe** many of **us** were killed in the last attack, for we **had plainly the** better of the enemy ; but our design being to **get off,** some shifted for themselves one way, and some another, in the best manner they could, and as their several fortunes guided them. Four hundred more of this body, as I afterwards understood, having broke through the enemy's body another way, kept together, and got into Pontefract Castle, and three hundred more made northward, and to Skipton, where the Prince afterwards fetched them off.

These few of us that were left together, with whom I was, being now pretty clear of pursuit, halted, and **began** to inquire who and what we were, and what we **should** do ; and on a short debate I proposed **we** should make to the first garrison of the king's that we could **recover, and** that we should keep together, lest the country-people should insult us upon the roads. With this resolution we pushed on westward for Lancashire ; but our misfortunes were not yet at an end : we travelled very hard, and got to a village upon the river Wharf, near Wetherby.   At Wetherby there was a bridge, but we understood that a party from Leeds had secured the town and the post, in order to stop the flying cavaliers, and that it would be very hard to get through there, though, as we understood afterwards, there were no soldiers there but a guard of the townsmen. In this pickle we consulted what course to take; to stay where we were till morning, we all concluded would not be safe; some advised to take the stream with our horses, but the river, which is deep, and the current strong, seemed to bid us have a care what we did of that kind, especially in the night. We resolved therefore to refresh ourselves and our horses, which indeed is more than we did, and go on till we might come to a ford or bridge, where we might get over. Some guides we had, but they either were foolish or false, for after we had rid eight or nine miles, they plunged us into a river at a place they called a ford, but it was a very ill one, for most of our horses swam, and seven or eight were lost, but we saved the men; however, we got all over.

We made bold with our first convenience to trespass upon the country for a few horses, where we could find them, to remount our men whose horses were drowned, and continued our march; but being obliged to refresh ourselves at a small village on the edge of Bramham-moor, we found the country alarmed by our taking some horses, and we were no sooner got on horseback in the morning, and entering on the moor, but we understood we were pursued by some troops of horse. There was no remedy **but** we must pass this moor; and though our horses were exceedingly tired, **yet** we pressed on upon a round trot, and recovered an **enclosed country on** the other side, **where we** halted. And here, necessity putting us **upon it,** we were obliged to look out for more horses, for several of our men were dismounted, and others' horses disabled **by** carrying double, those who lost their horses getting up behind them; but we were supplied by our enemies against their will.

The enemy followed us over the moor, and we having a woody enclosed country about us, where we were, I observed by their moving they had lost sight of us; upon which **I** proposed concealing ourselves till we might judge of their numbers. **We** did so, and lying close in a wood, they past hastily by us, without skirting or searching the wood, which was **what on** another occasion they would not have done. **I found they were** not above a hundred and **fifty horse,** and considering that to let them go before us, would **be to alarm** the country, and stop our design; I thought, since we might be able to deal with them, we should not meet with a better place for it, and told the rest of our officers my mind, which all our party presently (for **we** had not time for a long debate) agreed to. Immediately upon this I caused two men to **fire** their pistols in the wood, at two different places, as far asunder as I could. This I did to give them an **alarm,** and amuse them ; **for being in the** lane, **they** would otherwise have got through before we had been ready, and **I resolved to** engage them **there, as** soon as it was possible. After this alarm, we **rushed out** of the wood, with about **a** hundred horse, and charged them on the flank in a broad lane, the wood being on their right. **Our** passage **into** the lane being narrow, gave us some difficulty in our getting out ; **but** the surprise of the charge did our work ; for the enemy thinking we had been a mile or two before, had not the least thoughts of this onset, till they heard us in the wood, and then they who were before could not come back. We broke into the lane just in the **middle** of them, and by **that** means divided them ; **and** facing to the left, charged the rear. First our dismounted men, which were near fifty, lined the edge of the wood, and fired with their carabines upon those which were before, so warmly, that they put them into a great **disorder.** Meanwhile, fifty more **of our horse** from the farther part of the wood showed themselves in the lane upon their front ; this **put them** of the foremost party into **a great** perplexity, and **they** began to face about, to fall upon us who were engaged in the rear ; but their facing about in a lane where **there was** no room to wheel, and [as ?] one who **understands the** manner of wheeling **a** troop of horse must imagine, put them into a great disorder. Our party in the head of the lane taking **the** advantage **of** this mistake of the enemy, charged in upon them, and routed them entirely. Some found means to break into the enclosures on the other side of the land, and get away. About thirty were killed, and about twenty-five made prisoners, and forty very good horses were taken ; **all** this while not a man of ours was lost, and not above seven or eight wounded. Those in the rear behaved themselves better ; for they stood our charge with a great deal of resolution, and all we could do could not break them ; but at last our men, who had fired on foot through the hedges at the other party, coming to do the like here, there was no standing it any longer. The rear of them faced about, and retreated out of the lane, and drew up in the open field to receive and rally their fellows. We killed about seventeen of them, and followed them to the end of the lane, but had no mind to have any more fighting **than** needs must ; our condition at that time not **making** it proper, the towns round us being all in the **enemy's** hands, and the country but indifferently pleased **with** us ; however, we stood facing them till they thought fit to march away. Thus we were supplied with horses enough to remount our men, and pursued our first design of getting into Lancashire. As for our prisoners, we let them off on foot.

But the country being by this time alarmed, and **the** rout of our army everywhere known, we foresaw abundance of difficulties before **us** ; we were not strong enough to venture into any great towns, and we were too many to be concealed in small ones. Upon this we resolved to halt in a great wood, about three miles beyond the place where we had the last skirmish, and sent out scouts to discover the country, and learn what they could, either of the enemy or of our friends.

Anybody may suppose we had but indifferent quarters here, either for ourselves or for our horses; but, however, we made shift to lie here two days and one night. In the interim I took upon me, with two more, to go to Leeds to learn some news; we were disguised like country ploughmen; the clothes we got at a farmer's house, which for that particular occasion we plundered; and I cannot say no blood was shed in a manner too rash, and which I could not have done at another time; but our case was desperate, and the people too surly, and shot at us out of the window, wounded one man, and shot a horse, which we counted as great a loss to us as a man, for our safety depended upon our horses. Here we got clothes of all sorts, enough for both sexes; and thus, dressing myself up *a la paisant*, with a white cap on my head, and a fork on my shoulder, and one of my comrades in the farmer's wife's russet gown and petticoat, like a woman, the other with an old crutch like a lame man, and all mounted on such horses as we had taken the day before from the country, away we go to Leeds by three several ways, **and** agreed **to** meet upon the bridge. My pretended countrywoman acted **her part to the** life, **though the party was** a gentleman of **good** quality of **the** Earl of Worcester's family ; **and the** cripple did as well as he ; but I thought myself **very awkward in my dress,** which **made me** very shy, especially among **the soldiers.** We passed their sentinels and guards at Leeds un-observed, and **put** up our horses at several houses in the town, from whence we went up and down to make our remarks. My cripple was the fittest to go among the soldiers, because there was **less** danger of being pressed. There he informed himself of the matters of **war,** particularly that the enemy sat down again to the **siege** of York ; that flying parties were in pursuit of the cavaliers ; and there he heard that five hundred horse of the Lord Manchester's men had **followed a** party of cavaliers over Bramham-moor ; and that, entering a lane, the cavaliers, who were a thousand strong, fell **upon** them, and killed them all but **about fifty.** This, though it was a lie, was very pleasant **to us to** hear, knowing it was our party, because **of the other part of the** story, **which was** thus: that the cavaliers had taken possession of such **a wood** where they rallied all the troops of their fly-**ing** army ; that they had plundered the country as they came, taking **all the** good horses they could get ; that they had plundered Goodman Thompson's house, which was the farmer I mentioned, and killed man, woman, and child ; and that they were about two thousand strong.

My other friend in woman's clothes got among the good wives at an inn, where she set up her horse, and there she heard the same sad and dreadful tidings ; and that this party was so strong none of the neighbouring garrisons durst stir out ; but that they had sent expresses to York for a party of horse to come to their assistance.

I walked up and down the town, but fancied myself so ill-disguised, and so easy to be known, that I cared not to talk with anybody. We met at the bridge exactly at our time, and compared our intelligence, found it answered our end of coming, and that we had nothing to do but to get back to our men ; but my cripple told me he would not stir till he bought some victuals, so away he hops with his crutch, and buys four or five great pieces of bacon, as many of hung beef, and two or three loaves ; and, borrowing a sack at the inn (which I suppose he never restored), he loads his horse, and, getting a large leather bottle, he filled that of aqua vitæ instead of small beer ; my woman comrade did the like. I was uneasy in my mind, and took no care but to get out of the town ; however, we all came off well enough ; but it was well for me that I had no provisions with me, as you will hear presently. We

came, as I said, into the town by several ways, and so
we went out; but about three miles from the town
we met **again exactly where we** had **agreed.**   I being
about **a** quarter of **a mile from** the rest, I met three
country fellows on horseback; one had **a** long **pole
on his shoulder, another a** fork, the third no weapon
at all, **that I** saw; I gave them the road very orderly,
being habited like one of their brethren; but one of
them stopping **short at me,** and looking earnestly,
calls out, 'Hark thee, friend,' says he, in a broad
north-country tone, 'whar hast thou thilk horse?'   I
must confess I was in the utmost confusion at the
question, neither being able to answer the question,
nor to speak in his tone; so I made as if I did not
hear him, and went on.   'Na, but ye's not gang soa,'
says the boor, and comes up to me, and takes hold **of
the horse's** bridle to stop me; at which, vexed at
heart that **I could** not tell how to talk to him, I
reached him a great knock on the pate with my fork,
and fetched him off his horse, and then began to
mend **my pace.**   The other clowns, though it seems
they **knew not** what the fellow wanted, pursued me,
and, finding they **had** better heels than I, I saw there
was no remedy but to make use of my hands, and
faced about.   The first that came up with me was he
that had no **weapons,** so I thought **I** might parley
with him; and, speaking as country-like as I could, I
asked him what he wanted?   'Thou'st knaw that

soon,' says Yorkshire, 'and **I'se but** come **at thee.'** 'Then keep awa', man,' said I, 'or I'se brain thee.' By this time the third man came up, and the parley ended; for he gave me no words, but laid at me with his long pole, **and** that **with** such **fury that** I began to be doubtful of him. I was loath to shoot **the** fellow, though I had pistols under my grey frock, as well for that the noise of a pistol might bring more people in, **the** village being in our rear, and **also** because **I could** not imagine what the fellow meant, or would have; but at last, finding he would be **too many** for me **with** that long weapon, **and a hardy strong** fellow, I threw myself off my horse, and, running in with him, stabbed my fork into his horse; the horse, being wounded, staggered awhile, and then fell down, and the booby had **not** the sense to get down in **time,** but fell with him; upon which, giving him **a** knock **or two** with **my** fork, I secured him. The other, by this time, had **furnished** himself with a great stick out **of a** hedge, **and,** before **I was** disengaged from the last fellow, gave me two such blows, that if the last had not missed my head, and hit me on **the** shoulder, **I** had ended the fight and my life together. **It was** time to look about me now, for this **was a** madman; I defended myself with my fork, but it **would not** do; at last, in short, I was forced to pistol **him, and** get on horseback again, and, with all **the** speed I could make, get away to the wood to our men.

If my two fellow spies had not been behind, I had never known what was the meaning of this quarrel of the three countrymen, but my cripple had all the particulars; for he being behind us, as I have already observed, when he came up to the first fellow, who began the fray, he found him beginning to come to himself; so he gets off, and pretends to help him, and sets him upon his breech, and, being a very merry fellow, talked to him, 'Well, and what's the matter now?' says he to him. 'Ah, wae's me,' says the fellow, 'I'se killed!' 'Not quite, mon,' says the cripple. 'O that's a fause thief,' says he, and thus they parleyed. My cripple got him on his feet, and gave him a dram of his aqua vitæ bottle, and made much of him, in order to know what was the occasion of the quarrel. Our disguised woman pitied the fellow too, and together they set him up again upon his horse, and then he told them that that fellow was got upon one of his brother's horses who lived at Wetherby; they said the cavaliers stole him, but it was like such rogues (no mischief could be done in the country, but it was the poor cavaliers must bear the blame), and the like; and thus they jogged on till they came to the place where the other two lay. The first fellow they assisted as they had done the other, and gave him a dram out of the leather bottle; but the last fellow was past their care; so they came away. For when they understood that it was my horse they claimed, they began to be afraid that their own horses might be known too, and then they had been betrayed in a worse pickle than I, and must have been forced to have done some mischief or other to have got away.

I had sent out two troopers to fetch them off, if there was any occasion ; but their stay was not long, and the two troopers saw them at a distance coming towards us, so they returned.

I had enough of going for a spy, and my companions had enough of staying in the wood ; for other intelligences agreed with ours, and all concurred in this, that it was time to be going : however, this use we made of it, that, while the country thought us so strong, we were in the less danger of being attacked, though in the more of being observed ; but all this while we heard nothing of our friends, till the next day. We then heard Prince Rupert, with about a thousand horse, was at Skipton, and from thence marched away to Westmoreland.

We concluded now we had two or three days' time good ; for, since messengers were sent to York for a party to suppress us, we must have at least two days' march of them, and therefore all concluded we were to make the best of our way. Early in the morning, therefore, we decamped from those dull quarters ; and as we marched through a village we found the people very civil to us, and the women cried out, 'God bless them, it is a pity the round-heads should **make such work with such** brave men,' and the like. Finding we were **among our** friends, we **resolved to halt** a little and **refresh** ourselves; and, **indeed,** the people were very kind to **us, gave us victuals and** drink, and took **care** of our horses. It happened **to** be my lot to stop at a house where the good woman took a great deal of pains to provide **for** us; **but I** observed the good man walked about with **a** cap upon his head, and very much out of order. I took no great notice **of** it, being very sleepy, and having asked my landlady to let me have a bed, I lay down and slept heartily: when I waked I found my landlord on another bed, groaning very **heavily.**

When I came downstairs I found my cripple talking with my landlady; he was now out of his disguise, but **we** called him cripple still; **and** the other, who put **on** the woman's clothes, **we** called Goody Thompson. **As** soon as he saw me, he called me **out;** '**Do you know,**' says he, 'the man of the house you **are** quartered in?' 'No, not I,' says I. 'No, so I believe, nor they you,' says he; '**if they did,** the good wife **would** not have made you a posset, and fetched a white loaf for you.' 'What do you mean?' says I. 'Have you seen the man?' says he. 'Seen him,' says I, 'yes, and heard him too; the man is sick, and groans so heavily,' says I, '**that I could not** lie upon the bed any longer for him.' 'Why, this is the poor man,' says he, 'that you knocked down with your fork yesterday, and I have had all the story out yonder at the next door.' I confess it grieved me to have been forced to treat one so roughly who was one of our friends, but to make some amends we contrived to give the poor man his brother's horse ; and my cripple told him a formal story, that he believed the horse was taken away from the fellow by some of our men ; and, if he knew him again, if it was his friend's horse, he should have him. The man came down upon the news, and I caused six or seven horses, which were taken at the same time, to be shown him ; he immediately chose the right ; so I gave him the horse, and we pretended a great deal of sorrow for the man's hurt ; and that we had not knocked the fellow on the head as well as took away the horse. The man was so overjoyed at the revenge he thought was taken on the fellow, that we heard him groan no more. We ventured to stay all day at this town, and the next night, and got guides to lead us to Blackstone-Edge, a ridge of mountains which parts this side of Yorkshire from Lancashire. Early in the morning we marched, and kept our scouts very carefully out every way, who brought us no news for this day : we kept on all night, and made our horses do penance for that little rest they had, and the next morning we passed the hills, and got into Lancashire, to a town called Littleborough, and from thence to

Rochdale, a little market-town. And now we thought ourselves safe as to the pursuit of enemies from the side of York; our design was to get to Bolton, but all the country was full of the enemy in flying parties, and how to get to Bolton we knew not. At last we resolved to send a messenger to Bolton; but he came back and told us he had, with lurking and hiding, tried all the ways that he thought possible, but to no purpose; for he could not get into the town. We sent another, and he never returned; and some time after we understood he was taken by the enemy. At last one got into the town, but brought us word they were tired out with constant alarms, had been straitly blocked up, and every day expected a siege, and therefore advised us either to go northward, where Prince Rupert and the Lord Goring ranged at liberty; or to get over Warrington bridge, and so secure our retreat to Chester. This double direction divided our opinions; I was for getting into Chester, both to recruit myself with horses and with money, both which I wanted, and to get refreshment, which we all wanted; but the major part of our men were for the north. First, they said, there was their general, and it was their duty to the cause, and the king's interest obliged us, to go where we could do best service; and there were their friends, and every man might hear some news of his own regiment, for we belonged to several regiments; besides, all the towns to the left of us were possessed by Sir William Brereton; Warrington and Northwich garrisoned by the enemy, and a strong party at Manchester; so that it was very likely we should be beaten and dispersed before we could get to Chester. These reasons, and especially the last, determined us for the north, and we had resolved to march the next morning, when other intelligence brought us to more speedy resolutions. We kept our scouts continually abroad, to bring us intelligence of the enemy, whom we expected on our backs, and also to keep an eye upon the country; for, as we lived upon them something at large, they were ready enough to do us any ill turn, as it lay in their power.

The first messenger that came to us was from our friends at Bolton, to inform us that they were preparing at Manchester to attack us. One of our parties had been as far as Stockport, on the edge of Cheshire, and was pursued by a party of the enemy, but got off by the help of the night. Thus all things looking black to the south, we had resolved to march northward in the morning, when one of our scouts from the side of Manchester assured us Sir Thomas Middleton, with some of the parliament forces, and the country troops, making above twelve hundred men, were on their march to attack us, and would certainly beat up our quarters that night. Upon this advice we resolved to be gone; and getting all things in readiness, we began to march about two hours before night ; **and** having gotten a trusty fellow for a guide, a fellow that we found was a friend to our side, he put **a** project into my head which saved us all **for that** time ; and that was, **to give** out in the village **that we** were marched back to Yorkshire, resolving to **get into** Pontefract Castle ; and, accordingly, he leads **us out of the** town the same way we came **in ; and taking a** boy with him, he sends the boy back just at night, and bade him say he saw us go up the hills at Blackstone-Edge ; and it happened very well ; for this party were **so sure of us that** they had placed four hundred men on **the road** to the northward, to intercept our retreat that way, and had left no way for us, as they thought, to get away, but back again.

About ten o'clock **at night** they assaulted our quarters, but **found we** were gone ; and being informed which way, they followed upon the spur, and **travelling** all night, being moonlight, they found themselves the next day about fifteen miles east, just out **of** their way ; for we had, by the help of our guide, **turned short at** the foot of the hills, and through blind untrodden paths, and with difficulty enough, by noon the next day, had reached almost twenty-five miles **north**, near a town called Clithero. Here we halted **in** the open field, and sent out our **people** to see how things were in the country. This part **of** the country, almost unpassable, and walled round with hills, **was** indifferent quiet ; and we got some refreshment for ourselves, but very little horse meat, and so went on; but we had not marched far before we found ourselves discovered; and the four hundred horse sent to lie in wait for us as before, having understood which way we went, followed us hard; and, by letters to some of their friends at Preston, we found we were beset again. Our guide began now to be out of his knowledge; and our scouts brought us word the enemy's horse was posted before us; and we knew they were in our rear. In this exigence we resolved to divide our small body, and so amusing them, at least one might get off if the other miscarried. I took about eighty horse with me, among which were all that I had of my own regiment, amounting to above thirty-two, and took the hills towards Yorkshire. Here we met with such unpassable hills, vast moors, rocks, and stony ways, as lamed all our horses, and tired our men; and sometimes I was ready to think we should never be able to get over them, till our horses failing, and jack-boots being but indifferent things to travel in, we might be starved before we should find any road or towns, for guide we had none, but a boy who knew but little, and would cry when we asked him any questions. I believe neither men nor horses ever passed in some places where we went, and for twenty hours we saw not a town nor a house, excepting sometimes from the top of the mountains, at a vast distance. I am persuaded we might have encamped here, if we had had provisions, till the war had been over, and have met with no disturbance; and I have often wondered since how we got into such horrible places, as much as how we got out. That which was worse to us than all the rest was, that we knew not where we were going, nor what part of the country we should come into, when we came out of those desolate crags. At last, after a terrible fatigue, we began to see the western parts of Yorkshire, some few villages, and the country at a distance looked a little like England; for I thought before it looked like old Brennus's hill, which the Grisons call the grandfather of the Alps. We got some relief in the villages, which indeed some of us had so much need of that they were hardly able to sit their horses, and others were forced to help them off, they were so faint. I never felt so much of the power of hunger in my life, for having not eaten in thirty hours, I was as ravenous as a hound; and if I had had a piece of horseflesh, I believe I should not have had patience to have stayed dressing it, but have fallen upon it raw, and have eaten it as greedily as a Tartar.

However, I ate very cautiously, having often seen the danger of men's eating heartily after long fasting. Our next care was to inquire our way. Halifax, they told us, was on our right; there we durst not think of going; Skipton was before us, and there we knew not how it was; for a body of three thousand horse, sent out by the enemy in pursuit of Prince Rupert, had been there but two days before, and the country people could not tell us whether they were gone or no; and Manchester's horse, which were sent out after our party, were then at Halifax, in quest of us, and afterwards marched into Cheshire. In this distress we would have hired a guide, but none of the country people would go with us; for the roundheads would hang them, they said, when they came there. Upon this I called a fellow to me, 'Hark ye friend,' says I, 'dost thee know the way so as to bring us into Westmoreland, and not keep the great road from York?' 'Ay marry,' says he, 'I ken the ways weel enou.' 'And you would go and guide us,' said I, 'but that you are afraid the roundheads will hang you?' 'Indeed would I,' says the fellow. 'Why then,' says I, 'thou hadst as good be hanged by a roundhead as a cavalier; for, if thou will not go, I'll hang thee just now.' 'Na, and ye serve me soa,' says the fellow, 'I'se ene gang with ye; for I care not for hanging; and ye'll get me a good horse, I'se gang and be one of ye, for I'll nere come heame more.' This pleased us still better, and we mounted the fellow, for three of our men died that night with the extreme fatigue of the last service.

Next morning, when our new trooper was mounted and clothed, we hardly knew him; and this fellow led

us by such ways, such wildernesses, and yet with such
prudence, keeping the hills to the left, that we might
have the villages to refresh ourselves, that without
**him we had certainly either perished in those moun-
tains or** fallen into the enemy's hands. We passed
the great road from York so critically as **to** time, that
from **one of the hills** he showed us a party of **the**
enemy's horse who were then marching into Westmoreland. We lay still that day, finding we were not
discovered by them ; and our guide proved the best
scout that we could have had ; for he would go out
ten miles at a time, and bring us in all **the** news of
the country. **Here he** brought **us word** that York
was surrendered **upon** articles, and **that** Newcastle,
which had been surprised by the king's party, was
besieged by another army of Scots, advanced to help
their brethren.

Along the edges of those vast mountains we past,
with **the** help of **our** guide, till we came **into the**
forest **of** Swale ; and finding ourselves perfectly concealed here, for no soldier had ever been here all the
war, nor perhaps would not, if it had lasted seven
years, we thought we wanted a few days' rest, at least
for our horses, so we resolved to halt, and while we
did so, we made some disguises, and sent out some
spies into the **country ;** but, as here were no great
towns, nor no post road, we got very little intelligence.
We rested four days, and then marched again ; and,

indeed, having no great stock of money about us, and not very free of that we had, four days was enough for those poor places to be able to maintain us.

We thought ourselves pretty secure now; but our chief care was how to get over those terrible mountains; for, having passed the great road that leads from York to Lancaster, the crags, the farther northward we looked, looked still the worse, and our business was all on the other side. Our guide told us he would bring us out if we would have patience, which we were obliged to, and kept on this slow march till he brought us to Stanhope, in the county of Durham, where some of Goring's horse, and two regiments of foot had their quarters. This was nineteen days from the battle of Marston-moor. The prince, who was then at Kendal, in Westmoreland, and who had given me over as lost, when he had news of our arrival sent an express to me to meet him at Appleby. I went thither accordingly, and gave him an account of our journey; and there I heard the short history of the other part of our men, whom we parted from in Lancashire. They made the best of their way north. They had two resolute gentlemen who commanded; and being so closely pursued by the enemy that they found themselves under the necessity of fighting, they halted, and faced about, expecting the charge. The boldness of the action made the officer who led the enemy's horse

(which it seems were the county horse only), afraid of
them ; which they perceiving, taking the advantage of
his fears, bravely advance, and charge them ; and,
though they were above two hundred horse, they
routed them, killed about thirty or forty, got some
horses and some money, and pushed on their march
night and day ; but coming near Lancaster they were
so waylaid and pursued that they agreed to separate,
and shift every man for himself ; many of them fell
into the enemy's hands, some were killed attempting
to pass through the river Lune, some went back
again, six or seven got to Bolton, and about eighteen
got safe to Prince Rupert.

IV.—'COLONEL JACK'

(*The memory of* Colonel Jack *is preserved by one famous and admirable passage at the beginning, describing the Colonel's experiences as a youthful thief, which will be presently given in full. I have selected two others from later parts of the book because they illustrate very well the curiously unheroic view of life which distinguished Defoe, and which was, I think, more common among the English of the seventeenth and eighteenth centuries than it sometimes suits us to acknowledge. On the whole the novel is a sort of compound of the themes of* Moll Flanders *and of the* Memoirs of a Cavalier (*for Jack, though he cuts so bad a figure in the second of our extracts, afterwards served with credit abroad*), and it seems to me as a whole inferior to both. There can, however, be no doubt about the following account of Jack's initiation into pilfering.*)

The subtle devil, never absent from his business, but ready at all occasions to encourage his servants, removed all these difficulties, and brought him into an intimacy with one of the most exquisite divers, or pickpockets, in the town; and this, our intimacy, was of no less a kind than that, as I had an inclination to be as wicked as any of them, he was for taking care that I should not be disappointed.

He was above the little fellows who went about stealing trifles and baubles in Bartholomew fair, and ran the risk of being mobbed for three or four shillings. His aim was at higher things, even at no less than considerable sums of money, and bills for more.

He solicited me earnestly to go and take a walk with him as above, adding, that after he had shown me my trade a little, he would let me be as wicked as I would; that is, as he expressed it, that after he had made me capable, I should set up for myself, if I pleased, and he would only wish me good luck.

Accordingly, as Major Jack went with his gentleman, only to see the manner, and receive the purchase, and yet come in for a share; so he told me if he had success I should have my share as much as if I had been principal; and this he assured me was a custom of the trade, in order to encourage young beginners, and bring them into the trade with courage, for that nothing was to be done if a man had not the heart of the lion.

I hesitated at the matter a great while, objecting the hazard, and telling the story of Captain Jack, my elder brother, as I might call him. 'Well, colonel,' says he, 'I find you are faint-hearted, and to be faint-hearted is indeed to be unfit for our trade, for nothing but a bold heart can go through stitch with this work; but, however, as there is nothing for you to do, so there is no risk for you to run in these things the first time. If I am taken,' says he, 'you have nothing to do in it, they will let you go free; for it shall be easily made appear that whatever I have done you had no hand in it.'

Upon those persuasions I ventured out with him; but I soon found that my new friend was a thief of quality, and a pickpocket above the ordinary rank, and that aimed higher abundantly than my brother Jack. He was a bigger boy than I a great deal; for though I was now near fifteen years old, I was not big of my age, and as to the nature of the thing, I was perfectly a stranger to it. I knew indeed what at first I did not, for it was a good while before I understood the thing as an offence. I looked on picking pockets as a trade, and thought I was to go apprentice to it. It is true, this was when I was young in the society, as well as younger in years, but even now I understood it to be only a thing for which, if we were catched, we ran the risk of being ducked or pumped, which we call soaking, and then all was over; and we made nothing of having our rags wetted a little; but I never understood, till a great while after, that the crime was capital, and that we might be sent to Newgate for it, till a great fellow, almost a man, **one of** our society, was hanged for it; and then **I was terribly frighted, as** you shall hear by and by.

Well, upon the persuasions of this lad I walked **out with** him; a poor innocent boy, and (as I **re**member my very thoughts perfectly well) I had no evil **in** my intentions; I had never stolen anything in my life; and if a goldsmith had left me in his shop, with heaps of money strewed all round me, and bade me look after it, I should not have touched it, I was so honest; but the subtle tempter baited his hook for me, as **I** was a child, in a manner suitable to my childishness, **for** I never took **this** picking of pockets **to** be dishonesty, **but, as I have** said above, I looked **on it** as a kind of **trade** that I was to **be** bred **up** to, and so **I** entered upon it, till I became hardened in it beyond the power of retreating; and thus **I was made** a thief involuntarily, and went on a length **that few** boys do, without coming **to** the common period **of that** kind of life, I mean to the transport-ship, or to the gallows.

The first day I went abroad with my new instructor, he carried me directly into the city, and as **we went** first **to the** water-side, he led me into the long-room at the Custom-house; we were but a couple **of ragged** boys at **best,** but I was much the worse;

my leader had a hat on, a shirt, and a neckcloth ; as
for me, I had neither of the three, nor had I spoiled
my manners so much as to have a hat on my head
since my nurse died, which was now some years.
His orders to me were to keep always in sight, and
near him, but not close to him, nor to take any notice
of him at any time till he came to me ; and if any
hurlyburly happened I should by no means know
him or pretend to have anything to do with him.

I observed my orders to a tittle.   While he peered
into every corner, and had his eye upon everybody,
I kept my eye directly upon him, but went always at
a distance, and on the other side of the long-room,
looking as it were for pins, and picking them up out
of the dust as I could find them, and then sticking
them on my sleeve, where I had at last got forty or
fifty good pins ; but still my eye was upon my comrade, who, I observed, was very busy among the
crowds of people that stood at the board doing
business with the officers who pass the entries, and
make the cocquets, etc.

At length he comes over to me, and stooping as
if he would take up a pin close to me, he put something into my hand, and said, ' Put that up, and
follow me down stairs quickly ; ' he did not run, but
shuffled along apace through the crowd, and went
down, not the great stairs which we came in at, but
a little narrow staircase at the other end of the long

room; I followed, and **he** found I **did, and** so went
on, not stopping below as **I** expected, nor speaking
one word **to me,** till through innumerable narrow
passages, **alleys,** and dark ways, **we** were got up into
Fenchurch - street, **and through** Billiter - **lane into**
Leadenhall-street, and from thence into Leadenhall-
market.

It was not a meat-market day, so we had room to
sit down upon one of the butchers' stalls, and he bid
me lug out. What he had given me was a little
leather letter-case, with a French almanack stuck **in**
the inside of **it, and a** great many papers in it **of**
several kinds.

We looked them over, and found there were several valuable bills in it, such as bills of exchange, and
other notes, things I did not understand; but among
the rest was a goldsmith's note, as he called it, of one
Sir Stephen Evans, for £300, payable to the bearer,
and at demand; besides this, there was another **note**
for £12 : 10s., being **a** goldsmith's bill too, but I
forget **the name; there was** a bill or two also written
in French, which **neither** of us understood, but which
it seems were things of value, being called foreign
bills accepted.

The rogue, my master, knew what belonged to the
goldsmith's bills well enough, and I observed, when
he read the bill of **Sir** Stephen, **he said,** 'This is too
big for me to meddle with;' but when he came to the

bill £12 : 10s., he said to me, 'This will do, come hither, Jack;' so away he runs to Lombard-street, and I after him, huddling the other papers into the letter-case. As he went along, he inquired the name out immediately, and went directly to the shop, put on a good grave countenance, and had the money paid him without any stop or question asked; I stood on the other side the way looking about the street, as not at all concerned with anybody that way, but observed that when he presented the bill he pulled out the letter-case, as if he had been a merchant's boy, acquainted with business, and had other bills about him.

They paid him the money in gold, and he made haste enough in telling it over, and came away, passing by me, and going into Three-King-court, on the other side of the way; then we crossed back into Clement's-lane, made the best of our way to Cole-harbour, at the water-side, and got a sculler for a penny to carry us over the water to St. Mary-Over's stairs, where we landed, and were safe enough.

Here he turns to me; 'Colonel Jack,' says he, 'I believe you are a lucky boy, this is a good job; we'll go away to St. George's Fields and share our booty.' Away we went to the Fields, and sitting down in the grass, far enough out of the path, he pulled out the money; 'Look here, Jack,' says he, 'did you ever see the like before in your life?' 'No, never,' says

I, and added very innocently, 'Must we have it all?' 'We have it!' **says he,** 'who should have it?' 'Why,' says **I, 'must the** man **have** none of it again that lost **it?'** '**He** have it again;' says he, 'what d'ye mean by that?' 'Nay, I don't know,' says I; '**why** you said just now you would let him have the t'other bill again; that you said was too big for you.'

He laughed at me; 'You are but a little boy,' says he, 'that's true, but I thought you had not been such a child neither;' so he mighty gravely explained the thing to me thus: that the bill of Sir Stephen Evans was a great bill for £300, 'And if I,' says he, 'that **am but a** poor lad, should venture **to** go for the money, they will presently say, how **should** I come by such a bill, and that I certainly found it or stole it; so they will stop me,' says he, 'and take it away from me, and it may bring me into trouble for it too; **so,**' says he, 'I did say it was too big for me to meddle with, and that I would let the man have it again, **if** I could tell how; but for the money, Jack, the **money that we** have got, I warrant you he should have none of that; besides,' says he, 'whoever he be that has lost this letter-case, to be sure, as soon as he missed it, he would run to the goldsmith and give notice that if anybody came for the money they would be stopped; **but** I am too old for him there,' **says he.**

'Why,' says I, '**and** what **will you** do with the

bill; will you throw it away? if you do, somebody else will find it,' says I, 'and they will go and take the money.' 'No, no,' says he, 'then they will be stopped and examined, as I tell you I should be.' I did not know well what all this meant, so I talked no more about that; but we fell to handling the money. As for me, I had never seen so much together in all my life, nor did I know what in the world to do with it, and once or twice I was going to bid him keep it for me, which would have been done like a child indeed, for, to be sure, I had never heard a word more of it, though nothing had befallen him.

However, as I happened to hold my tongue as to that part, he shared the money very honestly with me; only at the end he told me that though it was true he promised me half, yet as it was the first time, and I had done nothing but look on, so he thought it was very well if I took a little less than he did; so he divided the money, which was £12 : 10s., into two exact parts, viz., £6 : 5s., in each part; then he took £1 : 5s., from my part, and told me I should give him that for hansel. 'Well,' says I, 'take it then, for I think you deserve it all:' so, however, I took up the rest; 'and what shall I do with this now,' says I, 'for I have nowhere to put it?' 'Why, have you no pockets?' says he; 'Yes,' says I, 'but they are full of holes.' I have often thought since that, and with some mirth too, how I had really more wealth than I knew **what to** do with, **for** lodging I had none, nor any box or drawer to **hide** my money in, nor **had** I any pocket, but **such as I** say was full **of holes**; I knew nobody in the world that I could go **and desire** them to lay it up for me; for being a poor naked, ragged boy, they would presently say, **I had** robbed somebody, and perhaps lay hold **of me, and** my money would be my crime, as they say it **often is** in foreign countries; and now, as I was full of wealth, behold I was full of care, for what to do to secure my money I could not tell; and this held me so long, **and was so vexatious to me the next day,** that I truly sat down and cried.

Nothing could be more perplexing than this money was to me all that night. I carried it in my hand **a** good while, for it was in gold, all but 14s.; and that **is** to say, it was in four guineas, and that 14s., was more difficult **to** carry than the four guineas; at last **I sat** down, and pulled off one of my shoes, and put the four **guineas into that;** but after I had gone a while, my shoe hurt me so I could not go, so I was fain to sit down again and take it out of my shoe, and carry it in my hand; then I found a dirty linen rag in the street, and I took that up, and wrapt it all together, and carried it in that a good way. I have often since heard people say, when they have been talking of **money** that they could not get in, 'I wish I had it in a foul clout:' in truth, I had mine in a foul clout; for it was foul, according to the letter of that saying, but it served me till I came to a convenient place, and then I sat down and washed the cloth in the kennel, and so then put my money in again.

Well, I carried it home with me to my lodging in the glass-house, and when I went to go to sleep I knew not what to do with it; if I had let any of the black crew I was with know of it, I should have been smothered in the ashes for it, or robbed of it, or some trick or other put upon me for it; so I knew not what to do, but lay with it in my hand, and my hand in my bosom, but then sleep went from my eyes : O, the weight of human care ! I, a poor beggar-boy, could not sleep so soon as I had but a little money to keep, who, before that could have slept upon a heap of brick-bats, stones, or cinders, or anywhere, as sound as a rich man does on his down bed, and sounder too.

Every now and then dropping asleep, I should dream that my money was lost, and start like one frighted ; then, finding it fast in my hand, try to go to sleep again, but could not for a long while, then drop and start again. At last a fancy came into my head that if I fell asleep I should dream of the money, and talk of it in my sleep, and tell that I had money, which if I should do, and one of the rogues should hear me, they would pick it out of my bosom, and of my hand too, without waking me ; and after that thought I could not sleep a wink more ; so that

I passed that night over in care and anxiety enough; and this, I may safely say, was the first night's rest that I lost by the cares of this life and the deceitfulness of riches.

As soon as it was day I got out of the hole we lay in, and rambled abroad in the fields towards Stepney, and there I mused and considered what I should do with this money, and many a time I wished that I had not had it; for, after all my ruminating upon it, and what course I should take with it, or where I should put it, I could not hit upon any one thing, or any possible method to secure it, and it perplexed me so, that at last, as I said just now, I sat down and cried heartily.

When my crying was over, the case was the same; I had the money still, and what to do with it I could not tell. At last it came into my head that I would look out for some hole in a tree, and see to hide it there till I should have occasion for it. Big with this discovery, as I then thought it, I began to look about me for a tree; but there were no trees in the fields about Stepney or Mile-end that looked fit for my purpose; and if there were any that I began to look narrowly at, the fields were so full of people that they would see if I went to hide anything there, and I thought the people eyed me as it were, and that two men in particular followed me to see what I intended to do.

This drove me farther off, and I crossed the road at Mile-end, and in the middle of the town went down a lane that goes away to the Blind Beggar's at Bednal-green; when I came a little way in the lane I found a footpath over the fields, and in those fields several trees for my turn, as I thought; at last, one tree had a little hole in it, pretty high out of my reach, and I climbed up the tree to get it, and when I came there I put my hand in, and found (as I thought) a place very fit, so I placed my treasure there, and was mighty well satisfied with it; but, behold, putting my hand in again to lay it more commodiously, as I thought, of a sudden it slipped away from me, and I found the tree was hollow, and my little parcel was fallen in quite out of my reach, and how far it might go in I knew not; so that, in a word, my money was quite gone, irrecoverably lost; there could be no room so much as to hope ever to see it again, for 'twas a vast great tree.

As young as I was, I was now sensible what a fool I was before, that I could not think of ways to keep my money, but I must come thus far to throw it into a hole where I could not reach it. Well, I thrust my hand quite up to my elbow, but no bottom was to be found, or any end of the hole or cavity; I got a stick of the tree, and thrust it in a great way, but all was one; then I cried, nay, roared out, I was in such a passion; then I got down the tree again, then up again, and **thrust in** my **hand** again till **I** scratched my arm **and made it** bleed, and cried all the while most violently ; then **I began to think I** had not so much **as a** halfpenny **of it left** for a halfpenny roll, and **I was hungry, and then I** cried **again** ; then **I came away in** despair, crying and roaring **like a little boy that had** been whipped ; then **I** went **back** again **to the tree, and up** the tree again, and **thus I did several** times.

The **last time I** had gotten up the tree **I** happened **to** come down not on the same side that **I** went up and came down **before, but on the other side** of the tree, and on the **other side of the bank** also ; and, behold, the tree had a **great** open place, **in the** side of it close to the ground, as old hollow trees often have ; and looking into **the** open place, to my inexpressible joy there lay my money and my linen rag, all wrapped up just as **I** had **put it** into the hole ; for **the tree being hollow** all **the** way up there had **been** some **moss** or light stuff, which **I** had not judgment enough to know, **was not firm,** and had **given** way **when it** came **to drop out of my** hand, **and so it** had slipped quite **down at once.**

I was but a child, and **I** rejoiced like a child, for **I** hollo'd quite out aloud when I saw **it** ; then I ran **to** it, and snatched it up, hugged and kissed the dirty **rag** a hundred times; then danced **and** jumped about, **ran** from one end **of** the field **to the** other, and, in short, I knew not what, much less do I know now what I did, though I shall never forget the thing either what a sinking grief it was to my heart, when I thought I had lost it, or what a flood of joy overwhelmed me when I had got it again.

While I was in the first transport of my joy, as I have said, I ran about, and knew not what I did; but when that was over I sat down, opened the foul clout the money was in, looked at it, told it, found it was all there, and then I fell a-crying as savourly as I did before, when I thought I had lost it.

It would tire the reader should I dwell on all the little boyish tricks that I played in the ecstacy of my joy and satisfaction, when I had found my money; so I break off here. Joy is as extravagant as grief, and since I have been a man I have often thought that had such a thing befallen a man, so to have lost all he had, and not have a bit of bread to eat, and then so strangely to find it again, after having given it so effectually over,—I say, had it been so with a man, it might have hazarded his using some violence upon himself.

Well, I came away with my money, and, having taken sixpence out of it, before I made it up again, I went to a chandler's shop in Mile-end, and bought a halfpenny roll and a halfpenny-worth of cheese, and sat down at the door after I bought it, and ate it very heartily, and begged some beer to drink with it, which the good woman gave me very freely.

S

Away I went then for the town, to see if I could
find any of my companions, and resolved I would try
no more hollow trees for my treasure. As I came
along Whitechapel, I came by a broker's shop, over
against the church, where they sold old clothes, for I
had nothing on but the worst of rags ; so I stopped
at the shop, and stood looking at the clothes which
hung at the door.

'Well, young gentleman,' says a man that stood at
the door, 'you look wishfully ; do you see anything
you like, and will your pocket compass a good coat
now, for you look as if you belonged to the ragged
regiment ?'   I was affronted at the fellow. 'What's
that to you,' says I, 'how ragged I am ? if I had seen
anything I liked I have money to pay for it ; but I
can go where I shan't be huffed at for looking.'

While I said thus, pretty boldly to the fellow,
comes a woman out, 'What ails you,' says she to the
man, 'to bully away our customers so ? a poor boy's
money is as good as my lord mayor's ; if poor people
did not buy old clothes what would become of our
business ?' and, then turning to me, 'Come hither,
child,' says she, 'if thou hast a mind to anything I
have, you shan't be hectored by him ; the boy is a
pretty boy, I assure you,' says she, to another woman
that was by this time come to her. 'Ay,' says the
t'other, 'so he is, a very well-looking child, if he was
clean and well dressed, and may be as good a gentle-

man's son for anything we know, as any of those that are well dressed. Come, my dear,' says she, 'tell me what is it you would have?' She pleased me mightily to hear her talk of my being a gentleman's son, and it brought former things to my mind; but when she talk'd of my being not clean, and in rags, then I cried.

She pressed me to tell her if I saw anything that I wanted; I told her no, all the clothes I saw there were too big for me. 'Come, child,' says she, 'I have two things here that will fit you, and I am sure you want them both; that is, first, a little hat, and there,' says she (tossing it to me), 'I'll give you that for nothing; and here is a good warm pair of breeches; I dare say,' says she, 'they will fit you, and they are very tight and good; and,' says she, 'if you should ever come to have so much money that you don't know what to do with it, here are excellent good pockets,' says she, 'and a little fob to put your gold in, or your watch in, when you get it.'

It struck me with a strange kind of joy that I should have a place to put my money in, and need not go to hide it again in a hollow tree; that I was ready to snatch the breeches out of her hands, and wondered that I should be such a fool never to think of buying me a pair of breeches before, that I might have a pocket to put my money in, and not carry it about two days together in my hand, and in my shoe, and I knew not how; so, in a word, I gave her two shillings for the breeches, and went over into the churchyard, and put them on, put my money into my new pockets, and was as pleased as a prince is with his coach and six horses. I thanked the good woman too for the hat, and told her I would come again when I got more money, and buy some other things I wanted ; and so I came away.

I was but a boy 'tis true, but I thought myself a man, now I had got a pocket to put my money in, and I went directly to find out my companion, by whose means I got it ; but I was frighted out of my wits when I heard that he was carried to Bridewell ; I made no question but it was for the letter-case, and that I should be carried there too ; and then my poor brother Captain Jack's case came into my head, and that I should be whipped there as cruelly as he was, and I was in such a fright that I knew not what to do.

But in the afternoon I met him ; he had been carried to Bridewell, it seems, upon that very affair, but was got out again. The case was thus : having had such good luck at the custom-house the day before he takes his walk thither again, and as he was in the long-room, gaping and staring about him, a fellow lays hold of him, and calls to one of the clerks that sat behind, ' Here,' says he, ' is the same young rogue that I told you I saw loitering about t'other day, when the gentleman lost his letter-case and his goldsmith's bills; I dare say it was he that stole them.' Immediately the whole crowd of people gathered about the boy, and charged him point blank; but he was too well used to such things to be frighted into a confession of what he knew they could not prove, for he had nothing about him belonging to it, nor had any money, but sixpence and a few dirty farthings.

They threatened him, and pulled and hauled him, till they almost pulled the clothes off his back, and the commissioners examined him; but all was one, he would own nothing, but said he walked up through the room only to see the place, both then and the time before, for he had owned he was there before; so as there was no proof against him of any fact, no, nor of any circumstances relating to the letter-case, they were forced at last to let him go; however, they made a show of carrying him to Bridewell, and they did carry him to the gate to see if they could make him confess anything; but he would confess nothing, and they had no *mittimus*; so they durst not carry him into the house, nor would the people have received him, I suppose, if they had, they having no warrant for putting him in prison.

Well, when they could get nothing out of him they carried him into an alehouse, and there they told him that the letter-case had bills in it of a very great value, that they would be of no use to the rogue that had **them, but** they **would** be of infinite damage to the gentleman that had lost them ; and that he had left word with the clerk, who the man that stopped this **boy** had called to, and who was there with him, that **he** would give £30 to any one that would bring them again, and give all the security that could be desired that **he would give** them no trouble, **whoever** it was.

He was just come from out of their hands when I met with him, and so he **told** me all the story ; ' but,' says he, ' I would confess nothing, and so I got off, and am come away clear.' ' Well,' says I, ' and what will you do with the letter-case, and the bills, will not you let the poor man have his bills again ?' ' No, not I,' says he, ' I won't trust them, what care I for their bills ?' It came into my head, as young as I was, that it was a sad thing indeed to **take a** man's bills away for **so much** money, and **not have** any advantage by it either ; for I concluded that the gentleman who owned the bills must lose all the money, and it was strange he should keep the bills and make a gentleman lose so much money for nothing. I remember that I ruminated very much **about** it, and, though I did not understand it very well, yet it lay upon my mind, and I said every now and then to him, ' Do let the gentleman have his **bills** again ; do, pray do ;' and so I teazed him with do, and pray do, till **at last I cried** about them. He said, 'What, would you have me be found out and sent to Bridewell, and be whipped, as your brother Captain Jack was?' I said, 'No, I would not have you whipped, but I would have the man have his bills, for they will do you no good, but the gentleman will be undone, it may be;' and then, I added again, 'Do let him have them.' He snapped me short, 'Why,' says he, 'how shall I get them to him? Who dare carry them? I dare not, to be sure, for they will stop me, and bring the goldsmith to see if he does not know me, and that I received the money, and so they will prove the robbery, and I shall be hanged; would you have me be hanged, Jack?'

I was silenced a good while with that, for when he said, 'Would you have me be hanged, Jack?' I had no more to say; but one day after this he called to me, 'Colonel Jack,' says he, 'I have thought of a way how the gentleman shall have his bills again; and you and I shall get a good deal of money by it if you will be honest to me, as I was to you.' 'Indeed,' says I, 'Robin,' that was his name, 'I will be very honest; let me know how it is, for I would fain have him have his bills.'

'Why,' says he, 'they told me that he had left word at the clerk's place in the long-room, that he would give £30 to any one that had the bills, and would restore them, and would ask no questions. Now, if you will go, like a poor innocent boy, as you are, into the long-room, and speak to the clerk, it may do; tell him, if the gentleman will do as he promised, you believe you can tell him who has it; and if they are civil to you, and willing to be as good as their words, you shall have the letter-case, and give it them.'

I told him, 'Ay, I would go with all my heart.' 'But, Colonel Jack,' says he, 'what if they should take hold of you, and threaten to have you whipped, won't you discover me to them?' 'No,' says I, 'if they would whip me to death I won't.' 'Well, then,' says he, 'there's the letter-case, do you go.' So he gave me directions how to act, and what to say; but I would not take the letter-case with me, lest they should prove false, and take hold of me, thinking to find it upon me, and so charge me with the fact; so I left it with him, and the next morning I went to the custom-house, as was agreed; what my directions were, will, to avoid repetition, appear in what happened; it was an errand of too much consequence indeed to be entrusted to a boy, not only so young as I was, but so little of a rogue as I was yet arrived to the degree of.

Two things I was particularly armed with, which I resolved upon: 1. That the man should have his bills again; for it seemed a horrible thing to me that he should be made to lose his money, which I supposed he must, purely because we would not carry the letter-case home. **2.** That whatever happened to me, I was never to tell the name of my comrade Robin, who had been the principal. With these two pieces of honesty, for such they were both in themselves, and with a manly heart, though a boy's head, I went up into the long-room in the Custom-house the next day.

As soon as I came to the place where the thing was done, I saw the man sit just where he had sat before, and it ran in my head that he had sat there ever since; but I knew no better; so I went up, and stood just at that side of the writing-board that goes upon that side of the room, and which I was but just tall enough to lay my arms upon.

While I stood there, one thrust me this way, and another thrust me that way, and the man that sat behind began to look at me; at last he called out to me; 'What does that boy do there? get you gone, sirrah; are you one of the rogues that stole the gentleman's letter-case on Monday last?' Then he turns his tale to a gentleman that was doing business with him, and goes on thus: 'Here was Mr. —— had a very unlucky chance on Monday last, did not you hear of it?' 'No, not I,' says the gentleman. 'Why, standing just there, where you do,' says he, 'making his entries, he pulled out his letter-case, and laid it down, as he says, but just at his hand, while he reached over to the standish there for a penful of ink, and somebody stole away his letter-case.'

'His letter-case!' says t'other, 'what, and was there any bills in it?'

'Ay,' says he, 'there was Sir Stephen Evans's note in it for £300, and another goldsmith's bill for about £12, and, which is worse still for the gentleman, he had two foreign accepted bills in it for a great sum, I know not how much, I think one was a French bill for 1200 crowns.'

'And who could it be?' says the gentleman.

'Nobody knows,' says he, 'but one of our room-keepers says he saw a couple of young rogues like that,' pointing at me, 'hanging about here, and that on a sudden they were both gone.'

'Villains!' says he again; 'why, what can they do with them, they will be of no use to them? I suppose he went immediately and gave notice to prevent the payment.'

'Yes,' says the clerk, 'he did; but the rogues were too nimble for him with the little bill of £12 odd money; they went and got the money for that, but all the rest are stopped; however, 'tis an unspeakable damage to him for want of his money.'

'Why, he should publish a reward for the encouragement of those that have them to bring them again; they would be glad to bring them, I warrant you.'

'He has posted it up at the door, that he will give £30 for them.'

'Ay, but he should add, that he will promise not to stop, or give any trouble to the person that brings them.'

'He has done that too,' says he, 'but I fear they won't trust themselves to be honest, for fear he should break his word.'

'Why, it is true, he may break his word in that case, but no man should do so; for then no rogue will venture to bring home anything that is stolen, and so he would do an injury to others after him.'

'I durst pawn my life for him, he would scorn it.'

Thus far they discoursed of it, and then went off to something else. I heard it all, but did not know what to do a great while; but at last, watching the gentleman that went away, when he was gone, I ran after him to have spoken to him, intending to have broke it to him, but he went hastily into a room or two, full of people, at the hither end of the long-room; and when I went to follow, the doorkeepers turned me back and told me, I must not go in there; so I went back, and loitered about, near the man that sat behind the board, and hung about there till I found the clock struck twelve, and the room began to be thin of people; and at last he sat there writing, but nobody stood at the board before him, as there had all the rest of the morning; then I came a little nearer, and stood close to the board, as I did before; when, looking up from his paper, and seeing me, says he to me, 'You have been up and down there all this morning, sirrah, what do you want? you have some business that is not very good, I doubt.'

'No, I han't,' said I.

'No? it is well if you han't,' says he; 'pray what business can you have in the long-room, sir; you are no merchant?'

'I would speak with you,' said I.

'With me,' says he, 'what have you to say to me?'

'I have something to say,' said I, 'if you will do me no harm for it.'

'I do thee harm, child, what harm should I do thee?' and spoke very kindly.

'Won't you indeed, sir?' said I.

'No, not I, child; I'll do thee no harm; what is it? do you know anything of the gentleman's letter-case?'

I answered, but spoke softly, that he could not hear me: so he gets over presently into the seat next him, and opens a place that was made to come out, and bade me come in to him; and I did.

Then he asked me again if I knew anything of the letter-case.

I spoke softly again, and said, Folks would hear him.

Then he whispered softly, and asked me again.

I told him I believed I did; but that, indeed, I
had it not, nor had no hand in stealing it, but it was
gotten into the hands of a boy that would have burnt
it, if it had not been for me; and that I heard him
say that the gentleman would be glad to have them
again, and give a good deal of money for them.

'I did say so, child,' said he, 'and if you can get
them for him he shall give you a good reward, no
less than £30, as he has promised.'

'But you said too, sir, to the gentleman just now,'
said I, 'that you was sure he would not bring them
into any harm that should bring them.'

'No, you shall come to no harm; I will pass my
word for it.'

Boy. Nor shan't they make me bring other people
into trouble?

Gent. No, you shall not be asked the name of
anybody, nor to tell who they are.

Boy. I am but a poor boy, and I would fain have
the gentleman have his bills, and indeed I did not
take them away, nor I han't got them.

Gent. But can you tell how the gentleman shall
have them?

Boy. If I can get them I will bring them to you
to-morrow morning.

Gent. Can you not do it to-night?

Boy. I believe I may if I knew where to come.

Gent. Come to my house, child.

Boy. I don't know where you live.

Gent. Go along with me now, and **you** shall see. So he carried me **up into** Tower-street, and showed me his **house, and** ordered me to come there at five o'clock at night; which accordingly I did, and carried **the** letter-case with me.

When I came the gentleman asked me if I had brought the book, as he called it.

'It is not a book,' said I.

'No, the letter-case, that's all one,' says he.

'You promised me,' said I, 'you would not hurt me,' and cried.

'Don't be afraid, child,' says he, 'I will not hurt thee, poor boy; nobody shall hurt thee.'

'Here it is,' said I, and pulled it out.

He **then** brought **in another** gentleman, who it seems owned the letter-case, and asked him if that **was** it? and he said, 'Yes.'

Then he asked me if all the bills were in it?

I told him I heard him say there was one gone, but I believed there was all the rest.

'Why do you believe so?' says he.

'**Because** I heard the boy that I believe stole them, say they were too big for him to meddle with.'

The gentleman, **then,** that owned them, said, 'Where is the boy?'

Then the other gentleman put in, and said, 'No, you must not ask him that; I passed my word that

you should not, and that he should not be obliged ı
tell it to anybody.'

'Well, child,' says he, 'you will let us see the
letter-case opened, and whether the bills are in it?'

'Yes,' says I.

Then the first gentleman said, 'How many bills
were there in it?'

'Only three,' says he, 'besides the bill of £12:10s.;
there was Sir Stephen Evans's note for £300, and
two foreign bills.'

'Well, then, if they are in the letter-case, the boy
shall have £30, shall he not?' 'Yes,' says the
gentleman, 'he shall have it freely.'

'Come then, child,' says he, 'let me open it.'

So I gave it him, and he opened it, and there
were all three bills, and several other papers, fair and
safe, nothing defaced or diminished, and the gentleman said, 'All is right.'

Then said the first man, 'Then I am security to
the poor boy for the money.' 'Well, but,' says the
gentleman, 'the rogues have got the £12:10s.; they
ought to reckon that as part of the £30.' Had he
asked me, I should have consented to it at first word ;
but the first man stood my friend. 'Nay,' says he,
'it was since you knew that the £12:10s. was received that you offered £30 for the other bills, and
published it by the crier, and posted it up at the
custom-house door, and I promised him the £30 this

morning.' They argued long, and I thought would have quarrelled about it.

However, at last they both yielded a little, and the gentleman gave me £25 in good guineas. When he gave it me, he bade me hold out my hand, and he told the money into my hand; and when he had done, he asked me if it was right? I said I did not know, but I believed it was: 'Why,' says he, 'can't you tell it?' I told him, No; I never saw so much money in my life, nor I did not know how to tell money. 'Why,' says he, 'don't you know that they are guineas?' No, I told him, I did not know how much a guinea was.

'Why, then,' says he, 'did you tell me you believed it was right?' I told him because I believed he would not give it me wrong.

'Poor child,' says he, 'thou knowest little of the world, indeed; what art thou?'

'I am a poor boy,' says I, and cried.

'What is your name?' says he—'but hold, I forgot,' said he; 'I promised I would not ask your name, so you need not tell me.'

'My name is Jack,' said I.

'Why, have you no surname?' said he.

'What is that?' said I.

'You have some other name besides Jack,' says he, 'han't you?'

'Yes,' says I, 'they call me Colonel Jack.'

'But have you no other name?'

'No,' said I.

'How came you to be called Colonel Jack, pray?

'They say,' said I, 'my father's name was Colonel.

'Is your father or mother alive?' said he.

'No,' said I, 'my father is dead.'

'Where is your mother then?' said he.

'I never had e'er a mother,' said I.

This made him laugh. 'What,' said he, 'had you never a mother, what then?'

'I had a nurse,' said I, 'but she was not my mother.'

'Well,' says he to the gentleman, 'I dare say this boy was not the thief that stole your bills.'

'Indeed, sir, I did not steal them,' said I, and cried again.

'No, no, child,' said he, 'we don't believe you did. This is a very clever boy,' says he, to the other gentleman, 'and yet very ignorant and honest; 'tis pity some care should not be taken of him, and something done for him; let us talk a little more with him.' So they sat down and drank wine, and gave me some, and then the first gentleman talked to me again.

'Well,' says he, 'what wilt thou do with this money now thou hast it?'

'I don't know,' said I.

'Where will you put it?' said he.

'In my pocket,' said I.

'In your pocket,' said he; 'is your pocket whole? shan't you lose it?'

'Yes,' said I, 'my pocket is whole.'

'And where will you put it, when you get home?'

'I have no home,' said I; and cried again.

'Poor child!' said he, 'then what dost thou do for thy living?'

'I go of errands,' said I, 'for the folks in Rose-mary-lane.'

'And what dost thou do for a lodging at night?'

'I lie at the glass-house,' said I, 'at night.'

'How, lie at the glass-house! have they any beds there?' says he.

'I never lay in a bed in my life,' said I, 'as I remember.'

'Why,' says he, 'what do you lie on at the glass-house?'

'The ground,' says I, 'and sometimes a little straw, or upon the warm ashes.'

Here the gentleman that lost the bills, said, 'This poor child is enough to make a man weep for the miseries of human nature, and be thankful for himself; he puts tears into my eyes.' 'And into mine too,' says the other.

'Well, but hark ye, Jack,' says the first gentleman, 'do they give you no money when they send you of errands?'

'They give me victuals,' said I, 'and that's better.'

'But what,' says he, 'do you do for clothes?'

'They give me sometimes old things,' said I, 'such as they have **to spare.**'

'Why, you have never **a** shirt on, I believe,' said **he,** 'have you?'

'No, I never had a shirt,' **said I, 'since my nurse** died.'

'How long ago is that?' said he.

'Six winters, when this is out,' said I.

'Why, how old are you?' said he.

'**I** can't tell,' said I.

'Well,' says the gentleman, 'now you have this money won't you buy some clothes, and a shirt with some of it?'

'Yes,' said I, I would buy some clothes.

'And what will you do with the rest?'

'I can't tell,' said I, and cried.

'What do'st cry for, Jack?' said he.

'I am afraid,' said I; and cried still.

'What art afraid of?'

'They will know I have money.'

'Well, and what then?'

'Then I must sleep no more in the warm **glass-**house, and I shall be starved with cold. **They** will take away my money.'

'But why must you sleep there no more?'

Here the gentlemen observed to one another how

naturally anxiety and perplexity attend those that have money. 'I warrant you,' says the clerk, 'when this poor boy had no money he slept all night in the straw, or on the warm ashes in the glass-house, as soundly and as void of care as it would be possible for any creature to do; but now, as soon as he has gotten money, the care of preserving it brings tears into his eyes, and fear into his heart.'

They asked me a great many questions more, to which I answered in my childish way as well as I could, but so as pleased them well enough; at last I was going away with a heavy pocket, and I assure you not a light heart, for I was so frighted with having so much money that I knew not what in the earth to do with myself: I went away, however, and walked a little way, but I could not tell what to do; so, after rambling two hours or thereabout, I went back again, and sat down at the gentleman's door, and there I cried as long as I had any moisture in my head to make tears of, but never knocked at the door.

I had not sat long, I suppose, but somebody belonging to the family got knowledge of it, and a maid came and talked to me, but I said little to her, only cried still; at length it came to the gentleman's ears. As for the merchant, he was gone. When the gentleman heard of me, he called me in, and began to talk with me again, and asked me what I stayed for?

I told him I had not stayed there all that while, for I had been gone a great while, and was come again.

'Well,' says he, 'but what did you come again for?'

'I can't tell,' says I.

'And what do you cry so for?' said he. 'I hope you have not lost your money, have you?'

No, I told him, I had not lost it yet, but I was afraid I should.

'And does that make you cry?' says he.

I told him, Yes, for I knew I should not be able to keep it, but they would cheat me of it, or they would kill me, and take it away from me too.

'They,' says he, 'who? what sort of gangs of people art thou with?'

I told him they were all boys, but very wicked boys; 'Thieves and pickpockets,' said I, 'such as stole this letter-case, a sad pack, I can't abide them.'

'Well, Jack,' said he, 'what shall be done for thee? Will you leave it with me? shall I keep it for you?'

'Yes,' said I, with all my heart, 'if you please.'

'Come, then,' says he, 'give it me; and that you may be sure that I have it, and you shall have it honestly again, I'll give you a bill for it, and for the interest of it, and that you may keep safe enough. Nay,' added he, 'and if you lose it, or anybody takes it from you, none shall receive the money but yourself, or any part of it.'

I presently pulled out all the money, and gave it to him, only keeping about 15s. for myself to buy some clothes ; and thus ended the conference between us on the first occasion, at least for the first time. Having thus secured my money to my full satisfaction I was then perfectly easy, and, accordingly, the sad thoughts that afflicted my mind before began to vanish away.

This was enough to let any one see how all the sorrows and anxieties of men's lives come about ; how they rise from their restless pushing at getting of money, and the restless cares of keeping it when they have got it. I that had nothing, and had not known what it was to have had anything, knew nothing of the care either of getting or of keeping it ; I wanted nothing, who wanted everything ; I had no care, no concern about where I should get my victuals, or how I should lodge ; I knew not what money was, or what to do with it ; and never knew what it was not to sleep till I had money to keep and was afraid of losing it.

I had, without doubt, an opportunity at this time, if I had not been too foolish, and too much a child to speak for myself ; I had an opportunity, I say, to have got into his service, or perhaps to be under some of the care and concern of these gentlemen ; for they seemed to be very fond of doing something for me, and were surprised at the innocence of my talk to them, as well as at the misery (as they thought it) of my condition.

But I acted indeed like a child ; and leaving my money, as I have said, I never went near them for several years after. What course I took, and what befel me in that interval, has so much variety in it, and carries so much instruction in it, that it requires an account of it by itself.

The first happy chance that offered itself to me in the world was now over ; I had got money, but I neither knew the value of it nor the use of it ; the way of living I had begun was so natural to me I had no notion of bettering it ; I had not so much as any desire of buying me any clothes, no, not so much as a shirt, and much less had I any thought of getting any other lodging than that in the glass-house, and loitering about the streets, as I had done ; for I knew no good, and had tasted no evil ; that is to say, the life I had led being not evil in my account.

In this state of innocence I returned to my really miserable life, so it was in itself, and was only not so to me, because I did not understand how to judge of it, and had known no better.

My comrade that gave me back the bills, and who, if I had not pressed him, designed never to have restored them, never asked me what I had given me, but told me if they gave me anything it should be my own ; for as, he said, he would not run the venture of being seen in the restoring them, I deserved the reward if there was any ; neither did he trouble his head with inquiring what I had, or whether I had anything **or no** ; so my title to what I had got was clear.

I went now up and down just as I did before ; I had money indeed in my pocket, but I let nobody know it ; I went of errands cheerfully as before, and accepted of what anybody gave me, with as much thankfulness as ever ; the only difference that I made with myself, was, that if I was hungry, and nobody employed me, or gave me anything to eat, I did not beg from door to door, as I did at first, but went to a boiling-house, as I said once before, and got a mess of broth and a piece of bread, price a half-penny ; very seldom any meat, or if I treated myself, it was a half-penny worth of cheese ; all which expense did not amount to above twopence or threepence a week ; for, contrary **to the** usage of the rest of the tribe, I was extremely frugal, **and I** had not disposed of any of the guineas which I **had at first** ; neither, as I said to the custom-house gentleman, could I tell what a guinea was made of, or what it was worth.

After I had been about a month thus, and had done nothing, my comrade, as I called him, came to me one morning ; 'Colonel Jack,' says he, 'when shall you and I take a walk again?' 'When you will,' said I. 'Have you got no business yet?' says he. 'No,' says I ; and so one thing bringing in another, he told me I was a fortunate wretch, and he believed I would be so again ; but that he must make a new bargain with me now ; 'for,' says he, 'Colonel, the first time we always let a raw brother come in for full share to encourage him, but afterwards, except it be when he puts himself forward well, and runs equal hazard, he stands to courtesy ; but as we are gentlemen, we always do very honourable by one another ; and if you are willing to trust it, or leave it to me, I shall do handsomely by you, that you may depend upon.' I told him I was not able to do anything, that was certain, for I did not understand it, and therefore I could not expect to get anything, but I would do as he bade me ; so we walked abroad together.

We went no more to the Custom-house, it was too bold a venture ; besides, I did not care to show myself again, especially with him in company ; but we went directly to the Exchange, and we hankered about in Castle-alley, and in Swithin's-alley, and at the coffee-house doors. It was a very unlucky day, for we got nothing all day but two or three handkerchiefs, and came home to the old lodgings at the glass-house ; nor had I anything to eat or drink all day, but a piece of bread which he gave me, and some water at the conduit at the Exchange-gate. So when he was gone from me, for he did not lie in the

glass-house as I did, I went to my old broth-house
for my usual bait, and **refreshed** myself, and the next
day early went to meet him again, as he appointed me.

Being **early in the morning, he** took his **walk to**
Billingsgate, where it seems two sorts of **people** make
a great crowd as soon as it is light, and at that time
a-year, rather before daylight; that is to say, crimps,
and **the masters** of coal ships, who they call collier-
masters; and, secondly, fishmongers, fish-sellers, and
buyers of fish.

It was the **first of** these people that he had his
eye upon. So he gives me **my** orders, **which was**
thus: 'Go you,' says he, 'into **all** the alehouses, as
we go along, and observe where any people are telling
of money; and **when** you find any, come and tell me.'
So he stood at the door, and I went into the houses.
As the collier-masters generally sell their coals at the
gate, as they call it, so they generally receive their
money in those alehouses; and it was not long before
I brought him word of several. Upon this he went
in, and made his observations, but found nothing to
his purpose; at length I brought him word that there
was a man in such a house who had received **a great**
deal of money **of** somebody, I believed of several
people, and that it lay all upon the table in heaps,
and **he** was very busy writing down **the** sums, and
putting it up in several bags. 'Is he?' says he, 'I'll
warrant him I **will have** some of it;' and in he goes.

He walks up and down the house, which had several open tables and boxes in it, and he listened to hear, if he could, what the man's name was; and he heard somebody call him Cullum, or some such name. Then he watches his opportunity, and steps up to him, and tells him a long story, that there were two gentlemen at the Gun tavern, sent him to inquire for him, and to tell him they desired to speak with him.

The collier-master had his money lying before him, just as I had told him, and had two or three small payments of money, which he had put up in little black dirty bags, and lay by themselves; and as it was hardly broad day, he found means, in delivering his message, to lay his hand upon one of those bags, and carry it off perfectly undiscovered.

When he had got it, he came out to me, who stood but at the door; and pulling me by the sleeve, 'Run, Jack,' says he, 'for our lives;' and away he scours, and I after him, never resting, or scarce looking about me, till we got quite up into Fenchurch-street, through Lime-street, into Leadenhall-street, down St. Mary-Axe, to London-wall, then through Bishopsgate-street, and down Old Bedlam into Moorfields. By this time we were neither of us able to run very fast, nor need we have gone so far, for I never found that anybody pursued us. When we got into Moorfields, and began to take breath, I asked him what it was frighted him so? 'Fright me, you fool,' says he, 'I have **got a** devilish great bag of money.' 'A bag!' said I. 'Ay, ay,' said he, 'let us get out into the fields where nobody can see us, and I'll show it you.' So away he had me through Long-alley, and cross Hog-lane, and Holloway-lane, into the middle of the great field, which, since that, has been called the Farthing Pie-house Fields. There we would have sat down, but it was all full of water; so we went on, crossed the road at Anniseed Cleer, and went into the field where now the great hospital stands; and finding a bye place, we sat down, and he pulls out the bag. 'Thou art a lucky boy, Jack,' says he, 'thou deservest a good share of this job truly, for it is all along of thy lucky news.' So he pours it all out into my hat, for, as I told you, I now wore a hat.

How he did to whip away such a bag of money from any man that was awake and in his senses I cannot tell; but there was a great deal in it, and among it a paper-full by itself. When the paper dropt out of the bag, 'Hold,' says he, 'that is gold!' and began to crow and hollow like a mad boy. But there he was baulked, for it was a paper of old thirteenpence - halfpenny pieces, half and quarter pieces, with ninepences, and fourpence-halfpennies, all **old** crooked money, Scotch and Irish coin; so he was disappointed in that; but as it was, there was about £17 or £18 in the bag, as I understood by him; for I could not tell money, not I.

Well, he parted this money into three ; that is to say, into three shares, two for himself, and one for me, and asked, if I was content ?   I told him, Yes, I had reason to be contented ; besides, it was so much money added to that I had left of his former adventure, that I knew not what to do with it, or with myself, while I had so much about me.

This was a most exquisite fellow for a thief ; for he had the greatest dexterity at conveying anything away, that he scarce ever pitched upon anything in his eye but he carried it off with his hands, and never, that I know of, missed his aim, or was caught in the fact.

He was an eminent pickpocket, and very dexterous at ladies' gold watches ; but he generally pushed higher, at such desperate things as these ; and he came off the cleanest, and with the greatest success imaginable ; and it was in these kinds of the wicked art of thieving that I became his scholar.

As we were now so rich he would not let me lie any longer in the glass-house, or go naked and ragged, as I had done ; but obliged me to buy two shirts, a waistcoat, and a great coat ; for a great coat was more for our purpose in the business we were upon than any other.   So I clothed myself as he directed, and he took me a lodging in the same house with him, and we lodged together in a little garret fit for our quality.

Soon after this we walked out again, and then we

tried our **fortune in** the places by the Exchange a second **time.** Here we began to act separately, and I undertook to walk **by** myself; and the first thing I did accurately **was a** trick I played that required some skill **for a new** beginner, for I had never seen any business of that kind done before. **I saw** two gentlemen mighty eager in talk, and one pulled out a pocket-book two or three times, and then slipt it into his coat-pocket again, and then out it came again, and papers were taken out, and others were put in; and then in it went again, and so several times; the man being still warmly engaged with another man, and two or three others standing hard by them. The last time he put his pocket-book into his pocket, he might be said to throw it in, rather than put it in with his hand, and the book lay end-way, resting upon some other book, or something else in his pocket; so that it did not go quite down, but one corner of it was seen above his pocket.

This careless way of men putting their pocket-books into a coat-pocket, which is so easily dived into by the least boy that has been used to the trade, can never be too much blamed; the gentlemen are in great hurries, their heads and thoughts entirely taken up, and it is impossible they should be guarded enough against such little hawk-eyed creatures as we were; and, therefore, they ought either never to put their pocket-books up at all, or to put them up more

secure, or to put nothing of value into them. I
happened to be just opposite to this gentleman in
that they call Swithin's-alley ; or that alley rather
which is between Swithin's-alley and the Exchange,
just by a passage that goes out of the alley into the
Exchange ; when seeing the book pass and repass
into the pocket, and out of the pocket as above, it
came immediately into my head, certainly I might get
that pocket-book out if I were nimble, and I warrant
Will would have it, if he saw it go and come to and
again as I did ; but when I saw it hang by the way,
as I have said ; ' Now it is mine,' said I to myself, and,
crossing the alley, I brushed smoothly, but closely, by
the man, with my hand down flat to my own side,
and, taking hold of it by the corner that appeared,
the book came so light into my hand, it was impossible the gentleman should feel the least motion, or
anybody else see me take it away. I went directly
forward into the broad place on the north side of the
Exchange, then scoured down Bartholomew-lane, so
into Tokenhouse-yard, into the alleys which pass
through from thence to London-wall, so through
Moorgate, and sat down on the grass in the second
of the quarters of Moorfields, towards the middle
field ; which was the place that Will and I had appointed to meet at if either of us got any booty.
When I came thither, Will was not come, but I saw
him a coming in about half an hour.

As soon **as** Will came to me, I asked him what booty he had gotten? He looked pale, and, as I thought, frighted; **but he** returned, **'I have got** nothing, not **I; but, you** lucky young dog,' says he, 'what have you got? Have not you got the gentleman's pocket-book in Swithin's-alley?' **'Yes,'** says I, and laughed at him; 'why, how did you know it?' 'Know it!' says he, 'why the gentleman is raving and half distracted; he stamps and cries, and tears his very clothes; he says he **is** utterly undone and ruined, and the folks in the alley say there is I know not how many thousand pounds in it; what can be in it?' says Will; 'come, let us see.'

Well, we lay close in the grass in the middle of the quarter, so that nobody minded us; and so we opened the pocket-book, and there was a great many bills and notes under men's hands; some goldsmiths', and some belonging to insurance offices, as they call them, and the like; but that which was it seems worth all the rest was that in one of the folds of the cover **of the** book, where there was a case with several partitions, there **was a** paper full of loose diamonds. The man, as we understood afterward, was a Jew, who dealt in such goods, and who indeed ought to have taken more care of the keeping of them.

Now was this booty too great, even for Will himself, **to** manage; for though by this time I was come to understand things better than I did formerly, when

I knew not what belonged to money; yet Will **was** better skilled by far in those things than I. But this puzzled him too, as well as me. Now were we something like the cock in the fable; for all these bills, and I think there was one bill of Sir Henry Furness's for £1200, and all these diamonds, which were worth about £150, as they said; I say, all these things were of no value to us, one little purse of gold would have been better to us than all of it. 'But come,' says Will, 'let us look over the bills for a little one.'

We looked over all the bills, and, among them, we found a bill under a man's hand for £32; 'Come,' says Will, 'let us go and inquire where this man lives.' So he went into the city again, and Will went to the post-house, and asked there; they told him he lived at Temple-bar: 'Well,' says Will, 'I will venture, I'll go and receive the money; it may be he has not remembered to send to stop the payment there.'

But it came into his thoughts to take another course; 'Come,' says Will, 'I'll go back to the alley and see if I can hear anything of what has happened, for I believe the hurry is not over yet. It seems the man who lost the book was carried into the King's-head tavern, at the end of that alley, and a great crowd was about the door.'

Away goes Will, and watches and waits about the place; and then, seeing several people together, for they were not all dispersed, he asks one or two what was the matter; they **tell** him a long story of a gentleman who had lost his pocket-book, with a great bag of diamonds in **it,** and bills for **a** great many thousand pounds, and I know not what; and that they had been just, crying it, and **had** offered £100 **reward to** any one who would discover and restore it.

'I wish,' **said** he, to one of them that parleyed with him, 'I did but know who has it, I don't doubt but I could help him to it again; does he remember nothing of anybody, boy, or fellow, that was near him? if he could but describe him, it might do.' Somebody that overheard him was so forward **to** assist the poor gentleman that they went up and let him know what a young fellow, meaning Will, had been talking at the door; and down comes another gentleman from him, and, taking Will aside, asked him what **he** had said about it? Will was a grave sort of a young man, that, though he was an old soldier at the trade, had **yet** nothing of it in his countenance; and he answered that he was concerned in business where a great many of the gangs of little pickpockets haunted, and if he had but the least description of the person they suspected he durst say he could find him out, **and** might perhaps get the things again for him. Upon this he desired him to go up with him to the gentleman, which he did accordingly; and there, he said, he sat leaning his head back to the chair, pale as a cloth; disconsolate to a strange degree, and, as Will described him, just like one under a sentence.

When they came to ask him whether he had seen no boy, or shabby fellow, lurking near where he stood, or passing, or repassing, and the like, he answered, 'No, not any;' neither could he remember that anybody had come near him. 'Then,' said Will, 'it will be very hard, if not impossible, to find them out. However,' said Will, 'if you think it worth while, I will put myself among those rogues, though,' says he, 'I care not for being seen among them; but I will put in among them, and if it be in any of those gangs, it is ten to one but I shall hear something of it.'

They asked him then, if he had heard what terms the gentleman had offered to have it restored; he answered, 'No' (though he had been told at the door); they answered, 'He had offered £100.' 'That is too much,' says Will; 'but if you please to leave it to me, I shall either get it for you for less than that, or not be able to get it for you at all.' Then the losing gentleman said to one of the other, 'Tell him, that if he can get it lower, the overplus shall be to himself.' William said he would be very glad to do the gentleman such a service, and would leave the reward to himself. 'Well, young man,' says one of the gentlemen, 'whatever you appoint to the young artist that has done this roguery (for I warrant he is an artist, let it be who it will), he shall be paid, if it be within the £100, and the gentleman is willing to give you £50 besides for your pains.'

'Truly, sir,' says Will, very gravely, 'it was by mere chance, that, coming by the door, and seeing the crowd, I asked what the matter was? but if I should be instrumental to get the unfortunate gentleman his pocket-book, and the things in it again, I shall be very glad; nor am I so rich neither, sir, but £50 is very well worth my while too.' Then he took directions who to come to, and who to give his account to if he learned anything, and the like.

Will stayed so long, that, as he and I agreed, I went home, and he did not come to me till night; for we had considered before that it would not be proper to come from them directly to me, lest they should follow him and apprehend me. If he had made no advances towards a treaty, he would have come back in half an hour, as we agreed; but staying late, we met at our night rendezvous, which was in Rosemary-lane.

When he came he gave an account of all the discourse, and particularly what a consternation the gentleman was in who lost the pocket-book, and that he did not doubt but we should get a good round sum for the recovery of it.

We consulted all the evening about it, and concluded he should let them hear nothing of them the next day at all ; and that the third day he should go, but should make no discovery, only that he had got a scent of it, and that he believed he should have it, and make it appear as difficult as possible, and to start as many objections as he could. Accordingly, the third day after he met with the gentleman, who he found had been uneasy at his long stay, and told him they were afraid that he only flattered them to get from them ; and that they had been too easy in letting him go without a further examination.

He took upon him to be very grave with them, and told them that if that was what he was like to have for being so free as to tell them he thought he might serve them they might see that they had wronged him, and were mistaken by his coming again to them ; that if they thought they could do anything by examining him, they might go about it, if they pleased, now ; that all he had to say to them was, that he knew where some of the young rogues haunted, who were famous for such things ; and that by some inquiries, offering them money, and the like, he believed they would be brought to betray one another, and that so he might pick it out for them ; and this he would say before a justice of peace, if they thought fit ; and then all that he had to say further to them was, to tell them he had lost a day or two in their service, and had got nothing, but to be suspected for his pains ; and that after that he had done, **and** they might seek their **goods where** they could **find them.**

They began to listen a little upon that, and asked **him if he could** give them **any** hopes of recovering their loss; **he** told **them** that he was **not afraid to tell them that he** believed he had heard some news of them, **and** that what he had done had prevented **all** the bills **being** burnt, book and all; but that now he **ought not to be** asked any more questions till they **should** be pleased to answer him a question or two. They told him they would give him any satisfaction they could, and bid him tell what he desired.

'Why, sir,' says he, 'how can you expect any thief that had robbed **you** to such a considerable value as this, would come and put himself into your hands, confess he had your goods, and restore them to you, if you **do not** give them assurance that you will not only give them the reward you agreed to, **but also** give assurance that they shall not be stopped, questioned, or called to account before a magistrate?'

They said they would give all possible assurance of it. 'Nay,' says he, 'I **do** not know what assurance you are able **to** give; for when a poor fellow is in your clutches, and has shown you your goods, you may seize upon him for **a** thief, and **it** is plain he must be so; then you go, take away your goods, send him **to prison, and what** amends can he have of you afterward?'

They were entirely confounded with the difficulty; they asked him to try if he could get the things into his hands, and they would pay him the money before he let them go out of his hand, and he should go away half an hour before they went out of the room.

'No, gentlemen,' says he, 'that won't do now. If you had talked so before you had talked of apprehending me for nothing, I should have taken your word; but now it is plain you have had such a thought in your heads, and how can I, or any one else, be assured of safety?'

Well, they thought of a great many particulars, but nothing would do; at length the other people who were present put in that they should give security to him, by a bond of £1000, that they would not give the person any trouble whatsoever. He pretended they could not be bound, nor could their obligation be of any value, and that their own goods being once seen, they might seize them; 'and what would it signify,' said he, 'to put a poor pickpocket to sue for his reward?' They could not tell what to say: but told him, that he should take the things of the boy, if it was a boy; and they would be bound to pay him the money promised. He laughed at them, and said, 'No, gentlemen, as I am not the thief, so I shall be very loath to put myself in the thief's stead, and lie at your mercy.'

They told him they knew not what to do then,

and that it would be very hard he would not trust them at all. He said, he was very willing to trust them, and to serve them ; but that it would be very hard to be ruined and charged with the theft, for endeavouring to serve them.

They then offered to give it him under their hands that they did not in the least suspect him ; that they would never charge him with anything about it ; that they acknowledged he went about to inquire after the goods at their request ; and that if he produced them, they would pay him so much money, at or before the delivery of them, without obliging him to name or produce that person he had them from.

Upon this writing, signed by three gentlemen who were present, and by the person in particular who lost the things, the young gentleman told them he would go and do his utmost to get the pocket-book, and all that was in it.

Then he desired that they would in writing, beforehand, give him a particular of all the several things that were in the book ; that he might not have it said, when he produced it, that there was not all ; and he would have the said writing sealed up, and he would make the book be sealed up when it was given to him. This they agreed to ; and the gentleman accordingly drew up a particular of all the bills that he remembered, as he said, was in the book ; and also of the diamonds, as follows :

One bill under Sir Henry Furness's hand for £1200.

One bill under Sir Charles Duncomb's hand for £800, £250 indorsed off.—£550.

One bill under the hand of J. Tassel, goldsmith, £165.

One bill of Sir Francis Child, £39.

One bill of one Stewart, that kept a wager-office and insurance, £350.

A paper containing thirty-seven loose diamonds, value about £250.

A little paper, containing three large rough diamonds, and one large one polished, and cut, value £185.

For all these things they promised, first, to give him whatever he agreed with the thief to give him, not exceeding £50, and to give him £50 more for himself for procuring them.

Now he had his cue, and now he came to me, and told me honestly the whole story as above; so I delivered him the book, and he told me that he thought it was reasonable we should take the full sum; because he would seem to have done them some service, and so make them the easier. All this I agreed to; so he went the next day to the place and the gentlemen met him very punctually.

He told them at the first word he had done their work, and, as he hoped, to their mind; and told them, if it had not been for the diamonds, he could have got all for £10, but that the diamonds had shone so bright in the boy's imagination that he talked of running away to France or Holland, and living there all his days like a gentleman ; at which they laughed. 'However, gentlemen,' said he, 'here is the book ;' and so pulled it out, wrapt up in a dirty piece of a coloured handkerchief, as black as the street could make it, and sealed with a piece of sorry wax, and the impression of a farthing for a seal.

Upon this, the note being also unsealed, at the same time he pulled open the dirty rag, and showed the gentleman his pocket-book ; at which he was so over-surprised with joy, notwithstanding all the preparatory discourse, that he was fain to call for a glass of wine or brandy to drink, to keep him from fainting.

The book being opened, the paper of diamonds was first taken out, and there they were every one, only the little paper was by itself; and the rough diamonds that were in it were loose among the rest ; but he owned they were all there safe.

Then the bills were called over, one by one, and they found one bill for £80 more than the account mentioned ; besides several papers which were not for money, though of consequence to the gentleman, and he acknowledged that all was very honestly returned ; 'And now, young man,' said they, 'you shall see we will deal as honestly by you ;' and so, in the first place, they gave him £50 for himself, and then they told out the £50 for me.

He took the £50 for himself, and put it up in his pocket, wrapping it in paper, it being all in gold: then he began to tell over the other £50; but when he had told out £30, 'Hold, gentlemen,' said he, 'as I have acted fairly for you, so you shall have no reason to say I do not do so to the end. I have taken £30, and for so much I agreed with the boy; and so there is £20 of your money again.'

They stood looking one at another a good while, as surprised at the honesty of it; for till that time they were not quite without a secret suspicion that he was the thief, but that piece of policy cleared up his reputation to them. The gentleman that had got his bills said softly to one of them, 'Give it him all;' but the other said (softly too), 'No, no, as long as he has got it abated, and is satisfied with the £50 you have given him, 'tis very well, let it go as it is.' This was not spoke so softly but he heard it, and said, 'No,' too; 'I am very well satisfied, I am glad I have got them for you;' and so they began to part.

But just before they were going away one of the gentlemen said to him, 'Young man, come, you see we are just to you, and have done fairly, as you have also, and we will not desire you to tell us who this cunning fellow is that got such a prize from this gentleman; but as you have talked with him, pr'ythee, can you tell us nothing of how he did it, that we may beware of such sparks again?'

'Sir,' says Will, 'when I shall tell you what they say, and how the particular case stood, the gentleman would blame himself more than anybody else, or as much at least. The young rogue that catched this prize was out, it seems, with a comrade, who is a nimble experienced pickpocket as most in London, but at that time the artist was somewhere at a distance, and this boy never had picked a pocket in his life before; but, he says, he stood over against the passage into the Exchange, on the east side, and the gentleman stood just by the passage; that he was very earnest in talking with some other gentleman, and often pulled out this book and opened it, and took papers out, and put others in, and returned it into his coat-pocket; that the last time it hitched at the pocket-hole, or stopt at something that was in the pocket, and hung a little out, which the boy, who had watched it a good while, perceiving, he passes by close to the gentleman, and carried it smoothly off, without the gentleman's perceiving it at all.'

He went on; and said, ' 'Tis very strange gentlemen should put pocket-books which have such things in them into those loose pockets, and in so careless a manner.' 'That's very true,' says the gentleman; and so, with some other discourse of no great signification, he came away to me.

(Jack returning from Virginia, whither he has been transported, marries a wife under evil stars (Defoe's heroes and heroines, though they marry very much, are seldom fortunate, Jack least of all), and his wife, after very ill behaviour, leaves him.)

I was extremely satisfied with this proceeding, and took care to let her hear of it, though I gave no answer at all to her letter; and as I had taken care before, that whenever she played such a prank as this she should not be able to carry much with her, so, after she was gone, I immediately broke up housekeeping, sold my furniture by public outcry, and in it everything in particular that was her own, and set a bill upon my door, giving her to understand by it that she had passed the Rubicon; that as she had taken such a step of her own accord, so there was no room left her ever to think of coming back again.

This was what any one may believe I should not have done, if I had seen any room for a reformation; but she had given me such testimonies of a mind alienated from her husband, in particular espousing her own unsufferable levity, that there was indeed no possibility of our coming afterwards to any terms again.

However, I kept a couple of trusty agents so near her that I failed not to have a full account of her conduct, though I never let her know anything of me but that I **was** gone over to France ; as to her bills which she said she would draw upon me, she was **as** good as **her** word in drawing one of £30, which I refused to accept, and never gave her leave to trouble me with another.

*	*	*	*	*	*

I lived retired, because I knew she had contracted debts which I should be obliged to pay, and I was resolved to be gone out of her reach with what speed I could ; but it was necessary that I should stay till the Virginia fleet came in, because I looked for at least three hundred hogsheads of tobacco from thence, which I knew would heal all my breaches ; for indeed the extravagance of three years with this lady had sunk me most effectually, even far beyond her own fortune, which was considerable, though not quite £1500, as she had called it.

But all the mischiefs I **met** with on account of **this** match were not over yet ; for when I had been parted with her about three months, and had refused to accept her bill of £30 which I mentioned above, though I was removed from my first lodgings too, and thought I had effectually secured myself from being found out, yet there came a gentleman well dressed to my lodgings one day, **and** was let in before I knew of it, or else I should scarce have admitted him.

He was led into a parlour, and I came down to him in my gown and slippers; when I came into the room, he called me as familiarly by my name as if he had known me twenty years, and pulling out a pocket-book, he shows me a bill upon me, drawn by my wife, which was the same bill for £30 that I had refused before.

'Sir,' says I, 'this bill has been presented before, and I gave my answer to it then.'

'Answer, sir!' says he, with a kind of jeering, taunting air; 'I do not understand what you mean by an answer; it is not a question, sir, it is a bill to be paid.'

'Well, sir,' says I, 'it is a bill, I know that, and I gave my answer to it before.'

'Sir, sir,' says he, very saucily, 'your answer! there is no answer to a bill, it must be paid; bills are to be paid, not to be answered; they say you are a merchant, sir; merchants always pay their bills.'

I began to be angry too a little, but I did not like my man, for I found he began to be quarrelsome; however, I said, 'Sir, I perceive you are not much used to presenting bills; sir, a bill is always first presented, and presenting is a question, it is asking if I will accept or pay the bill, and then whether I say Yes or No, it is an answer one way or other; after it is accepted, it indeed requires no more answer but payment when it is due; if you please to inform yourself this is the usage which all merchants, or tradesmen of any kind, who have bills drawn upon them, act by.'

'Well, sir,' says he, 'and what then? What is this to the paying me the £30?'

'Why, sir,' says I, 'it is this to it, that I told the person that brought it I should not pay it.'

'Not pay it!' says he, 'but you shall pay it; ay, ay, you will pay it.'

'She that draws it has no reason to draw any bills upon me, I am sure,' said I; 'and I shall pay no bills she draws, I assure you.'

Upon this he turns short upon me; 'Sir, she that draws this bill is a person of too much honour to draw any bill without reason, and it is an affront to say so of her, and I shall expect satisfaction of you for that by itself; but first the bill, sir, the bill, you must pay the bill, sir.'

I returned as short; 'Sir, I affront nobody, I know the person as well as you I hope, and what I have said of her is no affront; she can have no reason to draw bills upon me, for I owe her nothing.'

I omit intermingling the oaths he laced his speech with, as too foul for my paper; but he told me he would make me know she had friends to stand by her, that I had abused her, and he would let me know it, and do her justice; but first, I must pay his bill.

I answered in short, I would not pay the bill, nor any bills she should draw.

With that he steps to the door and shuts it, and swore by G—d he would make me pay the bill before we parted ; and laid his hand upon his sword, but did not draw it out.

I confess I was frightened to the last degree, for I had no sword, and if I had, I must own that, though I had learned a great many good things in France to make me look like a gentleman, I had forgot the main article of learning, how to use a sword, a thing so universally practised there ; and to say more, I had been perfectly unacquainted with quarrels of this nature ; so that I was perfectly surprised when he shut the door, and knew not what to say or do.

However, as it happened, the people of the house hearing us pretty loud, came near the door, and made a noise in the entry, to let me know they were at hand ; and one of the servants going to open the door, and finding it locked, called out to me, 'Sir, for God's sake open the door ! what is the matter? shall we fetch a constable ?' I made no answer, but it gave me courage, so I sat down composed in one of the chairs, and said to him ; 'Sir, this is not the way to make me pay the bill ; you had much better be easy, and take your satisfaction another way.'

x

He understood me of fighting, which upon my word was not in my thoughts, but I meant that he had better take his course at law.

'With all my heart,' says he; 'they say you are a gentleman, and they call you colonel; now, if you are a gentleman, I accept your challenge, sir, and if you will walk out with me, I will take it for full payment of the bill, and will decide it as gentlemen ought to do.'

'I challenge you, sir!' said I; 'not I, I made no challenge; I said, this is not the way to make me pay a bill that I have not accepted; that is, that you had better seek your satisfaction at law.'

'Law!' says he, 'law! gentleman's law is my law; in short, sir, you shall pay me or fight me;' and then, as if he had mistaken, he turns short upon me, 'Nay,' says he, 'you shall both fight me and pay me, for I will maintain her honour;' and in saying this he bestowed about six or seven dammes and oaths by way of parenthesis.

This interval delivered me effectually, for just at the word 'fight me, for I will maintain her honour,' the maid had brought in a constable, with three or four neighbours to assist him.

He heard them come in, and began to be a little in a rage, and asked me if I intended to mob him instead of paying; and laying his hand on his sword, told me if any man offered to break in upon him he would run me through the first moment, that he might have the fewer to deal with afterwards.

I told him he knew I had called for no help (believing he could not be in earnest in what he had said), and that, if anybody attempted to come in upon us, it was to prevent the mischief he threatened, and which he might see I had no weapons to resist.

Upon this the constable called, and charged us both in the king's name to open the door; I was sitting in a chair, and offered to rise; he made a motion as if he would draw, upon which I sat down again, and the door not being opened, the constable set his foot against it and came in.

'Well, sir,' says my gentleman, 'and what now? what is your business here?' 'Nay, sir,' says the constable, 'you see my business, I am a peace-officer, all I have to do is to keep the peace, and I find the people of the house frightened for fear of mischief between you, and they have fetched me to prevent it.' 'What mischief have they supposed you should find?' says he. 'I suppose,' says the constable, 'they were afraid you should fight.' 'That is, because they did not know this fellow here; he never fights; they call him colonel,' says he; 'I suppose he might be born a colonel, for I dare say he was born a coward; he never fights, he dares not see a man; if he would have fought, he would have walked out with me, but he scorns to be brave; they would never have talked to you of fighting if they had known him : I tell you, Mr. Constable, he is a coward, and a coward is a rascal ;' and with that he came to me, and stroked his finger down my nose pretty hard, and laughed and mocked most horridly, as if I was a coward.   Now, for aught I knew, it might be true, but I was now what they call a coward made desperate, which is one of the worst of men in the world to encounter with, for being in a fury, I threw my head in his face, and closing with him, threw him fairly on his back by main strength, and had not the constable stepped in and taken me off, I had certainly stamped him to death with my feet, for my blood was now all in a flame, and the people of the house were frightened now as much the other way, lest I should kill him, though I had no weapon at all in my hand.

The constable too reproved me in his turn ; but I said to him, 'Mr. Constable, do not you think I am sufficiently provoked ? can any man bear such things as these ?   I desire to know who this man is, and who sent him hither ?'

'I am,' says he, 'a gentleman, and come with a bill to him for money, and he refuses to pay it.' 'Well,' says the constable very prudently, 'that is none of my business, I am no justice of the peace to hear the cause ; be that among yourselves, but keep your hands off one another, and that is as much as I desire; and therefore, sir,' says the constable to him, 'if I may advise you, seeing he will not pay the bill, and that must be decided between you as the law directs, I would have you leave it for the present, and go quietly away.'

He made many impertinent harangues about the bill, and insisted that it was drawn by my own wife; I said angrily, 'Then it was drawn by a ——;' he bullied me upon that, told me I durst not tell him so anywhere else; so I answered, I would very soon publish her for a —— to all the world, and cry her down; and thus we scolded for near half an hour, for I took courage when the constable was there, for I knew that he would keep us from fighting, which indeed I had no mind to, and so at length I got rid of him.

I was heartily vexed at this rencounter, and the more, because I had been found out in my lodging, which I thought I had effectually concealed; however, I resolved to remove the next day, and in the meantime I kept within doors all that day till the evening, and then I went out in order not to return thither any more.

Being come out into Gracechurch-street, I observed a man follow me, with one of his legs tied up in a string, and hopping along with the other, and two crutches; he begged for a farthing, but I inclining not to give him anything, the fellow followed me still, till I came to a court, when I answered hastily to him, 'I have nothing for you! Pray do not be so troublesome!' with which words he knocked me down with his crutches.

Being stunned with the blow, I knew nothing what was done to me afterwards; but coming to myself again, I found I was wounded very frightfully in several places, and that among the rest my nose was slit upwards, one of my ears almost cut off, and a great cut with a sword on the side of the forehead, also a stab into the body, though not dangerous.

Who had been near me, or struck me, besides the cripple that struck me with his crutch, I knew not, nor do I know to this hour; but I was terribly wounded, and lay bleeding on the ground some time, till coming to myself I got strength to cry out for help, and people coming about me, I got some hands to carry me to my lodging, where I lay by. It was more than two months before I was well enough to go out of doors, and when I did go out, I had reason to believe that I was waited for by some rogues, who watched an opportunity to repeat the injury I had met with before.

This made me very uneasy, and I resolved to get myself out of danger if possible, and to go over to France, or home, as I called it, to Virginia, so to be out of the way of villains and assassinations; for every time I stirred out here I thought I went in danger of my life ; and therefore, as before, I went out at night, thinking to be concealed, so now I never went out but in open day, that I might be safe, and never without one or two servants to be my lifeguard.

*(Jack (who, by the way, had **not finally got rid of his wife**, but was to be reconciled **to her long** afterwards) improved considerably in his manner of dealing with the conjugal misfortunes which stuck to him constantly, and are quaintly celebrated on his title-page.   He ran a marquis through the **body abroad, and caned** a captain heartily at home, **for misdemeanours towards two** of his **spouses.   But he was** never either **a fire-**eater or a high-flier ; and the **account of his courtship** of his fourth wife is an inimitable **instance of Defoe's** kindly and unconscious Philistinism.)*

My wife being now dead, I knew not what course to take in the world, and I grew so disconsolate and discouraged, that I was next door to being distempered, and sometimes, indeed, I thought myself a little touched in my head.   But it proved nothing but vapours, and the vexation of this affair, and in about a year's time, or thereabouts, it wore off again.

I had rambled up and down in a most discontented unsettled posture after this, I say, about a year, and then I considered I had three innocent

' children, and I could take no care of them, and that I must either go away, and leave them to the wide world, or settle here and get somebody to look after them, and that better a mother-in-law than no mother, for to live such a wandering life it would not do ; so I resolved I would marry as anything offered, though it was mean, and the meaner the better. I concluded my next wife should be only taken as an upper servant, that is to say, a nurse to my children, and housekeeper to myself, 'And let her be —— or honest woman,' said I, 'as she likes best, I am resolved I will not much concern myself about that ;' for I was now one desperate, that valued not how things went.

In this careless, and indeed rash, foolish humour, I talked to myself thus : 'If I marry an honest woman, my children will be taken care of; if she be a slut, and abuses me, as I see everybody does, I will kidnap her and send her to Virginia, to my plantations there, and there she shall work hard enough, and fare hard enough to keep her chaste, I'll warrant her.

I knew well enough at first that these were mad hair-brained notions, and I thought no more of being serious in them than I thought of being a man in the moon : but I know not how it happened to me, I reasoned and talked to myself in this wild manner so long, that I brought myself to be seriously desperate ; that is, to resolve upon another marriage, with all the suppositions of unhappiness that could be imagined to fall out.

And yet even this rash resolution of my senses did not come presently to action; for I was half a year after this before I fixed upon anything; at last, as he that seeks mischief shall certainly find it, so it was with me. There happened to be a young, or rather, a middle-aged woman in the next town, which was but a half mile off, who usually was at my house, and among my children, every day when the weather was tolerable; and though she came but merely as a neighbour, and to see us, yet she was always helpful in directing and ordering things for them, and mighty handy about them, as well before my wife died as after.

Her father was one that I employed often to go to Liverpool, and sometimes to Whitehaven, and do business for me; for having, as it were, settled myself in the northern parts of England, I had ordered part of my effects to be shipped, as occasion of shipping offered, to either of those two towns, to which, the war continuing very sharp, it was safer coming, as to privateers, than about through the Channel to London.

I took a mighty fancy at last that this girl would answer my end, particularly that I saw she was mighty useful among the children; so, on the other hand, the children loved her very well, and I resolved to love her too; flattering myself mightily, that as I had married two gentlewomen and **one** citizen, and they proved all three **naught, I** should 'now find what I wanted in an innocent country wench.

I took **up** a world of time in considering of this matter; indeed scarce any of my matches were done without **very** mature consideration; the second was the worst in that article; but in this, I thought of it, I believe, four months most seriously before I resolved, and that very prudence spoiled the whole thing; however, at last being resolved, I took Mrs. Margaret one day as she **passed by my** parlour door, called her in, and told her I wanted **to** speak with her; she came readily in, but blushed mightily when I bade her sit down in a chair **just** by me.

I used no great ceremony with her, but told her that I had observed she had been mighty kind to my children, and was very tender to them, and that **they all** loved her, and that if she and I could agree **about it,** I intended to make her their mother, if she **was not** engaged to somebody else. The girl sat still, and said never a word, till I said those words, 'if she was **not** engaged to somebody else;' when **she** seemed struck. However, I took no notice of it, other than this, 'Look ye, Moggy,' said I (so they **call** them in **the** country), 'if you have promised yourself, you must tell **me.'** For **we** all knew that **a young** fellow, a **good** clergyman's wicked son, had **hung** about her **a** great while, two or three years, and made love to her, but could never get the girl in the mind, it seems, to have him.

She knew I was not ignorant of it, and therefore, after her first surprise was over, she told me Mr. —— had, as I knew, often come after her, but she had never promised him anything, and had, for several years, refused him; her father always telling her that he was a wicked fellow, and that he would be her ruin if she had him.

'Well, Moggy, then,' says I, 'what dost say to me? art thou free to make me a wife?' She blushed and looked down upon the ground, and would not speak a good while; but, when I pressed her to tell me, she looked up, and said, she supposed I was but jesting with her; well, I got over that, and told her I was in very good earnest with her, and I took her for a sober, honest, modest girl, and, as I said, one that my children loved mighty well, and I was in earnest with her; if she would give me her consent, I would give her my word that I would have her, and we would be married to-morrow morning. She looked up again at that, and smiled a little, and said, 'No, that was too soon to say Yes;' she hoped I would give her some time to consider of it, and to talk with her father about it.

I told her she needed not much time to consider about it; but, however, I would give her till to-morrow morning, which was a great while. By this time I had kissed Moggy two or three times, and she began to be freer with me; and, when I pressed her to marry me the next morning, she laughed, and told me it was not lucky to be married in her old clothes.

I stopped her mouth presently with that, and told her she should not be married in her old clothes, for I would give her some new. 'Ay, it may be afterwards,' says Moggy, and laughed again. 'No, just now,' says I, 'come along with me, Moggy;' so I carried her upstairs into my wife's room that was, and showed her a new morning gown of my wife's, that she had never worn above two or three times, and several other fine things. 'Look you there, Moggy,' says I, 'there is a wedding-gown for you; give me your hand now that you will have me to-morrow morning; and as to your father, you know he has gone to Liverpool on my business, but I will answer for it he shall not be angry when he comes home to call his master son-in-law, and I ask him no portion; therefore, give me thy hand for it, Moggy,' says I, very merrily to her, and kissed her again; and the girl gave me her hand, and very pleasantly too, and I was mightily pleased with it, I assure you.

There lived about three doors from us an ancient gentleman, who passed for a doctor of physic, but who was really a Romish priest in orders, as there

are many in that part of the country; and in the
evening I sent to speak with him. He knew that
I understood his profession, and that I had lived
in popish countries, and, in a word, believed me a
Roman too, for I was such abroad. When he came
to me, I told him the occasion for which I sent for
him, and that it was to be to-morrow morning; he
readily told me if I would come and see him in the
evening, and bring Moggy with me, he would marry
us in his own study, and that it was rather more
private to do it in the evening than in the morning;
so I called Moggy again to me, and told her, since
she and I had agreed the matter for to-morrow, it
was as well to be done over night, and told her what
the doctor had said.

Moggy blushed again, and said she must go home
first, that she could not be ready before to-morrow.
'Look ye, Moggy,' says I, 'you are my wife now,
and you shall never go away from me a maid; I
know what you mean, you would go home to shift
you. Come, Moggy,' says I, 'come along with me
again upstairs.' So I carried her to a chest of linen,
where were several new shifts of my last wife's, which
she had never worn at all, and some that had been
worn.

'There is a clean smock for you, Moggy,' says I,
'and to-morrow you shall have all the rest.' When
I had done this, 'Now, Moggy,' says I, 'go and

dress you;' so I locked her in, and went downstairs. 'Knock,' says I, 'when you are dressed.'

After some time, Moggy did not knock, but down she came into my room, completely dressed, for there were several other things that I bade her take, and the clothes fitted her as if they had been made for her; it seems she slipped the lock back.

'Well, Moggy,' says I, 'now you see you shall not be married in your old clothes;' so I took her in my arms, and kissed her, and well pleased I was, as ever I was in my life, or with anything I ever did in my life. As soon as it was dark Moggy slipped away beforehand, as the doctor and I had agreed, to the old gentleman's housekeeper, and I came in about half an hour after, and there we were married in the doctor's study, that is to say, in his oratory, or chapel, a little room within his study, and we stayed and supped with him afterwards.

When, after a short stay more, I went home first, because I would send the children all to bed, and the other servants out of the way, and Moggy came some time after.   *   *   *   *   *
The next morning I let all the family know that Moggy was my wife, and my three children were rejoiced at it to the last degree. And now I was a married man a fourth time; and, in short, I was really more happy in this plain country girl, than with any of all the wives I had had. She was not

young, being about thirty-three, but she brought me a son the first year ; she was very pretty, well shaped, and of a merry cheerful disposition, but not a beauty ; she was an admirable family manager, loved my former children, and used them not at all the worse for having some of her own. In a word, she made me an excellent wife, but lived with me but four years, and died of a hurt she got of a fall while she was with child, and in her I had a very great loss indeed.

V.—'ROXANA'

(Roxana, or the Fortunate Mistress, *is, on the whole, the least good of Defoe's minor novels, though there are good things in it; and it is one of the most puzzling. Its title-page speaks of the heroine as having been known as the Lady Roxana 'in the time of Charles the Second,' and there are passages which directly point to that king, and to the Duke of Monmouth; yet the opening words tell us that she only came to England in* 1683, *and the next page that she was then but ten years old. Moreover, in the latter part there are huge episodes and digressions which square very ill with the rest. The opening, however, though not suitable for selection here, contains remarkable passages, and the following extract is Defoe in his unmistakable vein. A very interesting parallel, or rather contrast, might be drawn between Roxana and Manon Lescaut, considerably to Roxana's disadvantage; for she is a cold-blooded creature, the most disagreeable of Defoe's heroines, without a touch of the natural and healthy animalism which redeems Moll Flanders, and with much more than Moll's scheming and calculation. She has, however, found favour in some eyes ; and the less edifying parts of her adventures have recently been translated into French, where they look well enough. This extract, as I have said, bears Defoe's mark on every line of it. Roxana and her maid Amy are journeying from France, where, as elsewhere, they have had adventures none too creditable, to England.)*

When I passed in the ship between Dover and Calais, and saw beloved England once more under my view; England, which I counted my native country, being the place I was bred up in, though not born there; a strange kind of joy possessed my mind, and I had such a longing desire to be there, that I would have given the master of the ship twenty pistoles to have stood over and set me on shore in the Downs; and when he told me he could not do it, that is, that he durst not do it, if I would have given him a hundred pistoles, I secretly wished that a storm would rise that might drive the ship over to the coast of England, whether they would or not, that I might be set on shore anywhere upon English ground.

This wicked wish had not been out of my thoughts above two or three hours, but the master steering away to the north, as was his course to do, we lost sight of land on that side, and only had the Flemish shore in view on our right hand, or, as the seamen call it, the starboard side; and then, with the loss of the sight, the wish for landing in England abated, and I considered how foolish it was to wish myself out of the way of my business; that if I had been on shore in England, I must go back to Holland on account of my bills, which were so considerable, and I having no correspondence there, that I could not have managed it without going myself. But we had not been out of sight of England many hours before the weather began to change, the winds whistled and made a noise, and the seamen said to one another that it would blow hard at night. It was then about two hours before sunset, and we were passed by Dunkirk, and I think they said we were in sight of Ostend; but then the wind grew high, and the sea swelled, and all things looked terrible, especially to us that understood nothing but just what we saw before us; in short, night came on, and very dark it was, the wind freshened, and blew harder and harder, and about two hours within night it blew a terrible storm.

I was not quite a stranger to the sea, having come from Rochelle to England when I was a child, and gone from London, by the river Thames, to France afterward, as I have said. But I began to be alarmed a little with the terrible clamour of the men over my head, for I had never been in a storm, and so had never seen the like, or heard it; and once offering to look out at the door of the steerage, as they called it, it struck me with such horror (the darkness, the fierceness of the wind, the dreadful height of the waves, and the hurry the Dutch sailors were in, whose language I did not understand one word of, neither when they cursed nor when they prayed), I say, all these things together filled me with terror, and, in short, I began to be very much frighted.

When I was come back into the great cabin, there sat Amy, who was very sea-sick, and I had a little before given her a sup of cordial waters to help her stomach. When Amy saw me come back and sit down without speaking, for so I did, she looked two or three times up at me ; at last she came running to me : 'Dear madam,' says she, 'what is the matter ? What makes you look so pale ? Why, you an't well, what is the matter ?' I said nothing still, but held up my hands two or three times. Amy doubled her importunities ; upon that I said no more but, 'Step to the steerage-door, and look out, as I did ;' so she went away immediately, and looked too, as I had bidden her, but the poor girl came back again in the greatest amazement and horror that ever I saw any poor creature in, wringing her hands and crying out, she was undone ! she was undone ! she should be drowned ! they were all lost ! Thus she ran about the cabin like a mad thing, and as perfectly out of her senses as any one in **such a** case could be supposed to be.   I was frighted myself, but when I saw the girl **in** such a terrible agony it brought me a little to myself, and I began to talk to her, and put her in a little hope.   I told her there was many a ship in **a** storm that was not cast away, and **I** hoped we should not be drowned ; that it was true the storm was very dreadful, but **I** did not see **that the seamen** were so much **concerned as we** were ; and so I talked to her as **well as I could,** though my heart was full enough of it, as well as **Amy's** ; and death began to stare in my face, ay, and something else too, that is to say, conscience, and my mind was very much disturbed ; but I had nobody to comfort me.

But Amy, being in so much worse a condition, **that is** to say, so much more terrified at the storm than **I** was, I had something to do to comfort her. She was, as I have said, like one distracted, and went raving about the cabin, crying out she was undone ! undone ! **she** should be drowned ! and the like ; and at last, the ship giving **a** jerk, by the force, I suppose, of some violent wave, it threw poor Amy quite down, for she was **weak** enough before with being sea-sick, **and** as it threw her forward, the poor girl struck her head against the bulk-head, as the seamen call it, of the cabin, and **laid** her as dead **as a** stone upon the floor or deck ; **that is** to say, **she** was so to all appearance.

I cried out for help, but it had been all one to
have cried out on the top of a mountain, where nobody had been within five miles of me, for the
seamen were so engaged, and made so much noise,
that nobody heard me or came near me. I opened
the great cabin door, and looked into the steerage to
cry for help, but there, to increase my fright, was two
seamen on their knees at prayers, and only one man
who steered, and he made a groaning noise too,
which I took to be saying his prayers, but it seems it
was answering to those above, when they called to
him to tell him which way to steer.

Here was no help for me, or for poor Amy, and
there she lay still so, and in such a condition that I
did not know whether she was dead or alive. In this
fright I went to her, and lifted her a little way up,
setting her on the deck, with her back to the boards of
the bulk-head; and I got a little bottle out of my
pocket, and I held it to her nose, and rubbed her
temples, and what else I could do, but still Amy
showed no signs of life, till I felt for her pulse, but
could hardly distinguish her to be alive. However,
after a great while, she began to revive, and in about
half an hour she came to herself, but remembered
nothing at first of what had happened to her for a
good while more.

When she recovered more fully she asked me
where she was? I told her she was in the ship yet,

but God knows how long it might be. 'Why, madam,' says she, 'is not the storm over?' 'No, no,' says I, 'Amy.' 'Why, madam,' says she, 'it was calm just now' (meaning when she was in the swooning fit occasioned by her fall). 'Calm, Amy,' says I, ''tis far from calm; it may be it will be calm by and by, when we are all drowned and gone to heaven.'

'Heaven, madam!' says she, 'what makes you talk so? Heaven! I go to heaven! No, no, if I am drowned I am damned! Don't you know what a wicked creature I have been? * * *
* * * I have lived a wretched abominable life of vice and wickedness for fourteen years. O madam, you know it, and God knows it, and, now I am to die; to be drowned! Oh! what will become of me! I am undone for ever! ay, madam, for ever! to all eternity! Oh! I am lost! I am lost! if I am drowned, I am lost for ever!'

All these, you will easily suppose, must be so many stabs into the very soul of one in my own case. It immediately occurred to me, 'Poor Amy! what art thou that I am not? What hast thou been that I have not been? Nay, I am guilty of my own sin and thine too.' Then it came to my remembrance that I had not only been the same with Amy, but that I had been the devil's instrument to make her wicked. * * * * *

*   *   *   *   *   *

that she had but followed me, I had been her wicked example; and I had led her into all; and that as we had sinned together, now we were likely to sink together.

All this repeated itself to my thoughts at that very moment, and every one of Amy's cries sounded thus in my ears; 'I am the wicked cause of it all! I have been thy ruin, Amy! I have brought thee to this, and now thou art to suffer for the sin I have enticed thee to! and if thou art lost for ever, what must I be? what must be my portion?'

It is true, this difference was between us, that I said all these things within myself, and sighed and mourned inwardly; but Amy, as her temper was more violent, spoke aloud, and cried, and called out aloud, like one in an agony.

I had but small encouragement to give her, and indeed could say but very little, but I got her to compose herself a little, and not let any of the people of the ship understand what she meant or what she said; but even in her greatest composure she continued to express herself with the utmost dread and terror on account of the wicked life she had lived, and crying out she should be damned, and the like, which was very terrible to me, who knew what condition I was in myself.

Upon these serious considerations, I was very

penitent too **for** my former **sins,** and cried out, though softly, two or three times, ' Lord have mercy upon me ! ' to this I added abundance of resolutions of what a life I would live if it should please God but to spare my life **but** this one time ; **how** I would **live** a single and a virtuous life, and spend a great deal of what I had thus wickedly got in acts of charity and doing good.

Under these dreadful apprehensions I looked back on the life I had led with the utmost contempt and abhorrence. I blushed, and wondered at myself how I could act thus, **how I** could divest myself of modesty and honour,   *   *   *   *   * and I thought if ever it should please God to spare me this one time from death it would not be possible that I should be the same creature again.

Amy went further ; she prayed, she resolved, she vowed **to** lead a new life, if God would spare her but this time. It now began to be daylight, for the storm held all night long, and it was some comfort to see the light of another day, which none of us expected ; but the sea went mountains high, and the noise of the water was as frightful to us as the sight of the waves ; **nor** was any land to be seen, nor did the seamen **know** whereabout they were. At last, to our great joy, they made land, which was in England, and on the coast of Suffolk ; and the ship being in the utmost distress, they ran **for** the shore at **all** hazards, and with great difficulty got into Harwich, where they were

safe, as to the danger of death ; but the ship was so
full of water, and so much damaged, that if they had
not laid her on shore the same day, she would have
sunk before night, according to the opinion of the
seamen, and of the workmen on shore too, who were
hired to assist them in stopping their leaks.

Amy was revived as soon as she heard they had
espied land, and went out upon the deck, but she
soon came in again to me : ' Oh, madam,' says she,
' there's the land indeed to be seen. It looks like a
ridge of clouds, and may be all a cloud for aught I
know ; but if it be land, 'tis a great way off, and the
sea is in such a combustion, we shall all perish before
we can reach it. 'Tis the dreadfullest sight to look
at the waves that ever was seen. Why, they are as
high as mountains ; we shall certainly be all swallowed
up, for all the land is so near.'

I had conceived some hope, that if they saw land
we should be delivered ; and I told her she did not
understand things of that nature ; that she might be
sure if they saw land they would go directly towards
it, and would make into some harbour ; but it was,
as Amy said, a frightful distance to it. The land
looked like clouds, and the sea went as high as
mountains, so that no hope appeared in the seeing
the land, but we were in fear of foundering before we
could reach it. This made Amy so desponding still ;
but as the wind, which blew from the east, or that

way, drove us furiously towards the land, so when, about half an hour after, I stepped to the steerage door and looked out, I saw the land much nearer than Amy represented it; so I went in and encouraged Amy again, and indeed was encouraged myself.

In about an hour, or something more, we see, to our infinite satisfaction, the open harbour of Harwich, and the vessel standing directly towards it, and in a few minutes more the ship was in smooth water, to our inexpressible comfort; and thus I had, though against my will, and contrary to my true interest, what I wished for, to be driven away to England, though it was by a storm.

Nor did this incident do either Amy or me much service, for the danger being over, the fears of death vanished with it, ay, and our fear of what was beyond death also. Our sense of the life we had lived went off, and with our return to life, our wicked taste of life returned, and we were both the same as before, if not worse. So certain is it, that the repentance which is brought about by the mere apprehensions of death, wears off as those apprehensions wear off; and death-bed repentance, or storm repentance, which is much the same, is seldom true.

However, I do not tell you that this was all at once neither; the fright we had at sea lasted a little while afterwards, at least, the impression was not quite blown off as soon as the storm; especially poor Amy, as soon as she set her foot on shore, she fell flat upon the ground and kissed it, and gave God thanks for her deliverance from the sea; and turning to me when she got up, 'I hope, madam,' says she, 'you will never go upon the sea again.'

I know not what ailed me, not I; but Amy was much more penitent at sea, and much more sensible of her deliverance when she landed and was safe, than I was. I was in a kind of stupidity, I know not well what to call it; I had a mind full of horror in the time of the storm, and saw death before me as plainly as Amy, but my thoughts got no vent, as Amy's did. I had a silent sullen kind of grief, which could not break out either in words or tears, and which was therefore much the worse to bear.

I had a terror upon me for my wicked life past, and firmly believed I was going to the bottom, launching into death, where I was to give an account of all my past actions; and in this state, and on that account, I looked back upon my wickedness with abhorrence, as I have said above; but I had no sense of repentance from the true motive of repentance; I saw nothing of the corruption of nature, the sin of my life, as an offence against God, as a thing odious to the holiness of His being, as abusing His mercy, and despising His goodness. In short, I had no thorough effectual repentance, no sight of my sins in their proper shape, no view of a Redeemer, or hope in Him.　I had **only such a** repentance as **a** criminal has at the place of execution, who is sorry, **not** that he has committed **the crime,** as it is a crime, **but** sorry that he is to be hanged for it.

(The most interesting part of the rest is a long and curious account of a splendid entertainment which Roxana gives to the King (Charles II.) and the **Duke** *of Monmouth.　The latter end of the book is—owing to the interpolations, as they most probably are, above referred to—nearly unreadable, and the bad ends to which both maid and mistress come, though sufficiently well deserved, are deferred too* **long, and** *brought on without dramatic propriety.)*

THE END

Printed by R. & R. CLARK, *Edinburgh*